SUZANNAH DUNN is the author of ten novels, all of which have been critically acclaimed. She has written three previous historical novels: *The Queen of Subtleties*, *The Sixth Wife* and *The Queen's Sorrow*.

Praise for *The Confession of Katherine Howard*

'Those who have fallen in love with the drama of the Tudor period will devour *The Confession of Katherine Howard* . . . an insightful foray into the life of one of Henry VIII's most misunderstood yet fascinating wives.'   *Scottish Sunday Herald*

'Dunn gives the story a vivid, contemporary feel, and Katherine's conversations with her closest friend, Cat Tilney, are gossipy and intimate, full of sly innuendo and confidences.'   *Marie Claire*

'Gripping, a page-turner, a thriller . . . Dunn's book has an incisive insight into how manipulative people work.'
    Dublin Evening Herald

Praise for *The Sixth Wife*

'My, what a story . . . utterly compelling.'   *The Times*

'Suzannah Dunn . . . weaves a kind of love story that is both moving and believable. This is the Tudor world as seldom seen.'   *Telegraph*

'Mesmerising and beautifully written.'   *Scotsman*

Praise for *The Queen of Subtleties*

'A stunningly refreshing way of retelling an old story. I often abandon historical novels nowadays, but I really could not put this one down. It brings Anne Boleyn to life as never before, and, probably for the first time ever in fiction, Henry VIII emerges as a truly credible character in an authentic setting.'

Alison Weir

By the same author

The Queen's Sorrow
The Sixth Wife
The Queen of Subtleties

The Confession of Katherine Howard

SUZANNAH DUNN

Harper
Press

Harper*Press*
An imprint of HarperCollins*Publishers*
77–85 Fulham Palace Road
Hammersmith
London W6 8JB

Visit our authors' blog at www.fifthestate.co.uk

This Harper*Press* paperback edition published 2011
1

First published in Great Britain by Harper*Press* in 2010

Copyright © Suzannah Dunn 2010

Suzannah Dunn asserts the moral right to be identified
as the author of this work

A catalogue record for this book is available from the British Library

ISBN 978-0-00-725830-7

Set in Bembo with Fairfield Display by
Palimpsest Book Production Limited, Falkirk, Stirlingshire

Printed and bound in Great Britain by Clays Ltd, St Ives plc

Mixed Sources
Product group from well-managed
forests and other controlled sources
www.fsc.org   Cert no. SW-COC-001806
© 1996 Forest Stewardship Council

FSC is a non-profit international organisation established to promote the
responsible management of the world's forests. Products carrying the FSC label
are independently certified to assure consumers that they come
from forests that are managed to meet the social, economic and
ecological needs of present and future generations.

Find out more about HarperCollins and the environment at
www.harpercollins.co.uk/green

Author's Note

Katherine Howard signed herself 'Katherine' on her letter
to Thomas Culpeper, so that is the spelling of her name
used in this book. The relationship between Cat Tilney and
Francis Dereham is my own invention. More information
on the historical background to the plot can be found at
www.suzannahdunn.co.uk

Acknowledgements

Many, many thanks to:

Antony Topping, coolest agent in town; and also at Greene and Heaton, those lovely foreign rights gals, Elizabeth Cochrane and Ellie Glason.

Clare Smith and Essie Cousins, at HarperCollins, for their clear-sighted, imaginative, unstintingly supportive and awesomely energetic [that's enough adjectives, ed] approach to making the most of my novels.

Anne O'Brien, for super-speedy yet gently-done copy-editing.

Sophie Goulden, Katherine Josselyn, Taressa Brennan, Elspeth Dougall, Julian Humphries and Kate Gaughran at HarperCollins, for doing so well what it takes to get the book on to the shelves.

Jo and Carol, for the home from home; and actually at home, David and Vincent, for smiling sweetly throughout the eighteen months that it took me to write this book, when all I did, frankly, was moan.

Contents

Contents

'Comet-like, brilliant yet transitory, Catherine Howard blazed across the Tudor sky.'

Lacey Baldwin Smith, *A Tudor Tragedy:*
The life and times of Catherine Howard, 1961

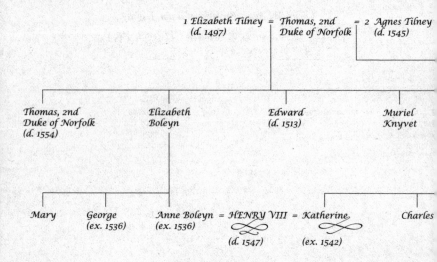

1 Elizabeth Tilney = Thomas, 2nd = 2 Agnes Tilney
(d. 1497)   Duke of Norfolk   (d. 1545)

Thomas, 2nd   Elizabeth   Edward   Muriel
Duke of Norfolk   Boleyn   (d. 1513)   Knyvet
(d. 1554)

Mary   George   Anne Boleyn = HENRY VIII = Katherine   Charles
        (ex. 1536)   (ex. 1536)   (ex. 1542)
                                   (d. 1547)   (ex. 1542)

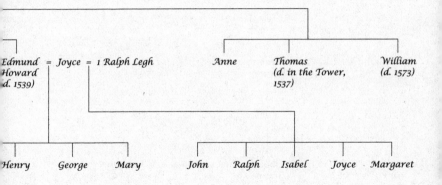

| Edmund Howard (d. 1539) | = Joyce = 1 Ralph Legh | | | Anne | Thomas (d. in the Tower, 1537) | William (d. 1573) |

| Henry | George | Mary | John | Ralph | Isabel | Joyce | Margaret |

November 2nd, 1541

The second of November was the last time when everything was all right, and of all days it was All Souls, the day of the dead. The day when, back in the old world, the bells rang for hours into the darkness to reach the souls in purgatory, to tell them we'd never forsake them, never stop pleading with God to take them in. Those bells clamoured on our behalf, too, though, I'd always felt: calling to the dead – so much more numerous than us – to spare a backwards glance. They couldn't resist it, creeping back to steal a look at us: we, the hapless living, ignorant of what was to come. They pressed in on us, after dark, coming in on the night air despite the closed doors, hovering among the rafters despite the flaring wicks, and drawing deep on our exhaled breaths. Much was made of their mischief, back in

Suzannah Dunn

the old days, but all I'd ever detected in the air on that one night of the year was despair.

As All Souls came to a close, that year, we were in the queen's private chamber. Soon to be free again of the doleful reproaches of the dead for a whole year, we'd already been reclaiming the world for the living. Life was never so much for the young as on the day that was soon to dawn and we in the queen's retinue were so much younger than everyone else at the palace, which the king and his company had acknowledged, leaving us to our dancing.

By around eleven o'clock we were reeling. Only a handful of us remained with the queen, having retreated at her invitation to her gorgeous private chamber, where we reclined on cushions around her vast, gold-canopied chair. Our pale faces were flushed with fireglow but the room could've been lit by our pearls and gems alone, the hundreds of them worked into the fabrics of our gowns and sleeves, collars and cuffs. England: firelight and fireblush; wine-dark, winking gemstones and a frost of pearls. Wool as soft as silk, in leaf-green and moss; satins glossy like a midsummer midnight or opalescent like winter sunrise.

To see us there, no one would ever have guessed that we were barely free of a decade of destruction: the stripping of churches and dismantling of monasteries, the chaining of monks to walls to die, the smash of a sword-blade into a queen's bared neck. None of it had actually happened to us, though; it'd passed us by as we'd sat embroidering alongside our housekeeper. Our parish church had been whitewashed, the local priory sold to a rich man, and we'd celebrated

2

fewer saints' days, but that, for us, had been the extent of it. The tumultuous decade had passed, the reforming queen was long gone and the reformations had ceased if not reversed, and there we were, grown up and at the palace as if nothing had ever happened: English girls, demure and bejewelled; Catholic girls, no less, half-asleep around an English Catholic queen.

My friend Kate: the queen. Little Kate Howard, my girl-hood friend, who'd been nobody much: she'd become England's queen. Just over a year on the throne, but from how she sat there under that shimmering canopy, she might've been born to it. Just nineteen years old, but doing a perfect job. At last, the king was happy again and life at the palace was, once again, fun: that's what everyone was saying. It was as if we'd gone back twenty years, people were saying, to the days of the first Catherine, the king's first queen, before all the trouble began. Before all the wives. And whoever would've believed that was possible? Kate looked to have a lifetime of queenship ahead of her: easing the king through his latter years before living on as dowager queen and – God willing – mother of his successor. Kate was the happy ending, of which – even better – we were, so far, only at the beginning.

Tiny Kate, in poppy-coloured silk, in the gold-glow of the canopy. With her eyes closed and head back, the Norfolk-family chin gave her – in spite of her repose – a teasing, testing look. Her silk-clad legs, outstretched, were crossed at the ankle and the sole of the uppermost shoe was visible: softest Spanish leather which was scuffed beyond repair by just one evening of dancing. Her fingers were laced in her lap, the rings numerous and their jewels so big that her little hands disappeared beneath them.

I was resting back on Francis; he was turning a skein of my hair in his fingers, his breath warm on the top of my head. Across the room, Alice and Maggie, my other girl-hood friends, were gazing into the smouldering sea-coal in the brazier. All of us were lost to the exquisite playing of one of Kate's favoured musicians, a doe-eyed boy of sixteen or seventeen, his head low over his lute.

It felt, to me, like the beginning, that night: finally, the real beginning of our future. I'd never had any reason to doubt it but – if truth be told – I'd always been sceptical of our sudden, unexpected success. That was the evening, though, when I finally let myself believe it, when I allowed it to work its magic on me. What I was thinking as I looked around that room was, *This is who we are*: the perfect queen and her faithful retinue. Now, I wish I could go back, patter over the lavish carpets to tap us on the shoulders, whisper in our ears and get us out of there alive. Little did we know it, but, that night, we were already ghosts in our own lives.

Just after the strike of eleven, Thomas Culpeper swaggered through the door, cloaked in raw night air but otherwise as polished as ever. He'd been around earlier but had gone off to see someone or do something and here he was again, with a sharp, meagre bow towards Kate. She slid down in her chair to reach him with her toes, to poke his shin, her playful kick an admonishment – *Don't* – because so perfunctory a bow was a provocation. He sat down at the foot of her chair, a halo of candlelight slipping on his chestnut hair as he looked up to whisper to her, 'You been sent for?'

The slightest shift of her head, the merest suggestion of a shake; and if the king hadn't sent for her by this time in the evening, he wouldn't do so. Strange, perhaps, that the king didn't want her on this night of all nights, when he'd spent the evening at a special service of his own devising to give thanks to God for his wonderful wife, for his late-flowering happiness. After four months on the road, showing her off around the country, he'd chosen for his homecoming this celebratory Mass from which modesty had demanded that she stay away. Yet he hadn't sent for her, afterwards.

Perhaps he wanted to think of her for that one night as God-given, as something like a miracle, which would've been tested by a tussle in the bed. And a tussle was surely what it would've been. Extraordinary though he was, whenever Kate was summoned to his bed I could only think of him as huge and old. To me, back then, he was already huge and old, even though actually he was only in his forties and not yet in particularly bad shape, only thickening as muscle softened to fat. He was more than twice my age, though, and had been ruler for longer than I'd been alive. To me, back then, older people seemed to have accumulated disappointment, to be weighed down by their disapproval for the rest of us – not unlike how I imagined the dead to be – and this was indeed the look of the king: the tight mouth; the eyes narrowed with distrust. The exception for him was

Kate: he shone whenever he looked at her; his features lifted and he looked alive, he looked relieved.

They made the oddest pair in every respect but most obviously in their physical mismatch: Kate tiny, and the king twice her size. She was only shoulder-high to most of the ladies at court but her husband was a head and shoulders taller than most of the men and half as wide again. He was twice as wide as Francis, who might've been considered girlish by those who didn't know him as I did. Francis's bones rose high in his silky boy-skin and I'd cupped each and every one. My hands had explored the configuration of him, edging along the shield of skull behind his ears, stroking down his breastbone, circling the knots of his wrists, spanning his hips, as if unwrapping a gift.

I couldn't help but wonder how Kate felt whenever she was summoned from her own bedroom to the one adjoining the king's apartment, the one they shared on those occasions when he asked for her and to which he came with a pair of attendants who'd wait outside for him. It seemed, to me, a hefty price to pay for all the deference, the egg-sized diamonds, the acres of cloth of gold that she wore and in which she draped her rooms – those river-view rooms occupied by the most talented young musicians and most knowledgeable chaplains and physicians. Then again, most of her ladies and maids would end up settling for situations that weren't so dissimilar, but for far less recompense. Not me, though: I was going to marry Francis, I'd make sure that happened and, now that he was the queen's private secretary, I was confident my parents could be persuaded.

There'd been no way, I knew, for Kate to refuse the king. He'd hadn't ordered her to marry him and he'd been careful to court her – for appearance's sake, for the sake of his pride – but all the same she could never have said no: he and her family would've seen to that. Whenever she went off to that shared bedroom, I didn't quite know what I was witnessing: coercion or compromise. She'd have known that it was what everyone was thinking but she let nothing slip, never even acknowledged the curiosity, which was quite something for a girl of knowing looks, the mistress of the cryptic confidence. She acted blithe when leaving for that shared bedroom and again when she returned, making clear that as far as she was concerned – and, thus, as far as everyone else should be concerned – it was nothing. I supposed she had to think of it that way for her to be able to endure it.

She lifted her head to catch my eye, and spoke quietly but emphatically: 'Room going free.' Thomas Culpeper's: she was offering me – and Francis – his bed for the night, as she did whenever she could. Thomas Culpeper would stay with her, and Francis and I would be able to spend a whole night alone together in his bed. Behind me, Francis tensed, making as if to decline. I knew why, I knew what he was thinking: *Not Thomas Culpeper's, anyone but Thomas Culpeper's.* But, as ever, I was quicker: 'Good, thank you.' Anyway, the offer had been made to me, not to Francis. Dutifully, I smiled my gratitude in Thomas Culpeper's direction but avoided meeting his eye, which wasn't hard because a glance at the likes of me was beneath him.

I, too, would've preferred that it wasn't Thomas Culpeper's

bed, but it was his or none. And although I'd over-indulged at supper and was tired from the dancing, and although I'd have loved to close my eyes and slide into oblivion, I wasn't going to turn down an all-too-rare night with Francis. Opportunities for even the swiftest encounter had been few and far between during the four long months on the road, but even in the palaces we too often had to suffer the embarrassment of begging time alone from room-mates or risk being discovered in the Office of Revels' storage rooms among papier-mâché unicorns. A couple of times, we'd even taken our chances in a window recess at the far end of the Queen's Gallery, flinching from distant footfalls. Very occasionally, when Kate and all her ladies were being elaborately entertained, she'd dare to slip me her bedroom key so that Francis and I could miss the show for some fun of our own. We'd sneak away to brave the line of yeomen on guard at the door to her apartment – the pair of us ostensibly on separate duties to prepare for the queen's eventual return – and hurry through room after room, ignoring any chamberers, until we reached the door of the most private room of all, and there we'd slip inside unseen. The first time, the bed itself almost did for us, that immense bed piled with furs and hung with gold cloth: we'd hardly dared clamber up on to it. And then there'd been the distraction of the star-gilded ceiling.

That night, All Souls, I rose and took Francis by the hand to draw him to his feet, keen not to waste time, anxious in case the offer was for any reason withdrawn. I led him out past the guards, down the stairs and into the gloom.

We were in step by the time we were skirting the inner courtyard, heading for the courtiers' rooms on the boundary of Fountain Court. We could've found Thomas Culpeper's rooms with our eyes closed, we probably knew the way better than he did: he was so rarely there. As a favoured Gentleman of the Privy Chamber, he was often required to sleep alongside the king's bed. If he wasn't, then – unbeknown to the king – there was a good chance he'd be in the queen's.

Francis went on ahead while I took cover in an adjacent stairwell. He was up the first two or three stairs with a single stride, then disappeared from view; but the rooms were on the first floor and I heard his knock, the answering cry and the opening of the door. Thomas Culpeper's attending man sounded disgruntled at having to shift so late. 'You're in here tonight?' No reply that I could hear from Francis; I pictured his apologetic shrug and lopsided smile, which in turn had me smiling. Then a clattering of footfalls on the steps: more than one pair; the attendant had had company. Two men bounced down into the stairwell but the laggard drew his companion back into shadow and they kissed. It was a momentary embrace, but savoured. A long moment, in which I couldn't quite make myself look away because I so envied them their passion, coming ahead of my own. Then they were crossing Fountain Court, heading for Base Court, as if it hadn't happened, and I was half-wondering if I'd imagined it.

I hurried up the stone steps. The door was closed, safeguarding the warmth. Inside, the fire was down to embers but the heat had built up solid. I took off my cloak, unaware until then of how I'd been tensed against the riverside chill. The inner door was open so that the bedroom could benefit from the fire. Thomas Culpeper was so privileged as to be allocated a pair of rooms, but still there was little space to accommodate two grown men. The rooms were in dire need of an airing, and I had to fight the urge to clear up the tankards and clothes that were strewn around. That wasn't what I was here for, I reminded myself.

I was here for Francis. My heart was thumping; it seemed to be saying, *Just us, just us.* He stood tall in front of the fireplace, yet also slightly hunched as if to make himself inconspicuous. As if that were possible. Which made me laugh, and then he was laughing, too, in response, although he couldn't have known why. He was already uncloaked; the top half of him a linen-clad glow. Brighter still was his hair. I had the sense again of knowing him to the very bones, his body given over to me in all its beguiling, disarming complexity so that I never knew where to start. I could take his face in my hands, feel how its smoothness was deceptive, detecting its invisible graininess: that daily undoing of him. Or I could cap his shoulders, relish their nudge into my palms. Ease my fingers through his tangled hair and rest the tips in the groove at the back of his neck. Lay a hand against his breastbone, the satisfying flatness of it.

I took a step towards him, picking up and breathing in his particular scent: piquant, like rainfall but not quite. We kissed. I'd only ever kissed one boy before Francis, but I knew – I just knew – that no one kissed as Francis did.

No one made love as he did, either: that, too, I knew. I'd heard plenty of talk which gave the impression that what others did together in bed was boisterous and fun. But for Francis and me, the act that brought us closest did so by pitching us against each other. Whenever I took him inside me, he'd move very slowly, edging his way towards my pleasure, resisting any rush, refusing to be swayed: his eyes on mine, almost defiant. I'd be hanging on his every move, matching him inch for inch in that slow dance, ekeing every sliver of sensation from his flex into me, a kind of despair assuaged but reinstated with each heartbeat. And it worked: his timing was faultless, which I knew – from talk – was far from the case for most men.

No one, I knew, had ever had what we had. Oh yes, he'd been the lover of a girl before me, but she was a carefree, curvy girl and their times in bed would've been bouncy and giggly. I was narrow-hipped and sharply articulated, and my heart, unlike hers, was diamond.

November 3rd

I don't know what time the men came for him, the next day; I didn't even know, until a whole day later, that anything untoward had happened. Odd to think how discreet an investigation it was, at first, in view of how rapid and brutal it became.

We'd parted at dawn, Thomas Culpeper arriving back and throwing open the bedroom door. Having dressed hurriedly, we'd left the rooms – still unacknowledged by Culpeper, who, in the absence of his attendant, made himself busy with the fireplace – and gone our separate ways from the foot of the stairs.

Back in my room, Alice and our irritatingly madonna-faced maid, Thomasine, were still asleep, so I slipped beneath the bedclothes for an extra hour. Kate wasn't an early riser, particularly after a night spent with Thomas Culpeper.

Later, when I arrived at Kate's apartment, I couldn't spot Francis. He didn't turn up for Mass, either, and, when there was no sign of him by late morning, I assumed he'd been sent on an errand.

The king hadn't been evident in chapel, either, and I'd glimpsed Kate register his absence. No surprise in itself, his absence: on days that weren't feast days, he preferred to worship in private in his closet adjoining the chapel. Which meant work, mostly, if rumour was correct: catching up on papers whilst only half-listening to Mass. Usually, though, Kate would've been informed of his absence – of the fact of it, if not the reason, unless the reason was ill-health. She wasn't expected to trouble her pretty little head with matters of state, and she made quite clear that she had no interest in doing so. All she ever wanted to know of the king was his whereabouts, even if only vaguely. Actually, what she wanted to know was when to anticipate his return.

Whenever he came to her rooms to see her, he'd eschew the royal chair that was there for him, lowering himself instead on to a bench – his huge thighs braced – so that she could settle herself beside him. She'd rest her head against his fur-rich shoulder and he'd ask her, 'What have you been doing, today?' the miracle being that he sounded genuinely interested, if not in the substance of what she had to say, then in her telling of it. He hung on her every word. She might have very little to say, but she could make something of nothing with her eye for detail and her word-perfect recall ('So *then* he said –'). She made it funny for him, with that dry delivery of hers. He even giggled – he did have a giggle, that great big man. Or with her, he did. So, there he'd be: a king with decades of rule, interested in the daily doings of a girl who professed no interest in anything much but clothes. Often he'd have a new acquisition to show her, perhaps a wind or string instrument or some ingenious item of percussion that he'd explain and demonstrate, and she'd just laugh at the nakedness of his enthusiasm, but he didn't seem to mind and in no time he'd be laughing, too.

Watching him with her, it was unimaginable to me that the jocular, twinkly man had, within the past five years, exiled one wife to a lonely death and signed an execution order for her successor.

That day, dinner was cleared away by twelve, and still no word from the king. I could see that Kate was dithering, unsure whether she should remain available, even less able than usual to make something of the daylight hours left to us. It looked a fine day, too: ripe for having something made of it outside the confines of her rooms, such as a game of bowls on the green down by the river or perhaps even a trip on the water. We couldn't be sure that this wouldn't be the last sunshine of the year.

I had no time for Kate's procrastination on such an after-noon. I was biding my time before my escape, planning a walk through Kate's private garden and then back along the moat and through her orchards. I wasn't needed, and could slip from under the expectation that I'd be around. I was good at that. The proper ladies-in-waiting did enough waiting around for the rest of us. I doubted that I'd ever get the hang of it. I was a maid-in-waiting in name only.

Of my fellow maids-in-waiting, Maggie, was poring over her little Book of Hours, as she so often was – I had no idea how she found so much in it – and Alice was ostensibly sewing but more often staring into space, an activity for which she had an extraordinary capacity. On the far side of the room, Lady Margaret – head of we maids and ladies – was in discussion with Sir Edward, head of Kate's household: in full flow, she was talking and nodding, frowning and smiling all at once as only she could do. She was the king's niece and the family resemblance was strong except in size: she was a slip of a girl. She looked scrappy in whatever finery she wore, a fault not just of her skinniness and pallor but also her anxious manner and its physical counterpart, the sore hands and abrasions beneath her collar and band of her hood. Hers was an onerous position for someone so young, no doubt foisted upon her as rehabilitation after her disgrace of a few years ago, the romantic entanglement for which, after her lover's death in the Tower, she'd apologised and been pardoned.

At the fireside, the Parr sisters were reading. My mother had taught me to read but then, when I'd grown up alongside Kate in the Duchess of Norfolk's house, there'd been little tutoring and I'd never progressed, had perhaps even regressed. I had no trouble with individual words but became lost if there were a lot of them: I could read a letter, but not a book. Kate sometimes ridiculed the Parr sisters to me for their book-reading, catching my eye and raising her eyebrows, referring to them in private as the po-faced Parrs, although in fact they were a cheerful enough pair. As queen, Kate had books of her own, but for her they were decorative, leather- and silk-bound, gold-enamelled, studded with turquoise and rubies. I didn't understand the precise nature of Kate's objection to the Parr sisters' absorption in books: she might've regarded it as a waste of time, she might've regarded it as presumptuous. Both, probably. For me, it was a source of fascination: how a book could hold them absorbed as if they were praying but with none of the subjugation of prayer. They had their heads bowed but I had a clear sense of them rising to those printed words with pleasure.

In the middle of the room, Jane Rochford was playing the lute in a business-like way. I kept waiting for Kate to say, *That's enough for now, thanks, Roch*, but she didn't; she didn't seem to hear it, whereas, unfortunately, it was all I could hear. There was never any respite from Jane Rochford: that dissatisfied but self-satisfied face was ever present in the queen's rooms. She never went off as everyone else sometimes did, for dog-walks or flower-picking or bowls-games, and – understandably – no one ever asked her along to any music practice. She was forever hanging around, imposing herself on whomever she could find and sighing hugely as she did so, under the mistaken impression that her affected languor was comical. She was never off duty because unlike all the other ladies she had no home to go to; no one had re-married her in the four years since her husband's execution.

Kate was mooching at the windows, sunlight snagging on her new brooch – a lover's knot of diamonds which the king had given her – but suddenly, 'Oh!' and she whirled around, finding me first. 'Look!'

I laid aside the letter I was writing to my cousin, and rose, craning to see the king's party beyond the moat.

'Looks as if he's off hawking, but why didn't he say?' She had no love of the outdoors, and probably would've declined an invitation to join him, but she resented not having been asked. Also, Thomas Culpeper would be gone all day because not only was he one of the king's favoured gentlemen, but he was a skilled hawker and even though we couldn't spot him at such a distance, we knew he'd be there.

'Where's Francis?' I asked her.

'Well, not there,' she replied, cocking her head towards the hawkers, amused by the prospect, the absurdity of it. Francis was firmly in her retinue, as I was; we were unknown to the king's household. Francis's place, like mine, was here, in her household. We'd come with her from home: we were hers.

I persisted: 'So, where is he, then?'

She didn't know. 'Perhaps he's ill.'

'He was fine, this morning.'

She gave me a look – *I bet he was* – but her flippancy rankled. 'I'm serious.'

She shrugged, expansively, turning it into a hugging of herself, turning herself away from the window.

Later, increasingly intrigued by Francis's whereabouts, I slipped into the second sitting of dinner in the Great Hall in search of his room-mate, Rob, who was able to tell me that Francis hadn't ever returned, that morning, to his room. Not ill, then, but up to something. There'd been mention, I recalled, of some clothes that he was considering buying from someone: perhaps that was what he was doing, busy trying to raise or retrieve the cash. Back in Kate's rooms, I spent a while longer expecting him to arrive before giving up and going for my walk. Maggie asked if she could come, and as always I was glad of a chance to lose myself in her cheery company. She tripped along at my side, chattering endearingly about some of the New Year gifts that she'd soon be sewing, and impressing upon me the various achievements of her little godson, before embarking upon a lengthy account – to which, admittedly, I only half-listened – of her family's dispute with the mason who was supposed to be building her grandfather's tomb. Maggie: two years my junior but in many ways old for her years. There was a gem-like shine to the river and cloud cover was no heavier than breath condensing on the surface of the sky.

I was surprised not to see Francis on my return. Still no one remarked on his absence, but, then, despite his position as usher to Kate's rooms, he did tend to come and go. Loyal to Kate though he was, he often disappeared – horse-riding, tennis-playing, tavern-frequenting with friends or his brothers – and managed to square it with her afterwards. I wasn't overly concerned. If anything was amiss, he would – I was sure – have told me.

Prayers, supper, and some music-making: the afternoon and evening drifted on. At six o'clock, as usual, Sir Thomas

Heneage came along with news of the king for Kate. He was a funny little man, goofy and chinless; Kate didn't often take to funny little men but Sir Thomas was an exception and she always invited him to stay for a drink and a gossip. This evening he told her that the king had gone off to London. London, suddenly, by barge, late on a November afternoon: something had come up, we might've surmised. Some*one*, perhaps: a troublesome nobleman or cleric; someone fallen from favour and being taken to task. But that was if we thought about it at all, and it's just as likely that we didn't.

Eventually, the evening livened up. Only a few of the king's gentlemen had accompanied him to London and just before eight o'clock the others turned up at Kate's door, ring-led by her brothers who were as delighted as ever with themselves. Their merry band was vying for an invitation, which, as usual, was forthcoming, albeit being issued under the ever-watchful eye of Lady Margaret. The men were eager to be entertained, although the day's hawking had helped deplete some of the ebullience that was often a problem after the end of the hunting season. In the end, good-natured gambling sufficed, the knight-marshal kept busy with the tallies.

November 4th

✥

The following morning, Francis was back in attendance, carrying on as if he'd never been away. I felt I was owed an explanation. Kate was keeping him busy, presumably with the usual mix of tasks. He was both her usher – gate-keeper to her rooms – and her secretary. The pair of them never worked together in a closet – that would've been too serious for her – but would merely retreat to a corner of whichever room we were all in. There, he'd read aloud the clutch of letters that arrived daily for her, and they'd discuss how he should respond on her behalf. They'd go through any appointments that needed to be made, and he'd set about making them. Then there were the thank-you letters for gifts – from silverware and sumptuous fabrics to baskets of fruit and jars of preserve – which came from people in every walk of life who, for their various reasons, were anxious to curry favour. Then perhaps they'd work on formal renditions of any pleas for clemency which the king had already heard from her in private and indicated that he'd permit. I'd never anticipated what a soft touch she would become in that respect, although, upon reflection, there was nothing soft about it. She was genuinely unnerved to think of the hard and fast nature of the law: its drastically impersonal, inflexible nature. What drew her to particular cases – what she had a feeling for – was the minutiae of personal circumstances, and I could well imagine that she made them compelling when relaying them to her husband.

All that morning, she and Francis made quite a spectacle with their industry. She was elaborately pinned and tucked, every inch the girl-queen, as good as gold, and he had an officious air. Habitually, he listened to her with only half his attention, polite but vague, but that particular morning he was frowning with concentration. He'd often make much, to me, of how he'd have been nothing without her, of how he owed his success to her – here he was, private secretary to the queen of England – but I wasn't so sure. When we girls had first come across him, he was a gentleman pensioner of the Duke of Norfolk's, an enviable position, and had he stayed in the duke's household, he'd have done very well for himself. He was following Kate's lead in that her own rise had been something of a fairytale, but she too, I sensed, had chosen to believe in the inevitability of it.

For her, the obscurity of her earlier life had been the mistake and the recent elevation her due. A natural enough attitude to take, I supposed, but I'd expected something different from her – from her of all people, so impatient with others' pretensions.

At last, late on during the afternoon – too late, in my opinion – Francis came to find me in the gallery, where I'd got drawn into music practice with Alice and Anne Basset. He came slinking over, all smiles, attempting to slide his way back into my favour. 'Hello, you.'

I said nothing although I did tilt my face for his kiss, which then struck me as a gesture typical of Kate – that showy petulance that she affected with men.

'Been busy?' He was keen to make amends.

Was I ever? But he'd asked, he'd given me the opportunity to knock him back, so I launched laboriously into a list of the day's decidedly unspectacular activities: I'd written to my cousin and my father; tackled a new piece on the virginals; been entrusted to choose a gown and some jewellery for Kate from The Wardrobe and The Jewel House, settling on an indigo satin gown and sapphire-and-pearl necklace; managed to catch Liz Fitzgerald's favoured tailor when he was visiting her, to ask if he could make a cloak for my little cousin in time for New Year; and dropped in at the Duchess of Richmond's rooms to check the progress of the puppies, one of which, when weaned, would be Kate's. I related all this in a deliberately flat tone, staring him down as I did so. Understandably, when he'd listened politely, he backed off.

Later still, when the evening's dancing began, I relented and took him aside, finally asking him outright, 'So, where were you, yesterday?'

He turned his big eyes to mine. 'My mother wasn't well.'

'What's wrong?' It must've been something serious, I thought, for him to have gone all the way to London, and my stomach clenched at the prospect of what he might be facing. Then again, he'd come all the way back, so whatever was wrong hadn't been serious enough to detain him.

'I don't really know.'

That struck me as vague, but, then, Francis was so often vague.

'Well, is she any better?'

'A bit.'

I began to suspect he was lying, so I delved: 'Were your brothers there?'

He nodded.

'Both of them?'

'Yes.' A touch of impatience, now: *I said so, didn't I?*

And thus I had him: 'You told me your younger brother was in York.' He'd told me that his brother had gone up there the previous week for a month of work.

He narrowed his eyes, he was cross. 'Well, he came back,' and he protested, 'I don't tell you everything.'

I sighed. 'Clearly not, Francis.' York and back inside a week? There'd barely have been time to turn around. He was definitely lying.

'*Look . . .*' but then he dropped whatever further protest

24

he was about to make and settled instead for, 'I've had a really, really long day,' and I saw how that, at least, was the truth. He looked exhausted. Tenderness washed over me and I let it drop.

November 5th

I shouldn't have, though, because in the early hours of the following morning a couple of handfuls of soil hissed at my window. Alice didn't stir but both Thomasine and I were woken. Thomasine occupied the side of the bed nearest the window and with a lot of muttering – *Bound to be Mr Dereham, what's the betting it's Mr Dereham* – she raised herself to it, prised it open, and peeked – 'Yup' – before flopping back down and yanking the bedclothes over her head. Anxious to put a stop to the disturbance, I rose and – night-gown over nightshirt, and shoes on – hurried down there.

He'd ducked inside the stairwell to hide from the night-watch. Despite the darkness, somehow I could see he was huge-eyed. His breathing skittered over the silence. He said nothing. He was terrified, I realised, and terror of my own leapt up inside me to meet his because I'd never seen him like this. He was here on the run from something or someone. This – here, this dark stairwell – was his refuge, yet clearly it was no refuge at all.

I couldn't – just couldn't – take him in my arms; something held me back, a dread perhaps of making him vulnerable. And he, too, held himself separate, trying to hold himself together. And so we stood there, looking at each other in the darkness. Still he said nothing – he couldn't say it, I understood, he couldn't bring himself to say that earlier he'd lied to me. It was obvious now but it had been obvious at the time, too, and I had to quell my fury that we'd ever had to go through that charade of his mother's supposed illness.

He confided, 'It was Wriothesley,' his breaths uneven and raucous in the silence.

Thomas Wriothesley, secretary of state to the king. I didn't understand: 'What was Wriothesley?'

'Had me in for questioning.'

Still nothing: it made no sense whatsoever, to me. 'About what?' Why on earth would Thomas Wriothesley be questioning Francis? And all day? And in such a way as to cause this terror in him? Francis was no one, he'd know nothing about anything. He was harmless: he was an innocent if I'd ever known one.

He urged, 'About *before*,' as if that should mean something.

'Before?'

'When we lived at the duchess's.'

What was there to know? What could possibly be of interest to a man such as Wriothesley? Or indeed anyone. I could barely recall our time there, myself, not least because there was nothing to remember: that was its distinguishing feature, for me. Nothing had ever happened at the duchess's. '*What* about the duchess's?'

Despite the darkness, I knew he'd given me a very direct look: loaded, in warning. 'Kate,' he whispered.

'Kate?' Kate had been nobody when she'd lived at the duchess's: she was just a girl. That was her virtue. All those previous complicated queens with their connections, but Kate was no one – a Howard, yes, but a minor one – and she had no history.

'Kate and me,' he said, and then suddenly I knew what he meant and my heart shrank. I tried to keep myself steady. He was looking at me – of course he was – and I resented it, I wanted not to be there under his scrutiny; I wanted to be away, by myself, alone.

'And' – he sounded wondrous – 'he knew it all.'

All: well, I didn't want to think about that. A tiny word encompassing so much, none of which I wanted to remember. I'd assumed we'd left it long behind.

'I don't know *how*,' he continued. 'But it was just, "We have information."'

'You didn't do anything wrong,' I said, because that was the point, pure and simple, and we needed to keep to the point. 'She wasn't married to the king, then.' Why, though, then, had Wriothesley questioned him about it? 'You did nothing wrong, there's no law against it.'

I was right, I knew I was right, so Francis's scepticism — a puff of dismissal — riled me. There was some reluctance from him — a held breath — before he ventured, 'But if there was pre-contract —'

'But there wasn't.' My insides were tight. 'Was that what Wriothesley was asking about?'

'Yes.'

'Well, there wasn't.'

We stood staring at each other in the darkness. I was listening hard to his silence; I could hear he was thinking of saying something. Then it came, tentatively: 'Some people would say there was.'

I held my temper, and was straight back at him: 'Some people will say anything, but Wriothesley's not asking them, is he. He's asking you. What did you tell him?'

'I said no, *of course*.' Now making something of being offended that I should even ask.

If he and Kate had been pre-contracted — if they'd promised themselves to each other — then they'd have been as good as married, they'd have been married in all but name and the king's marriage to her, coming afterwards, would be no marriage at all. Francis would be married to the queen, and — worse — he'd have known it. Kate would be a bigamist, and Francis would at the very least be an accessory to the hoodwinking of the king. So, the answer had to be no.

He and Kate had been a couple, at the duchess's, and almost everyone in the household had, in the end, known it. Here, now, Maggie and Alice — our old housemates —

knew. Francis and Kate had been lovers. He used to call her 'wifey', 'wifelet': it was a joke, but also it wasn't. A joke and no joke. I said, 'You should've been more discreet,' regretting it even as I said it because it was ridiculously unhelpful and even in the shadows I detected him giving me a despairing look. Quickly, I changed the subject: 'Kate doesn't know, does she, that Wriothesley had you in?' I didn't think so because – I was pretty sure – if she knew, I'd know.

'No.'

'Good. Look, this is nothing, Francis, is it. They just have to check. If someone's said something, they have to check, that's all.' And they'd have had to go to him because no one would dare approach the queen with it.

'Who, though?' he urged. 'Who's the someone? And why, and why now?'

That, I didn't know and didn't want to contemplate and it didn't matter. What mattered was that there was no pre-contract and that Wriothesley was able to establish the fact. What a blessing, in a sense, that he was investigating the past, his attention turned hard from what was currently happening with Thomas Culpeper. This was the luckiest escape ever, for Kate. She should stop what she was doing with Thomas Culpeper, though; she really had to stop it and I was going to have to say so.

He read my mind. 'Don't tell her,' he insisted. 'Don't say anything. Wriothesley said I'm to tell no one at all, *no one*, *understand?* Or this'll get nasty: that's what he said.'

'Nasty?' I was taken aback. *Nasty?* How dare he! Suddenly I felt sick to think of how the questioning might've been for Francis: the tone and the content of it. Yet in a sense the threat was a good sign, surely: under no circumstances was the queen to hear of any of this; it could be resolved without her ever having to hear of it. I returned to what mattered: 'Did he – Wriothesley – believe you? About the pre-contract?' – the lack of one.

'I don't know.'

Not the answer that I'd wanted, but at least he was being honest with me. 'Francis, *listen*: he has to believe you. You have to tell him. You have to tell him it was nothing, that you were just two silly kids . . .'

He said, 'Yes,' but I heard the anger in it. He didn't like me being dismissive of whatever it was that he'd had with Kate in the past. *Look at us*, I despaired: it wasn't each other with whom we should be angry. Then the realisation, ringing with the clarity of a bell: I must protect him. He was incapable of doing it himself: he didn't think ahead. But I did, it was as natural as breathing to me and now I could do it for him. I'd do anything to protect him. I took his arms, ran my hands up and down his arms: not much of a touch, but something, and enough, because he gave in, stepped forward and folded himself down over me. 'Go back to bed,' I whispered against his chest. 'Get some sleep.' And saying so, I could make an end to it, at least for now. 'Whatever this is about,' I said with utter certainty, 'it'll blow over.'

And I believed it, absolutely I did. I was right to think that Francis had done nothing illegal, and I was naïve enough, back then, to believe that what mattered was the truth. Worried, though: yes, I was, and of course I was. Wriothesley was secretary to the king: he was the man who, effectively, ran everything. Not, presumably, someone with time to waste on anything unimportant. But I'd heard nothing to suggest he was an unreasonable man, as some of the king's men were known to be. He was one of the new men: a capable administrator. Presumably, his hands were as good as any for Francis to be in, although I didn't like what those hands had already done to him, he who was usually so sweetly devil-may-care. But, I reminded myself, Wriothesley would've had to be thorough. Someone had let something slip and it'd come to the attention of the king's own secretary who was duty-bound to investigate and then, finding it unsubstantiated, get rid of it. Which he would, because Francis had done nothing. Yes, he and Kate had messed about, but who hadn't? Well, to some extent, anyway. What mattered was the future: that's what I kept reminding myself, all through that night. The king adored Kate. Even if he did ever hear of what she'd got up to in her earlier years, he'd turn a blind eye because he was looking to the future, to – at long last – a successful marriage and, God willing, a second male heir. He was getting on in years; he hadn't the time for quibbling over details of the past. He'd finally found what – or *who* – he'd been looking for. He'd never been happier – everyone said so – and Kate was doing such a good job. She was ideal: uncontroversial, with no strong religious affiliation – simply a traditional girl – and the Howards were stalwarts, not newcomers. And in any case her ties to her family were comfortably loose. And she was English, too, not foreign like the first queen and the latter. She was everything he needed. True, she wasn't yet pregnant, but these were still fairly early days and she was young and healthy. She was entirely trouble-free except for what went on, sometimes, in her bed behind her closed door on nights when the king hadn't asked for her. But no one knew about that, except me and Francis and Jane Rochford, and anyway it'd stop, soon enough, despite what Kate claimed; I knew it would; it always did, although probably she'd then take up with someone else. I wished she'd stop it, now that she was queen. Why couldn't she stop it?

I did manage some sleep, in the small hours – I must've, because before I knew it, I was up against the morning and there was nothing for it but to drag myself out of bed. I was slower than the brisk, ever-organised Alice: she was gone even before I'd placed both feet on the floor. Dressing under Thomasine's brisk supervision, I was dogged by unease, slipping free of it only whenever she snared my attention. Francis had been terrified: the fact was inescapable. I didn't want to think about how he'd looked; I'd never seen him like that before. Every time I closed my eyes, there he was, but he wasn't the Francis I knew.

Outside, a fine rain pulsed in gusts. Again I arrived at Kate's rooms later than usual; later than everyone, I established instantly, except Francis. *No Francis*. I steadied myself in the doorway, told myself that perhaps he was sleeping late, as I'd done. Perhaps, like me, this morning, he was befuddled and slow to emerge. Perhaps, though, he'd gone on the run. Would he? If he ran, they'd chase him. I willed him: *Be sensible*. But that was a lot to ask of Francis.

I was barely across the threshold before Kate was heading

for me, which had my heart catch before I registered her expression. Amused, she looked, and my blood surged because perhaps she was going to laugh and say, *You'll never guess what* . . . and, *I told them* . . ., and everything would be fine and she'd given Francis the day off to recover. I hardly dared hope it. She gestured that I should join her in the gallery: we were to talk privately. I followed her train of rosy velvet stitched with gold-thread swirls and studded with pearls, and the others in the room barely glanced our way; they'd think nothing of Kate going off to gossip with her oldest friend.

In the gallery, she led me into a window recess hung with a cage of songbirds.

'Francis is in for questioning about tax,' she said, cheerfully. 'Did you know?'

My heart contracted. Something else, something more? Was someone, for some reason, out to get him?

'They sent a man to tell me,' and it was this, apparently, that had amused her, the formality of it. She quoted the officious man: '"He will be unavailable for duties, today."' I understood it differently, though, this despatching of a messenger. This was nothing to do with tax. Wriothesley had Francis for a second day and had gone to the trouble, this time, of putting Kate off the scent. A second day of it? How many ways were there to ask the same question?

'What's he been up to, then?' she was asking, affectionate. As if she cared. 'I hope they don't drag me into it, because he did give me that money, once, to look after.'

What money?

35

'When he went off to Ireland, that time.' She smirked. 'I'm queen, see: good strongboxes.'

Yes: as queen, she'd have been the safest option. I'd said it before I could stop myself: 'You should be careful, Kate.'

She tipped her head to one side, teasing. 'About what?'

I glanced around, first. 'About –' I didn't even like saying his name – 'Thomas.' 'Thomas Culpeper' would've sounded ridiculously formal, but I'd hated having to say the familiar 'Thomas'. He wasn't 'Thomas' to me.

'Thomas?' A whispered, incredulous laugh. 'But I am. You know I am.' In the same tone, 'What's brought this on?'

A pinch of panic, because, of course, I'd promised not to say. 'I don't know, just –'

Francis was mine, Thomas Culpeper was hers: that's how, I hoped, she'd account for it.

And presumably she did, because she didn't pursue it. 'Of course I'm careful.' She dipped her head, quizzical, to bring my gaze back up to hers. 'There's only you who know.'

I was about to correct her but she said it for me, dismissively, as a kind of chant: 'Oh, and Francis, and Jane Rochford,' *I know, I know.* 'And –' laughing again in that whispered way as she swept back across the gallery to the door – 'it's not as if any of you are going to tell, are you.'

All morning I waited with mounting disbelief for Francis to appear, sometimes thinking he might've been released but gone elsewhere: to chapel, or to his room. Several times I came close to confiding in Maggie – sweet Maggie, who'd have been so concerned for me, I knew, and would've tried her very best to reassure me – but I couldn't face explaining everything. Kate didn't mention Francis again. She decided to hold a tennis tournament on the covered courts. While the king was away, she'd keep his gentlemen busy. Summoning Oliver Kelly, keeper of the courts, she made him cancel all prior bookings. Francis was on his list: 'Your Mr Dereham,' as Mr Kelly referred to him, scanning the page.

So, I spent most of that long afternoon sitting on a hard bench between equally bored Maggie and Alice with rain puffing through the wire-netted window at my back while, in front of me, various gentlemen exerted themselves on opposing sides of a taut, fringed rope. Despite the pretence of playfulness, they took themselves seriously: red-faced and clamp-jawed as they wielded their leather racquets and disputed points. Thomas Culpeper was down to his cambric shirt in no time. Kate cheered him on whenever he played; and whenever he scored a point, she blew him a kiss. She was enjoying scandalising the more staid of her ladies but I was in no mood for such games.

As soon as I could, I went directly to Francis's room – but there was no sign of him. Then, just as I'd done two days before, I went in search of Rob, his room-mate, when I was fairly sure where he'd be: dining in the Great Hall. He told me that the last he'd seen of Francis was when they'd left their room together in the morning, and he'd assumed Francis was on his way to the queen's rooms. ('Didn't he – ? Is something up?') I returned to their room and used some of their firewood ration, hoping they wouldn't mind, and sat there, then lay there on the bed that he and Rob had to share.

Francis turned up sometime after the strike of six. I'd
expected him to be pleased or at least relieved to see me,
but he didn't even look at me – bar one stinging glance –
and turned his back to tend the fire, which needed no tending.
I held my breath and steadied myself; there was nothing else
I could do. This was new to me, this contempt from him,
and I was going to have to feel my way. He was obviously
exhausted: whey-faced, and his eyes red-tinged. I supposed
he was dreading any further questioning. I had to question
him, though, if I were to be able to help; I had to know
what had happened.

He, though, was the first to speak: 'It was Mary.' He was
hunkered down on the little hearth, poking his fire-iron
into the incandescence. I'd got to my feet and was standing
awkwardly behind him, above him, longing to put my
fingers into his hair, to soothe him, to crouch down and
cover him with myself.

'Mary?'

'Wriothesley's information comes from Mary.' Still he
didn't look around; still jabbing into the fire.

Which Mary? I knew countless Marys.

'From the duchess's,' he said.

Mary Lassells. My old room-mate Mary. But she'd been
gone for years. Gone back home and probably into some
marriage, pity her poor husband. And anyway, no one ever
listened to Mary: that was who Mary was, the girl to
whom no one ever listened. True, she'd be quite likely to
want to cause trouble for Kate, and certainly she'd know
enough to be able to do so, but how on earth would she

– silly Mary Lassells – ever get her information to Wriothesley?

'Her brother,' Francis said, answering my unasked question. He turned around but made no other move towards me; on the contrary, he sat back on the hearth and hugged his knees. My hovering over him felt even more conspicuous and, reluctantly, I returned to the edge of the bed. 'Mary Lassells?' I said, pointlessly. 'Her brother?'

He said nothing; I'd got it right. I didn't remember any brother of Mary's, but why would I? I'd lived alongside Mary for years, but only alongside: she'd been nothing, really, to me; I hadn't ever known her and if she'd mentioned a brother, I wouldn't have been listening.

'He's come to Wriothesley with these stories of what Kate was up to.'

'But why?' The risk he'd taken was unthinkable: allegations about the adored queen.

He shrugged.

Mary's revenge, at last, and she'd found someone who'd listen to her, if only via someone else. Whatever his reasons, this brother of hers had gambled on finding an ear for his allegations. And, worryingly, he had.

'Wriothesley told you, though.' He hadn't had to tell Francis of the source. Was it a good sign, then, that he had? Wouldn't he have been in a stronger position if he hadn't – if he'd stuck with that mysterious, *We have information*. But, then, perhaps he had no need for any added strength.

'Oh, we're pretty frank with each other,' Francis said. 'We've no secrets from each other.' This was in a bitter tone

– the like of which I'd never heard from him and of which I'd never have guessed he was capable. He stared at me as if with a challenge.

I guarded against rising to it. 'What did he want to know about, today?'

'When it stopped.'

I didn't like that, either: the bluntness of *it*. But, anyway, the fact was that *it* – their romance, or however else Francis liked to think of it – had stopped when she'd lost interest and moved on.

'And why she gave me the job here.'

'But she gave us all jobs here.' Her family – sister and stepmother, aunt and cousin – and her old friends: me, Maggie and Alice.

He splayed his hands – *exactly* – but there was defeat in the gesture.

'What?' – it dawned on me – 'he thinks it was . . .' but I didn't know how to put it, '. . . more than that?'

Francis said nothing.

'But that's ridiculous,' I protested. 'And in fact she gave you your job because of me, so I could have you here with me –'

He frowned and I saw that he'd never thought of it that way.

'– and I'm going to go and tell him.'

He snapped, 'Don't go anywhere near him.'

'But if I –'

'Remember what he said: no one else should know, or it'll get nasty. It's not just me who's in trouble, here, it's

Kate, too, and I won't do anything to endanger her, do you understand that?'

Oh, perfectly. He'd made himself quite clear. I doubted his loyalty would be reciprocated if the situation were reversed, but he'd never been able to see that. Anyway, *would* I go to Wriothesley? He should be coming to me. But he wouldn't even know of my existence. I was no one.

Francis asked, 'Who's Manox?'

The name shot through me. 'Henry Manox?'

He shrugged. 'Manox' was evidently all he knew.

Wriothesley knows about Henry Manox. But of course he did, because Mary knew about Henry Manox.

Francis said, 'He's brought him in for questioning, that's what he said. Manox. Who is he?'

Why would Wriothesley be interested in Manox? Did he think Kate might've been pre-contracted to *him*, as well? 'He was our music teacher. At the duchess's. Before you came.' To my shame, I couldn't quite resist making it clearer: 'He was before you.' *Did you really think you were the first?*

Poor Manox – it hadn't ended all that well for him at the time, and now this, years later. But what was Wriothesley looking for? Why on earth would it matter, a long-ago dalliance with Henry Manox? I dreaded to think that Wriothesley's enquiries might not be solely about pre-contract but Kate's conduct in general.

Then Francis was asking me to stay, his rancour gone all of a sudden as if it had never been, replaced by a heart-breaking hopefulness. Rob wouldn't mind, he said: he'd go over to one of his friends when he found us here together.

My instinct, though, was to rush to warn Kate. Questions were being asked of more than one man, now, and there had to be a way – if only I could think of it – to warn her while protecting Francis from any more trouble. I needed time to think, though. What else could happen before morning? All that would occur, if I told her now, was that she'd suffer a bad night's sleep. There'd be nothing she could do, at this hour. And, anyway, Francis did need me. Besides, I was exhausted: I doubted I could even make it over to her rooms or, if I did, make much sense when I reached there.

So, I ended up crawling into bed with Francis, stepping out of my clothes and leaving them where they fell. We didn't talk; I'd thought we might, but we didn't, not a word. I'd assumed that sleep would elude him but within a few breaths he was dead to the world. Perhaps an hour or so later, the door opened, then closed: Rob, presumably, gone on his way to someone else's room to cadge some space in a bed or, unfortunately more likely, on a floor. I stayed awake for hours longer, listening to Francis's breaths, guardian of them, all the time conscious of lying very still as if under observation and afraid of giving myself away. Conscious of it, but unable to remedy it. Nor did I seem able to use the time to think through what I could say, in the morning, to Kate. Instead, I pondered what she might do when she knew that questions were being asked about her past. What *could* she do? Go to the king? She'd been told he was in London. Was Wriothesley taking the opportunity of the king's back being turned? Or had the king absented himself to allow this to happen, in the hope that it'd be cleared up before his return? His departure, I recalled, had been unexpected and Kate had been offered no explanation for it.

I lay there thinking how the king was Kate's only supporter. She'd come from nowhere. The king had chosen her, to everyone's complete surprise. No one could've predicted it; she'd been no one's project. The king alone had chosen her – liking what he saw and not looking any closer – and he'd championed her: she was only here on his whim. She had no friends with influence. Family, yes: her uncle, the Duke of Norfolk, was the country's most powerful nobleman and the king's right-hand man; but that was all the more reason for him to drop her fast if she were in trouble, and he was wily and heartless enough to do so. Five years previously, he'd done exactly that to his other queen-niece, Anne Boleyn: turning prosecutor, even, in that case; conducting the trial and then, at its conclusion, declaring the death sentence.

First at the flattering and fair persuasions of Manox . . . I suffered him at sundry times to handle and touch the secret parts of my body . . .

Never had I thought that Kate would one day become queen – she was a Howard but from the bottom of the Howard pile, the motherless tenth child of the disappointing second son, and empty of ambition. At the duchess's, though, she was queen of a kind from the day she arrived.

When I first ever saw her, I'd been momentarily blinded from a dash indoors and only as my eyes adjusted did I see that I'd run in on our Mrs Scully and that she was standing beside a girl. The girl wasn't quite standing but reclining against a hefty wooden chest. One hip on, one off. I recognised her as about my own age – twelve – but otherwise she was unlike any girl I'd ever encountered. The sling of that hip, perhaps. None of we girls at the duchess's would've dared sit like that, or indeed sit at all in the presence of an adult who was standing, even if that adult was only our own dear Mrs Scully.

Mrs Scully said to me, 'This is Katherine,' and she sounded very correct, as if addressing me in the presence of another adult.

She hadn't said, Catheryn, this is Katherine.

'The new girl,' she said. I was the new girl, though. Or had been, until now.

Any other girl, having dimpled, would've bitten her lip and glanced away, but this Katherine held me in her gaze, the glitter of which, I understood, was to be taken as a smile. Faintly amused, was how she looked. It struck me, even at the time, as an adult look, knowing and appraising. Unnerved, I'd murmured the requisite greeting and scarpered back to my friends.

I'd been at the duchess's for six months, by that time. It would be the making of me, my parents had said, to grow up in the household of Dowager Duchess of Norfolk, the widowed matriarch of England's foremost family. We were so lucky that she'd agreed to take me on. The duchess had been plain Agnes Tilney before she'd become the old duke's second wife, and she and my grandfather had been second cousins. We were the poor relations.

Aim high, my mother had been telling me ever since I could remember: *Don't settle*, she'd say. There were no lullabies, for me: only *Aim high. Don't settle.*

'*I* didn't settle,' she'd say, and look at me.

Back in those days I did only have eyes for her; there was no one else in my little world. What I saw of her, usually, was that long straight back of hers as she strode busily around our house. If she'd have settled, she – farmer's daughter – would've become a farmer's wife; she'd have married a tenant farmer and had a big, busy farmhouse to run. But she'd aimed high and married a gentleman's son who himself was aiming high and had become a successful lawyer. So, she had a big, busy manor house to run, with tenants to farm our land.

I grew up with the belief that there was work to do in the world: the work of bettering oneself. Our chaplain talked of having one's God-given place in the world, yet we as a family seemed intent on leaving our place behind. My mother's way around it was to believe that it was our place to better ourselves. Bettering ourselves, she said, was what God intended for the poor-relation Tilneys. 'God has been kind to us,' she'd say, 'and enabled us to work hard and we've done well, we've been able to make a good life for ourselves.' She never looked happy when she said it, though, she never looked pleased; she looked as if there was always so much more to do.

'All this,' she'd say sometimes, in wonder, when she paused in the garden and looked back at our house. But try as I might, I couldn't see what she saw. The house was all I'd ever known, and, beautiful though it was, it was just a house. If there was no house, what would there be? Nothing: just grass and mud; openness, emptiness, a clearing. The wonder in her voice scared me, the implication that what we had – *all this* – was unexpected, accidental, just as likely to not be. Grass and mud and wind and no shelter were just as likely. From how she said it, *all this* had been built by my parents' will alone, and the strength of their will alone kept it standing. But for how much longer? Whenever my father was home from his lodgings in London, I overheard tense exchanges on the rising cost of the stables, the expense of ordering new livery for the servants.

I grew up knowing that I had a part to play in keeping that house standing: I could make a good marriage, make connections. A good marriage – mine – would shore us up; we'd no longer be the poor relations isolated in our beautiful house in that clearing. I was my parents' only child and their fear for me was that I'd slide away into obscurity. Little did they know that there'd come a time when my obscurity was all we'd wish for.

Back then: Watch and learn, they urged me of my forth-coming time at the duchess's; soak everything up and do your utmost best at all times. I'd be working hard to help run a big household, as well as learning Latin and Greek, mathematics, music and astronomy, but the reward, ultim-ately, would be my own wealthy, well-connected household in which – God willing – I'd be raising my husband's heir and our many other eminently marriageable children. It all sounded good to me, or certainly good enough. At eleven years old, I knew of nothing else to wish for.

Make people want you, Catheryn, my mother said. Make yourself the girl who people want for their family, she said. Because, yes, it's all down to money, in the end, to dowry and social standing and there's nothing, she'd tell me, that you can do about any of that: that's for us to worry about, and we're doing the very best for you that we can. But there is something else: character. There are so many girls, Catheryn – more and more, these days – and so little to choose between those of you with your kind of dowry and background, but you can tip the balance in your favour. You can make yourself the girl who people want as their daughter-in-law, their son's wife, the mother of their grand-children. You can be the girl who lights up the room, catches eyes, warms hearts. Make yourself the girl that people want to be running their son's household. You'll need to show an eye for beauty and quality, she said, but a nose for value. A head for figures and a good hand for letter-writing. You'll need to give the impression you can deal with servants – keeping them in line whilst winning them over – and keep a good name with merchants and suppliers. Don't stand for nonsense but curb your tongue and keep your temper, and never take sides. Have a ready smile, be quick to lend an ear, a helping hand, and have an eye for who's to be trusted. Keep your counsel, but don't be secretive.

Be respectful to your elders and betters, she insisted. Never waiver in that, never be tempted for a single moment to think that you're quicker-witted or clearer-eyed than your elders and betters, because once you start that, you'll never be able to stop, and no one's interested in clever girls. Wittiness never got a baby to sleep, or a draper paid.

Make sure you're always looking neat and tidy and clean, she'd say, but other than that, don't worry about your appear-ance. You're not bad-looking, as it happens, she'd tell me, but looks fade before you know it, and then what are you left with? Beauty draws the eye but for all the wrong reasons. Keep your eyes down, Catheryn. Don't look at boys. Don't even look. Don't get distracted. Don't let any silly girls fill your head with talk of romance. Girls can be very silly, Catheryn, when they haven't had what you've been lucky enough to have: a proper upbringing. It's a silly girl who gets her head turned. Get your head turned, she said, and you're lost.

You're no one's fool, she'd say to me, and there was something in how she said it that suggested it was a secret between us and, for reasons I couldn't fathom, not an entirely comfortable one. A burden, almost, perhaps.

There was such a lot to remember about how I should be; I worried I'd never remember it all, let alone one day actually manage to *be* it. None of this would ever have been said to Katherine: she had no mother to say it and, because she'd been born into England's principal family, there was no need anyway for it to be said. And so she came unencumbered to the duchess's; whereas for me, my mother had spoken so compellingly that, in my mind's eye, I could see the woman I was to strive to become, the calm and capable, well-loved and much-valued lady, warm-hearted and cool-headed. She was a wonderful prospect, that lady, but always at a distance from me; such a distance that she seemed to have nothing to do with me, striding away into the future, and when I arrived at the duchess's I didn't know if I'd ever keep up or even ever dare take a step in her direction.

All that talk at home of the Howards' wealth, but when, on my journey from home to the duchess's, the leading rider called back that we'd arrived, I assumed we were stopping off somewhere for an overnight stay of which I hadn't been informed. We were approaching a timber gate-house, behind which was a moat and what appeared to be a jumble of barns. Hours earlier, we'd ridden away from the family home that my father had had built: a symmetrical, brick-built house gazing big-windowed over formal gardens. Clattering over that old drawbridge, I craned enquiringly towards my old nursemaid, Mrs Kent, but received only a smile in return. The drawbridge took us to a porters' lodge, beyond which was a courtyard like a farmyard: a flock of ewes being shepherded across it, and a dozen or so labourers yelling and hammering, hauling and slamming down plough-shafts, scythes, cartwheels and crates.

A couple of labourers took our horses, and a liveried man arrived to greet us, requesting that we accompany him. Duly, we tottered across cobblestones, avoiding the smears and dollops of dung. The man's grey jerkin had a subtle shimmer to it. My own servants were dressed in a flat, glaring blue. Someone wealthy, then, was staying here: a party from the duchess's, perhaps, to meet us and then take us on with them in the morning to her splendid, elegant house. I asked Mrs Kent, 'Where is this?'

'It's where the duchess lives.' She sounded surprised that I'd asked.

I was weary from the ride, lacking patience. Servants will

believe anything, I'd been told often enough. 'No, it isn't,' and I laughed to muffle my irritation.

She laughed, too. 'Yes, it is.'

Poor old Mrs Kent, I felt, who knew so little of the world.

We and our handful of attending men followed the well-dressed servant down a passageway into a courtyard which, to my relief, was serene. This, then, was where people lived, although I noticed that the windows, which were unshuttered, had linen in the frames instead of glass. Still, the place would do for an overnight stop, and, anyway, I was won over by the rich aroma of roasting meat. The servant ushered us through vast double-doors into a hall: a Great Hall, no less, the hammerbeam roof holding its decorative detail – coats of arms and sparring beasts – high above us, and the walls fortified by tapestries, their silken characters wan and fey among vines and waterfalls. The room could've come from stories that Mrs Kent used to tell me: stories of knights and damsels. No doubt this place had once been home to a noble family. Our own Hall was merely a room in which our staff put up a couple of tables at mealtimes for themselves and anyone visiting on household business, while my mother and I dined in the privacy of an adjacent parlour. This old Great Hall, although as yet deserted apart from a skulking wolfhound, was about to seat perhaps as many as a hundred people at several long tables: we'd stumbled upon a feast. At the far end, up on a platform, a linen-bright table bristled with silverware. 'The duchess's table,' Mrs Kent whispered, delighted. She'd know, I realised: she was old enough to have grown up in just such a house. *Was* this the duchess's house, then? It was impressive in here, but barely over the threshold was that farmyard with its mud and flies and indignant livestock. I would have to get word to my parents: they should know that the duchess had been misrepresented. We'd been tricked, hoodwinked. My mother's plans for me didn't include my growing up in a house no better than those of which she'd spoken as haunting her own childhood, the olden times before the coming of our bright new king and his subjects so keen to make better lives for themselves.

Distraction, though, came in the form of the household steward who blundered in, twinkly-eyed and bulbous-nosed, to introduce himself – 'Mr Scully' – and, having apprehended the hound, congratulated us on arriving just in time for supper. I wondered whether I'd be sitting with any of the other girls. My mother had told me there were four other girls in the duchess's care but she didn't know exactly who they were. She'd explained to me that any who weren't Howards – daughters, instead, of family friends – were in the household to be companions to those who were: that was how it worked, she'd said, as it had for hundreds of years in all the important households. Which, though, I now wondered, was I – family or friend? My parents considered me to be a blood relation of the duchess's, but, standing there in that huge old room, stroking a hound whose collar was embroidered with the Howard coat-of-arms, the relationship seemed so tenuous as to be negligible.

Nothing in how the duchess addressed me was enlightening on the matter. She'd followed her steward; I hadn't known whether to expect personal word from her but suddenly there she was, stepping from behind rotund Mr Scully to express polite concern for my welfare after the journey. I'd know now to describe her as a handsome woman: lean, with strong features, the most striking being her bird-black eyes. At the time, her silvered hair had me thinking of her as old; in fact, she probably wasn't even fifty. Wiry and brisk, she wore a gown of serviceable fustian and her fingers were stained with berry-juice. Presumably she'd come from the kitchen or still-room.

The girls were a further surprise: I would never have guessed them to be my companions if they hadn't been introduced as such, on their way into supper. I'd been anticipating composed, exquisitely dressed young ladies; but these were wide-eyed girls in barely passable worsted. Alice, Dottie and Mary were about my own age and Maggie looked to be a couple of years younger. To my relief, no distinction was made as to whom was related to the duchess, and all four were ushered to places on the high table, as was I.

Supper was plain fare – bird pie – which was welcome after the ride, and, as soon as we'd finished, the steward's wife – dumpy and smiley like her husband, but much younger – asked the girls to show me to their bedroom, waving us off with her babe-in-arm snatching at her coif. On the way across the courtyard to the staircase, the girls buzzed around me, full of questions. Their concerns were my horse at home – her name, her temperament – and whether I had brothers and sisters, and what was the latest I'd ever stayed up. I'd been anticipating serious-minded young ladies with firm marriage plans in place, ladies about to step up into their future lives; and me joining the ranks, the back of the queue, falling into line and following in their footsteps. Instead, there was Dottie telling me that Alice had been unwell and had an invalid's licence allowing her to eat meat on fish days and fast days, and Alice raising her eyebrows in acknowledgement of her good fortune. That, it seemed, counted as the big news around here.

And that I didn't mind, but when I saw the bedroom, it was all too much – or, rather, too little. My bed at home was cosy inside hangings, deep with covers and cushions, but here were five straw mattresses on the floor, each bearing a single blanket. Moreover, the suspiciously clean fireplace was clearly seldom – if ever – lit, and skimpy bolts of ox-blood-coloured fabric failed to hide bare-plastered walls. Detecting my disappointment, Dottie asked, 'What is it? What's the matter?' Ashamed of myself, I couldn't quite say, and merely gestured at the room. Dutifully, her big brown eyes followed my hand, but – I saw – she just couldn't see it, the drabness. Confounded, she tried to reassure me with, 'But we're all in here together,' and, giving me my first glimpse of that lovely, guileless smile of hers, 'It's great, you wait and see.'

My first full day at the duchess's began no differently from how my days began at home: prayers at six. No Mrs Kent, now, though, to get me dressed. Harried by the tolling bell, we girls fumbled with one another's pins and ribbons,

Mary complaining vociferously that no one was helping her enough or not fast enough, then scrunching her hair up under her hood with the furious admission that she'd just have to plait it later. By the time we arrived at the duchess's closet, the lady herself was already kneeling at the little altar. I'd soon learn that she was always well into her day before the opening of the house gates at five. After prayers came the basic household tasks – the emptying of chamberpots, and the sweeping of our own room and the Scullys', the duchess's bedchamber and her day room, the long gallery and Hall. Everywhere in the house bloomed the heady fragrance of baking bread. It was a bake day but not a Mass day, so, after a breakfast of rolls and cheese fetched to our room by Alice, we were to go to the duchess's day room for some tutoring by Mrs Scully. She despatched her step-daughter, Trudie – a scrappy, nine-year-old redhead – to take care of her various babies (I'd counted four, so far) before giving us a passage from Aesop's Fables to copy. My companions began on it laboriously, each individual letter a challenge, but I plucked up courage to whisper to Mrs Scully that I already knew how to write and to ask if I could perhaps write a letter home, a request which was gladly granted. I settled to it for an hour – but then that was it, apparently, for schoolwork, for the day. No reading, no translation, no maths, no music.

What there was, instead, was dancing tuition from a well-dressed girl who sauntered into the room on the stroke of nine and introduced herself to me as Polly. She'd not been at supper the previous afternoon, she said, because she'd been locked in her room for being naughty. When everyone else laughed, I realised she was joking. 'Kidding,' she confirmed: 'Headache.' Clearing a little dance floor by kicking aside the rushes, she informed me that in the duke's Norfolk home the rushes were scented with saffron – 'Nice touch' – and explained that that was where she'd lived until the previous year: she'd been a Howard ward since the age of seven, and she was now sixteen. I wondered why she'd been moved at this late stage to the duchess's. Possibly for exactly this, though: to teach the duchess's girls to dance. It would have to be done, but the duchess wouldn't have danced for decades and Mrs Scully – a housekeeper, not a noblewoman – would never have learned the finer points. Polly, though, seemed very much in the know. I wondered why she was still unmarried. She'd have been a considerable catch for her quick wits and prettiness – wide-spaced eyes, snub nose and full lips – let alone for the prized Howard connection. Most likely the duke was holding out for the best price; perhaps he was in the very process of driving a hard bargain and that was why she'd been sent to the duchess, safely out of the way while her future was decided, tantalisingly beyond the reach of whoever was bidding for her. During the hour before dinner, she put us through our paces, clapping rhythms and bellowing instructions, unstinting in her enthusiasm, laughing good-naturedly at our ineptitude, until we were flushed and exhilarated and Mary had slipped over and had had to be sat to the side on cushions and wrapped in a blanket.

Afternoons at the duchess's were mainly given over to

sewing, again under Mrs Scully's supervision but with the added good company of cheerful, know-all Polly. The duchess's was a big household so there was a mound of patching and darning to be tackled, lots of buttons and hooks-and-eyes to be re-attached, all to be rushed through, which was a relief because I've never been anything but poor with a needle. During these sessions, we gossiped. Dottie's sister was due to be married, that autumn, so, for those first afternoons of mine, the talk was of the match and the eagerly anticipated celebrations. Occasionally we'd be interrupted by Trudie and the trio of household pages with the more mobile of the Scully toddlers in tow, but they'd be sent back soon enough to the gallery or gardens.

After the daily load of repairs, we moved on to more challenging needlework, supposedly of better quality and intended by Mrs Scully to be improving for us. I'd come with something that I'd been working on: a little bag for dried lavender which I was stitching, slowly and badly, with a simple, repeating lavender-head design in blackwork. Luckily, no one even so much as glanced at it. Mrs Scully and Polly were working together on a superb altar cloth, and of my companions some were better at embroidery than others. Alice, working on a pair of sleeves, was unadventurous with her geometric pattern, but neat. Mary was stitching a whitework feather pattern on to a coif and was bitterly vocal on the subject of her own perceived shortcomings, which kept Mrs Scully and Polly busy issuing reassurances. Dottie was mired in a complicatedly florid cushion cover, but her frequent declarations of helplessness

– 'Oh, I just can't do this!' – gave the impression that being unable to do it made it all the more fun. Maggie loved to tidy up the sewing box of silks and needles, and Mrs Scully left her to it.

Every few days, Mrs Scully would remember that we should practise the lute and virginals and then there would be an afternoon of music. What we very rarely did was ride. My own horse had gone back home with Mrs Kent but I'd assumed that the duchess would have extensive stables. Hers was a thrifty household, though, and she didn't travel – never going to court because, Mrs Scully cheerfully said, 'She has no time for all that nonsense' – and disapproved of girls riding to hunt. The only way we ever had venison on the table, unless it came as a gift, was if servants went into the parkland and drove the deer into nets. Except for gifts, I'd soon learn, we had no fresh meat at all in winter – only salted – because, to save the cost of winter feed, the household followed the old tradition of the annual Martinmas slaughter. Indeed, most of the few horses that the duchess did own were released into the woods to fend for themselves in winter, the survivors re-captured in the spring.

The duchess spent her days busy either with household business – consulting with her secretary and steward, her caterer and the cooks – or spiritual matters with a bevy of chaplains. Sometimes there were visits from her stepson – the small, wily-looking duke, who was actually older than her – or her own two sons, one of whom had a lot of her in how he swung himself down from his horse and strode smiling into Hall, but the other pallid and pained-looking. Whenever the duchess came across us, we had to curtsey, which I loved to do, having the notion that I curtseyed particularly well. Most days, she took a couple of us with her into her meetings with senior household staff so that we'd learn about purchasing and menu-planning. She'd also take one of us on visits to those on the estate who were sick or in need, delivering them firewood, milk and bread, eggs and perhaps a hunk of cheese, perhaps some cast-off clothing and her famous tonic of breadcrumbs and rose-water. I savoured those rare opportunities for a ride.

Dottie was probably my favourite of the girls: shy, spindly and sparkly-eyed Dottie with her silk-scarf rosy-brown hair. Alice was the opposite – matronly and taciturn – but she was dependable. Mary, unfortunately, was hard work: so nearly appealing, bouncy and rosy-cheeked, keen to please and quick to laugh but, unfortunately, quicker to cry, easily riled and noisily aggrieved, perpetually on the crest of indignation. Maggie was a joy, the smallest of us but the biggest character. I loved her sometimes comical efforts to keep up with us, and anyway I only had to look at her to laugh: that unruly black hair, thick and wiry, growing outwards rather than down.

Yet for all it was wonderful to have companions, I was unused to it. It was a surprise, to me, how much solitude I could find for myself in that big, busy household, and how much – despite my newfound love of company – I still wanted it. It was there for the taking and I got better at finding it and bolder at taking it. The best times for going alone were just before or just after supper: two of the busiest times but coming when everyone's energy was running low, and so there was a slipping and sliding, the household unravelling a little, a hint of abandon in the air and, later, a resignation. A lurching and drifting towards nightfall. A good a time as any for cutting loose.

I'd cross the drawbridge and head for the gardens. That first autumn of mine at the duchess's was wonderful, a St Luke's Little Summer. Crusty sea-green lavender heads bobbed under burly bees, and everywhere was strung with barely visible spider webs of improbable spans, individual threads turned into tiny lightning bolts by the low sun. The air was somehow always cooler than I'd anticipated, like water, and moving through it gave me the pleasurable sensation of being dowsed. High above me and above the indignant rooks, birdsong tweaked at the sky as if pulling it flat in readiness for lowering it down, and dusk rose around me as rich as woodsmoke. Secluded at the far end of the flower garden was a banqueting house where, in the grand old days, favoured guests would have retreated after feasts for confectionery and spiced wine. It had long since fallen into disrepair, and my friends avoided it. I, though, found myself drawn to it. Its oak pillars and posts – now woodbine-clogged and fringed with tatty blossoms – were carved with sprightly little fleur-de-lys, sinuous vines and bold bunches of grapes; it had once been really quite something. It was even glazed, and, sometimes, having eased open the door and braved the cloth-like webs to climb the ladder-staircase, I'd peer through those sea-green diamonds of glass at the duchess's house:

buildings that, despite their decrepitude, didn't look in any danger of falling down, not least because there was nowhere much further to fall. I used to fantasise that over the years I'd furnish that banqueting house with a cosy bed and carpets and no one would know. It'd be for me alone and I felt something of a princess, I suppose, to have even the faintest possibility of it.

Evenings were nothing much at the duchess's. Apart from on the eve of an important feast day and then on the day itself, she eschewed the dancing and masques that were popular in most noble households and instead we had to be content with card and board games in the company of Polly and Mrs Scully and whichever Scully-children had yet to be put to bed. Later, though, in the privacy of our own room, gazing up at roofbeams barely visible in the glow of the solitary wick, and ignoring Mary's snores (mercifully, she fell asleep as soon as her head went down), the rest of us talked about boys. We discussed our future husbands: what we hoped they'd be like and what our lives with them might be like. It was as if we imagined those husbands – whoever they were – waiting patiently for us; as if, by having to take our time to grow up, we were inadvertently keeping them waiting. My mother might not have despaired, because there was nothing silly in our talk. We were careful to speak respectfully of those men: it was a serious undertaking even to speak of them, these men to whose selection our parents would give so much consideration. There was nothing resigned in our attitude towards the marriages for which we were heading. We had expectations of which we spoke spiritedly, understanding ourselves to be taking them along with us into the future – if not meeting our spouses halfway, then at least part of the way.

We all pitied Mary's future husband.

We didn't only talk, at bedtime: sometimes we sang. Or Dottie, Maggie and I did; Alice was no singer, she maintained a dignified silence. Dottie, Maggie and I sang love songs that we'd filched from the adult world and which we didn't fully understand, but we'd picked up threads from visiting musicians and from Polly and managed to make something of them, something that captivated us. In our bedroom and also sometimes when we were left alone in the gallery, in the gardens or the stillhouse, we offered up these little incantations – even Mary, sometimes, welcoming the opportunity to make a noise – as if trying to summon futures for ourselves.

Despite the talk of whom our parents would choose for us, we didn't shy away from speculating which boys in the household or neighbourhood we'd marry if by some chance we had the choice. Harmless, this talk, and liberating: a choice unburdened by the various considerations which, we knew, our parents had to take into account. Liberating, but never frivolous: we relished the choice that in fact we would never have, and chose carefully. Careful, as well, to avoid any conflict between one another. By negotiation, we parcelled out the better of the boys in the household and the neighbourhood: the trio of pages, and the sons of the higher-status members and retainers of the duchess's household such as her secretary and doctor. Not so much a choice, then, perhaps, as an allocation. Mine, that first autumn and winter, was the doctor's second son, fourteen-year-old Rufus: a watchful lad, by all accounts a clever boy. We kept our boys to ourselves and even they themselves – especially them – knew nothing of our interest in them.

We didn't idolise them. Our attitude to them was one of tolerance – as if they were merely, in some way, necessary. We took an interest in them, but there was no passion. What was important to us was the act of choosing. Looking back, I'm struck that our attitude to them was rather superior. In my daydreams, Rufus would be struck down, it didn't matter how, it mattered only that he was in desperate need and that I, grave and efficient, worked wonders. I found, in my daydreams, that I had a talent for it.

Bright-button-eyed Dottie had been right, that very first night: *It's great, you wait and see.* The only problem was that, in so enjoying myself, I couldn't shake a suspicion that I was betraying my mother: my mother, by whose very best efforts I was there at the duchess's. It wasn't only the talk of boys of which she would've disapproved, or the lack of schooling. Worse than that: she'd drummed into me that I'd have to be on my best behaviour at the duchess's, but to my surprise, I realised that it was at home that I'd been on my best behaviour. Both of us – my mother and me – had been forever on our best behaviour, whereas life in the duchess's household wasn't the ceremonial business that she'd believed it would be. At the duchess's, I was free of all that: I was free and every day was one long sigh of relief freighted with the shame of my disloyalty. However happy I was, I lived day by day with a catch in my breath, a lump in my throat, a hitch to my heartbeat: the sense that I was getting away with something and the day would come when I'd have to answer for it.

Katherine Howard arrived at the duchess's six months after I did, on the eve of Lady's Day. That first evening, she said very little; just regarded us all with that gaze of hers, that half-smile, answering our questions which, from shyness, were limited to practical considerations. Only Mary was more personal – 'Are your parents alive?' – but was answered at first less readily and then rarely, Katherine giving an impression of being unable to hear while she unpacked her chest and her bags. When we woke in the morning, Katherine's mattress lay square on to the wall in our higgledy-piggledy room and, shutting the door behind us, glancing back, I saw that it was our five that looked out of place.

Her first morning, she showed a similar effortless efficiency in the day room, copying letters as if it were nothing and gazing into space while waiting for the others to catch up. Mrs Scully was full of praise for her – 'Very good, Katherine!' – which rather dismayed me because it was only copying, after all, and she showed no signs of actually being able to write. When Mrs Scully left the room at the end of the lesson, Katherine remarked expressionlessly and to no one in particular, 'What do you think she was thinking when she put that dress on this morning? "Oh, this blue'll look good"?'

It'd been phrased as a question, but I knew full well that no actual response was required. Or none that wasn't in accord. The new girl's opinion was that the colour of Mrs Scully's dress was wrong and Mrs Scully should not only have known it but also cared.

Infuriatingly, ever-eager Dottie rushed in with an excuse: 'Not much else fits her –' as if Mrs Scully had lots of dresses from which to choose – 'because she's expecting again.'

'Yes.' Katherine bit a nail, then examined it. 'I can see she's been busy.'

Busy?

At that, Alice almost caught my eye but seemed to think better of it. I didn't like it that this new girl – or anyone, but especially this blank-faced, glittery-eyed new girl – should be passing comment on Mrs Scully. What was wrong with blue, anyway? True, it was more often the colour of servants' livery, and, true, it was more often worn by men than by women, but so what? What did it matter? The duchess's wasn't a fashionable household, and Mrs Scully was a busy countrywoman distracted by children.

More to the point, who was this girl to judge? From what I'd seen of her own clothes, they were plain and well used, handed down, even if she wore them as if they were something special, with cuffs turned back, buttons unfastened. In fact, she was plain herself, not that you'd know it from the way she walked around with that glittering half-smile. She walked tall despite her lack of stature.

Purposefully, too, her pace measured. Like an adult. None of our scampering or dawdling. She was thin-lipped and big-nosed; her eyes were small and grey, her hair not Tudor-gold but bronze. She wasn't a patch on any of us, I didn't think, with perhaps – if I was honest – the exception of double-chinned Alice. This colourless little new girl was nothing special but she acted as if she were. Polly would've put her in her place but she'd gone, having left us at Christmas to be married.

Later that morning, on our way into Hall for dinner, the new girl's eyes trailed the imposing figure of Mr Wolfe, the caterer, and – again – to no one in particular, matter-of-fact, she remarked, 'That one looks a lot like one of my sister's ex-lovers.' This time, no one responded. Little Maggie bit her lip. *That one* was a disturbingly casual way to refer to Mr Wolfe, who held considerable respect in the house-hold. And *lover*? Not a word we used, probably not a word we'd ever heard. *Ex-*, too, which made clear that there'd been others. And, anyway, even to think of our respectable – indeed, married – Mr Wolfe in that way . . .

When we were leaving Hall, though, and passed Jay-jay, one of the page boys, just as he spat copiously on to the cobblestones, Katherine muttered, 'You're nice,' for us to hear but for him to fail to catch, and it was this snipe of hers – pointless but pointed – that had us smiling among ourselves. The page boys were a wily trio and we'd never have admitted it but we were in awe of them, so it was good, for once, to feel superior.

Sewing, that afternoon, Katherine had barely clapped eyes

on Mrs Scully's stepdaughter before coming up with 'Oddbod', and nothing could've been more apt. Skin and bone, with birthmark-red hair and venous-blue eyes, Trudie was a girl of sudden revelations: a moth from the palm of her hand, a milk-tooth dredged from her pocket, a shrew's skeleton shrouded in her handkerchief. 'Oddbod,' decreed Katherine, her tone neutral, just as it was safe to do so, just as Trudie flitted away over the threshold ahead of her step-mother, and in that instant, it was done: Trudie became – affectionately, and only among us – Oddbod. As for Mrs Scully herself: later that afternoon, having asked us to fetch cheeses for the Lady's Day supper and rushing into the dairy to supervise us, she slipped but managed to correct it before it had properly happened, perhaps even before she'd consciously registered it. Respectfully averting my gaze, I came up against Katherine's, which showed no such compunction. That evening, Katherine relayed a message to me with, '"Skid" Scully's asking for you,' and by bedtime, Mrs Scully was, to all of us, without discussion, as if she had never been anything else, simply 'Skid'.

Despite myself, I began listening for Katherine's asides, anticipating them. We all did. Desultory though they were, they drew us in, they drew us to her in our efforts to catch them. I don't think it had ever occurred to us to pass judge-ment on anyone, but in the new girl's eyes everyone was fair game. I saw how adults took the light in those eyes as evidence of keenness and interest. Little did they know she was on the lookout, and that the smallest detail was up for comment: for speculation, or dismissal, or ridicule. The smaller, the better: the bigger the prize. People's appearance, their behaviour, their relationships, and what she saw – accurately – as their pretensions. Sometimes she was cutting, unkind, petty; sometimes, droll; often intriguing. Of the duchess's maid, Mrs Barber: *She needs one*, and a single tap of a fingertip to her top lip (which, later, had me surreptitiously and anxiously dabbing my fingertip to my own). Of Mr Wolfe and his wife: *No love lost there, bet the last time they did it was their wedding night.* Did what? Danced together? Of the bad-tempered farrier's wife, sometimes: *Probably due her monthly.* Monthly what? Confession? Of our chaplains, whispered in their wake: a flat-eyed, derisory, *God loves you, Fathers,* for which, I worried, we'd all be struck down.

I began catching myself thinking in asides, but mine were merely reflex, nothing but tics: *Nice one, Mr Scully; Don't trouble yourself, Mrs Barber; Is that really necessary, Mr Wolfe?* With the exception of Mary, who could never reign herself in, we girls began talking together in asides, too – our girlish exuberance dampened down. Within a week, we'd become watchers, turning self-conscious, guarded, judgemental. What had happened to the ready smile that my mother had insisted was so important? What had happened to *Be respectful?*

And still none of the adults seemed to notice; on the contrary, they regarded Katherine as the very model of diligence. Something to do with how high she held her head, perhaps; her meeting of their eyes with her own, and the confident half-smile. She hoodwinked everyone. *See that it's done, please, Katherine*: they were addressing everything to her, as if she were in charge of us. And thus she became so. Certainly my friends seemed to concur: there was a seriousness to their gathering around her, a respect in it – even from Mary, sometimes, in the early days – as if something important were to be gleaned from her very presence.

One morning, heading along the gallery towards the household office with a letter to my mother, I glanced down through a linen-screened window to see my friends following Katherine across the courtyard. Not that she was actually leading them, nor even walking in front of them: her pace was too stately for that, her swaying hips partnered by her swirling of a lavender head by its long stem. She was in the middle of them and it was Alice who was ahead, although turned around and pacing backwards. Still, I knew that whatever they were doing had been Katherine's idea – perhaps a casually thrown *Let's go to the gardens* – and even from a distance, and through that thick cloth, my friends' readiness was palpable. To my mind, everyone was being taken in, as I might so easily have been when I'd first set eyes on her. What pained me particularly was that Dottie was falling for those superior-sounding asides. I could understand it of Maggie, because she was young and thereby could be said to be impressionable, although actually she wasn't; and Alice because, as far as I could tell, despite her seriousness she was – frankly – empty-headed; and, well, anything could be expected of Mary. But Dottie: I was angry at Katherine for taking advantage of Dottie's readiness, and disappointed with Dottie for being naïve. For no reason that I could fathom, I'd expected more of Dottie.

I, alone, was standing my ground. My mother was wrong again, and this time spectacularly so: *Be the girl who warms hearts.* Well, despite her cold eyes and cutting comments, it was Katherine whom everyone wanted.

My mother had claimed that character was what distinguished a girl: she'd said not to pay attention to mere appearances. Yet Katherine did and everyone was in thrall to it. Each day, there was something different in how she dressed, so minor as to escape notice and censor by busy adults but for that reason looming large in our little world. A plaited ribbon slung around her wrist. Her sleeves rolled back as if she'd just finished doing something, which she hadn't. Her hood worn further and further back, and a loose knot in its veil which could've been there by mistake except that she didn't make mistakes. For me, it rankled: she'd given thought to how she dressed, as if it mattered, when – I knew, I just *knew* – that it didn't. Because how could it? Clothes were just cloth. Yet we looked for them, found ourselves looking for them, these additions and adaptations: I saw my friends sneaking looks, even as I did. Her own studied lack of regard, by contrast, implied they were nothing much, a momentary diversion: it was we who were in thrall to them, said her indifference, not she. Even noticing them – let alone commenting on them – should be beneath us, said that indifference of hers. So, we were reduced to a surreptitious keeping track of them, which was how they established their hold.

One morning, Dottie fixed a band of red cloth across her forehead, under the front of her hood, covering the parted hair that would usually be visible. She looked lovely – but, then, she always did; she didn't need a piece of cloth to make her so. Presumably she'd taken it from the basket of scraps. It was what Katherine had done earlier in the week – hers had been black satin – but Dottie wasn't wearing hers with Katherine's insouciance. Instead, adjusting her hood, she shone with shy pride. Seeing this, my heart sank in anticipation of her exposure, and sure enough: 'What's that?' asked Katherine, as we left for the duchess's closet. Caught off-guard, Dottie stammered, 'A piece of chamlet.' Reduced to being spelt out as such, that little red sash lost any magic that it might possibly have possessed. A scrap of chamlet: why wear it? Katherine appraised it with those almost-smiling eyes of hers, before pronouncing, unconvincingly and damningly, 'It's nice.' By dinner-time, it was gone and Dottie never again attempted anything similar.

My instinct, from the very first day, had been to resist Katherine, coupled in time by a stinging realisation that I'd be going it alone. She must've sensed my truculence, but never during that difficult first year when we lived alongside each other did she try to win me over. Nor, though, did she make any move to exclude me. It simply became accepted that I'd go for my walk in the gardens before supper while she and Dottie gossiped in our room, and that I'd loll on my mattress while, last thing, in their nightshirts, she, Dottie and Maggie practised their dance steps. I sensed that Katherine was keeping her distance from me: glittering back at me over the space that had opened up between us. But I didn't feel any freer. In fact, I couldn't shake a suspicion that I remained my own person only because she was allowing it.

Mary was faring less well. Katherine took everything in her stately stride with the exception of Mary. Mary was her stumbling block. I'd seen it on her very first evening and it had only worsened. I'd once overheard Skid sighing to her husband that Mary would try the patience of a saint but, before Katherine's arrival, our own tolerance of Mary had been less to do with saintliness than with being at an utter loss. Whenever she'd blundered in on us, bursting with greetings and expecting fulsome reciprocation, forgetting an appalling scene that she'd created a mere hour before, we'd find ourselves offering the required response just because she was impossible to ignore. Not for Katherine, though, and she showed us how easy it was. She simply didn't look at her. She'd continue doing whatever she was doing, or talking or listening to whomever had been talking to her, fixing her companion with a stare so that there was a clear obligation to continue. Pausing and turning to Mary would have been to drop Katherine: a choice between Mary and Katherine, which, for anyone, even me, was no choice at all because Mary would give you no thanks and would be likely to give you grief. So, Mary had to weather her rejection and sit disgruntled, fuming, learning her place.

One evening at supper, that first spring of ours at the duchess's, Katherine dipped a fingertip into the residue of sauce on her plate and began a sinuous sliding, rarely broken and then only with precision. She was writing. When finished, she looked momentarily pleased with it – head cocked, appreciative – before paying it no further mind. Quite a display in itself, her abandonment of it, as if this – writing in her sauce – was something she did all the time. And so there it was, the word, the *name*, staring up at us, staring us down: OTIS, and, framing it, the twin lobes of a heart.

Otis: charcoal-burner and – taking advantage of being out there in the woods – beekeeper. Long eyelashes and cowslick hair, and missing his two front teeth, which – happily – didn't make him any less ready to smile. Otis was nice enough. But too old – perhaps as old as twenty – and anyway he was a charcoal-burner. Charcoal-burning was a skilled job, and there was the added attraction of his honey, but he'd never have been parcelled out, previously, in our negotiations because he was a labourer, which was a step too far.

Katherine and Otis: from then on, we were spectators, whether we liked it or not. And there was plenty to watch, even if it was Katherine, in turn, watching. This was something to see, though: Katherine, previously so purposeful, now lingering at windows and doorways. As she looked for him, I noticed, her eyes changed. Before, they'd been how she'd faced down the world, they'd been reflective; but now that she was preoccupied, they had a darkness to them.

She didn't merely watch but began searching for him, too, covering a lot of ground even at her unhurried pace: making sure she was everywhere, taking the long way around buildings and courtyards in the hope of coming across him as he delivered fuel to the kitchen or smoke-house, bakery or wash-house. She'd go to places she'd previously tended to avoid, going more often to the dreaded jakes and volunteering for such unglamorous errands as taking wilted flower-arrangements to the compost heaps, even braving returning pitchers to the brewhouse where, once, it was said, a brewer's boy had fallen into a vat of boiling liquid and died. Never far behind her were Alice, Dottie and Maggie, slaves to this passion of hers; but whereas she held her head high, they looked flustered and fluttery.

Whenever she did come across Otis, all I ever saw her do was smile at him, if you could even call it a smile: a rueful twist to her lips, as if she and he were in something together, as if something had befallen them. He was always surrounded by the men with whom he worked, and these woodcutters showed no such reserve: they'd halt, startled to see her there – and to see that smile of hers – before acknowledging her presence with their own big, broad, congratulatory smiles. And there would be Otis himself in his filthy buffin doublet or perhaps just his rough buckram shirt, receiving the unsought attention with good humour – shrugs, smiles – in recognition of the absurdity of it. Before Katherine had singled him out, I'd have considered him nice enough if I'd considered him at all. Now, I found myself giving him some thought, intrigued as to what she saw in him. Try as I might, though, I just couldn't see it; and, worse, any of my encounters with him, however perfunctory, now suffered from a regrettable unease and I was left pining for the old lack of self-consciousness of which, I felt, I'd been robbed by Katherine.

Adding to my dismay, Dottie was soon following Katherine's lead with a crush of her own: hers for Harry, the wheelwright's assistant. She was vocal about her longing, unlike Katherine who said nothing of hers. *He's so lovely*, she'd sigh, although I didn't how she'd know, because we never saw him when he wasn't prone beneath a cart. Dottie couldn't keep her cool, she floundered whenever she spotted him, involuntarily holding her breath and blushing. There was none of Katherine's parading around the house and grounds; no slow smile. It didn't seem to give her pleasure, her fixation, but terror.

With hindsight, it was no coincidence that my own first-ever falling for someone was at this time, although, incredibly, I didn't make the connection, experiencing it instead as a bolt from the blue. Back in the days before Katherine, the linking of my name with Rufus – the doctor's son – had been nothing personal. This, though – my swooning over Stephen, kitchen-clerk, caterer's assistant – I kept very much to myself. Determined that my head shouldn't be turned – *It's a silly girl who gets her head turned, Catheryn* – I resisted even looking at him, but that was no escape because whenever I closed my eyes, there he was, waiting for me. It was his reserve that drew me: he was above and beyond all that was going on – that's what I told myself – and I alone would be able to reach him. His was a deliciously melancholy air – coming, actually, from his longish, oval face, his dark, heavy-lidded eyes – and I dreamed of his quiet, considered words in my ear. I didn't aim to turn his head but, to my surprise, my body went ahead and did it, walking around as if I were going somewhere and someone there had an interest in my arrival. That was all it was, but it worked, and on people other than Stephen, too: people followed me with their eyes, which were lit with approval. A new sensation, that: people's eyes on me, and the approval. *This is easy*, I'd think, and the ease itself was pleasurable. No wonder Katherine did as she did, I realised: this was how she lived her whole life, swanning around like this, garnering people's interest.

My little, unreciprocated romance kept going for several months, before succumbing to a suspicion that I'd mistaken Stephen's diffidence for depth. My attentions had lingered, perhaps, from a misguided sense of duty: I'd taken him up so, I felt, I shouldn't simply drop him. Katherine's obsession with Otis had ended, but – because she'd never spoken of it – we'd taken a while to notice. Eventually, we realised that she'd stopped walking around the grounds or writing his name in dust or condensation, and we turned our attention away because there was no longer anything for us to watch. He, too, turned away, just as accepting. If he was disappointed, he didn't show it. He'd had his time; ordinary life resumed and perhaps there was even some relief for him in that. He was off the hook.

Later that spring, on the last day of May, came news of another romance. We were sewing in the duchess's day room to the rhythmic trundle of runners, Skid rocking her sleeping newborn's cradle with her foot, when, suddenly, she laid aside her voluminous sewing – an old gown that she was turning into a kirtle – and, flashing us a smile, made an extraordinary announcement: 'Girls, we have a new queen.' She spoke brightly, but, I detected, falsely, making an effort towards enthusiasm. My world lurched. A glance around – Dottie, Alice – showed me that they assumed as I did: Queen Catherine had died. She'd died and been replaced and I hadn't known it. I hadn't known it because I'd been shut away here: my friends and me, we'd been shut away here. I almost cried out with frustration. If I'd been at home, my mother would've told me, she would've made sure I knew, she would never have let this happen: my not-knowing, my unconscious neglect of the lovely Queen Catherine. We'd often talked about the queen, my mother and me: how gentle and godly she was, and charitable and motherly, and how lucky we were to have her as our queen. From my mother I'd learned that she'd come many years ago from abroad – Spain – but we, the English people, had taken her as our own. Suddenly, I missed my mother, painfully.

Dottie was aghast: 'The queen's died?'

'No –' Skid answered readily, she was prepared, 'but she can't be queen any more.' Gently, breaking it to us.

What? How did that happen? I hadn't realised that *could* happen: that a queen could stop being a queen. Could it happen, then, to the king, too? The queen had been queen forever, or so it seemed to me: longer, anyway, than I'd been alive.

'Why can't she?' asked Alice.

Katherine was looking down at her hands and fiddling with one of her rings, but she was listening: that was how she listened, looking down. Mary and Maggie looked confused and concerned: Mary quiet for once, Maggie unusually circumspect.

Skid pushed on, but still barely audible over the grumble of the runners: 'There was a mistake.' Adding, 'That's what the king says. The king says she shouldn't ever have been made queen.'

A pretty big mistake, then: the wrong queen, for all this time.

'Why?' asked Maggie, wide-eyed. 'Was she bad?'

'Oh!' Skid laid a hand to her chest, as if to steady herself. 'No, no. Oh no, no, not at all. She's a good –' She stopped herself, returned to the point: 'It's just that – the king says, and his lawyers say – there was a problem because she'd been married before. To the king's brother.'

Dottie was incredulous: 'Didn't he know?'

Skid half-laughed, taken aback. Her face was blotchier than usual. 'Well, yes, he did know, but he didn't realise it was a problem. It's since come to light that it's a problem. So, anyway –' keen to move on – 'she'll be going to live in a castle in the countryside – perhaps she'll end up going back to Spain again after all these years, and wouldn't that be nice for her! – and the king has to start all over again with a new queen.' She added, 'This one's an English lady.'

English: blonde, I saw in my mind's eye, and polite-looking. I asked, 'What happens to Princess Mary?' The queen's daughter. The king's daughter. Like me, an only child.

Skid turned to me. 'Well, Catheryn, I'm glad you brought that up, because from now on we'll be calling her The Lady Mary.'

Maggie was thrown. 'Not Princess Mary?'

'No, because she's no longer a princess. Just as her mother is no longer queen, she's no longer a princess.' Were those tears in Skid's eyes? She'd been prone to tears since the baby – nicknamed Lilyflower – had been born.

'She was, though, wasn't she?' said Maggie, puzzled.

Skid opened her mouth to say something, then closed it but started again in that over-bright tone: 'Our new queen – Queen Anne – is a Howard! Well, her *mother's* a Howard, the duchess's stepdaughter, the sister of our own good duke. The duke's niece is our new queen! Isn't that marvellous? And –' she beamed at Katherine – 'Katherine, here, is her cousin!'

Katherine glanced up, but expressionless, giving nothing away, merely acknowledging the mention. I had a strong sense that it was all news to her. *Of course*, though, was what I was thinking, as if I'd been missing something which was now in my grasp: Katherine would have something to do with this lamentable state of affairs, even if she didn't know it. I pictured the new queen again but this time she was freckled and had a glint in her eyes.

'Do you know her?' Mary demanded of Katherine.

'No.'

But Mary, of course, didn't leave it. 'Have you ever seen her?'

'No.' Impatient, now.

'Oh,' Skid stepped in, conciliatorily, 'the Howard family is a very big family, there are a lot of –' she paused, here, to consider – 'different parts to it.'

Mary persisted. 'Do you think you'll be called to court, to serve her?'

Skid shushed her; but there'd been something, I felt, to her question. Katherine was too young to serve at court but she wouldn't always be. I could see it: I could definitely see Katherine at court, sitting around in attendance with a lot of other ladies, putting that composure of hers to perfect use. I pitied her. Court would never be an option for me and I recognised this for the liberation that it was. Confirmed for me was something I'd always suspected: that Katherine was of an entirely different ilk, that the two of us belonged to separate worlds and quite soon we'd be going our own ways. I didn't know how I'd lost sight of it, but one day, one day quite soon, I was going to be free of Katherine.

The coming of the new queen wasn't marked in any way in the duchess's household – but, then, nothing much ever was. We were informed of the new queen's coronation, the obligatory prayers being said for her on the day. She was heavily pregnant, by that time, not that we girls would know that for years to come. We knew only what we'd been told, which was that there'd been a mistake about queens that had been corrected. We believed what we were told; why wouldn't we? The king – had he known – would've been proud of us. How he must've been wishing that everyone could be as accommodating.

For a while, I was bracing myself for Katherine to make something of her connection to the new queen, but she didn't. In fact, I never heard her mention it. Once, though, during a verbal skirmish with the pages, Dottie's unwise parting shot was a puffed up, 'Anyway, Katherine's cousin is the queen,' to which Jay-jay retorted, '– is a *slut*.' It was a breathtakingly bad thing to say about the queen, of course, which, fortunately for him, neither Dottie nor Alice seemed to have heard: they were already bustling off with an air of vindication, Alice in the lead and Dottie pattering behind. What struck me, though, was not only that he'd dared voice it aloud, but the ring that it had had to it: of confidence, of authority. This, I suspected, was something that was being said: incredibly, this was something that people might well be saying.

Katherine, too, was walking away, eyes down, but at this she looked up, although the habitual half-amused expression didn't falter; the insult might've knocked her gaze upwards, but this was no flinch. Rather, she looked as if something was occurring to her. It was news to her, too, I saw, what people were saying about the queen, and she was taking stock. But there was no surprise in that taking stock, nor indignation. And, I saw, she wasn't to be cowed by it.

That midsummer, we had our own big change with which to contend, when a girl called Jo Bulmer came to live with us. She arrived escorted by her mother, who was clearly desperate to see inside the duchess's house and didn't appear dismayed by what she found, her boggling eyes silvered with reflection of the duchess's tableware. Mother and daughter stood side by side in Hall to be introduced to us, both of them fussily dressed in taffeta and in every other respect, too, strikingly alike. The angular face – all nose and chin – was odd on a twelve-year-old, as was the smile: broad and brash, fully expectant of a response in kind. Neither of them showed the slightest understanding that we girls might be too shy, initially, to rise to it.

Jo Bulmer's apeing of her mother extended to her conversation. Viewing our room, she kept up a commentary bristling with opinions and pronouncements, all of them adult in content and tone.

This room could do with a bit of time and money spent on it.

At least the servants look smart.

I'm sure this'll be an excellent place to be brought up.

With the exception of Mary, none of us said much. What was there to say? It was indeed an excellent place to be brought up: it was true, but not our kind of talk. Mary embarked on her questions, to which Jo Bulmer replied fulsomely, firmly, evidently embracing the challenge: *No, Mary, absolutely not, because . . .*

Her own burning question had already been asked, immediately after supper, with her very first step across the threshold from Hall: 'Which of you is the Howard girl?' Katherine hadn't been first to respond, although her reticence hadn't held the contempt that it would've if the question had come from Mary. It had been shiny-eyed Dottie who'd piped up, 'That's Katherine, here!'

Jo Bulmer smiled at Katherine as if this were good news for both of them, 'Ah, yes,' and nodded as if concluding a business deal, 'It's you, is it, Kate?'

The following day, she persisted in subjecting us to her mother's views. On the way to the duchess's closet, she started on saints, the worship of whom, she informed us, had just been banned. She relished the word 'banned', nostrils flaring with disapproval, then used the word 'idolatory'. Mary asked her what 'idolatory' was, for which I was grateful because I knew nothing of any religious changes. 'False idols,' Jo Bulmer answered. 'Don't worship them, is what we're being told. Get on with worshipping God Himself. Don't be distracted by saints. It's a lot of fuss about nothing,' she pronounced, 'because saints are a comfort to people, and where's the harm in that?' Then, 'Our parish priest is a nice man but he spends rather too much time on the poor.'

All that day, she berated herself as readily and cheerfully as she tackled everyone else – *Manners, Miss Bulmer!* – and even declared herself, a couple of times, *a bossy so-and-so*, but none of it helped: all of it blared her mother's approval and drove home our helplessness in the face of it. The back of my head was feeling heavy. Alice was even more grim-faced than ever, Dottie glowered, and Mary's colour was rising to dangerous heights. Maggie had seemed for a while to appreciate the new company, which, for her, took the form of being chivvied – *Look lively, little one!* – but by mid-afternoon she was despondent. Even the dogs were fractious, Pippin snapping at Ace on their afternoon walk.

Only Katherine appeared unbothered, as poised and unreadable as ever.

Just before supper, Skid sent us to the laundry to fetch the necessary items for the following day. Jo Bulmer was ahead of us through the door. 'Kate and I'll see to these petticoats, and Mary –' she indicated some shirts – 'you help Dottie with those. Catheryn, hosiery; Alice and Maggie, tablecloths.'

Mary, you help Dottie with those: this was more than Mary could take, but unfortunately, Dottie was the one to suffer for it. Mary raced her for the shirt on top of the pile, snatching it and letting fly with invective that had little Maggie turn back in the doorway, horrified, clamping her hands to her ears. Frazzled, Dottie did something I'd never before seen her do: she flailed at Mary in retaliation, deflected only by a deft move from Alice. Jo Bulmer stepped up to say her piece but Mary wasn't having it: she whirled around and slammed her against the wall. A stunned silence ensued, probably because each of us had longed all day to do exactly that. All of us except Katherine, perhaps, who'd already begun folding the petticoats and continued as if nothing had happened. Dusting herself down, Jo Bulmer then made it worse with a mere, motherly, 'No need for that, Mary.'

Mary stormed from the laundry and it was me who ended up folding the shirts with Dottie while Jo Bulmer took her self-appointed place beside Katherine. She'd latched on to Katherine – literally, positioning herself as right-hand girl – on her first evening, at the first opportunity, shouldering

Alice aside on our way into chapel for prayers, and there, clearly, she was determined to stay.

As time passed, I was increasingly dismayed that Katherine never tried to shake her off. Jo Bulmer was tenacious but Katherine could've done it: she'd never shrunk from putting Mary in her place. Jo Bulmer's grating deference did hold one benefit for us, though: she shut up, sharp, whenever Katherine had something to say. It was only a pity that Katherine said so little – although that had a compensation of its own, showing up Jo Bulmer's deference for the misjudgement that it was because an aside isn't an aside when it's heralded with a fanfare.

Jo Bulmer's principal misjudgement, though, was to fall for Katherine being a Howard, to fail to grasp that she was a nobody-Howard. Katherine herself was wise enough never to make anything of her lineage. Her father was the second son: a hard-enough position for any titled man – inheriting nothing save expectations and obligations – but one of which, I'd learn in the future, he made a spectacular hash. Edmund Howard was a miserable failure: he failed to ingratiate himself with the king, failed to make friends, failed to make a living. Reduced to begging for money or favour, he put everyone's backs up. When, on a trip home, I'd reported Katherine's arrival to my mother, she'd wrinkled her nose and said, 'Oh, she'll be one of that Edmund's children,' but she didn't know how many children – ten? – from how many wives – three? – and, if she was to be believed, few people did. Katherine's was an embarrassing mess of a family. So, more fool Jo Bulmer.

Maddening, too, though, was the sheer gall of the appropriation. It surprised me to feel it, but I did, very much: *Who is she, this Jo Bulmer, to come in like this and take over Katherine?* Katherine, who, for all her faults, I was beginning to feel, was ours.

At the end of my first summer at the duchess's, England gained a new princess. Or, officially, a first, as the previous one – 'The Lady Mary' – no longer counted. Skid came to tell us. We were in the orchard, filling baskets with apples while Oddbod reclined in the long grass with the dogs and endured the toddlers' pummelling. It was a stunning afternoon, extravagant with ermine-bright cloud and there was a blue sheen to the air itself. Skid had stayed at the house to rest – pregnant, again – but then there she was, barrelling through the flower garden towards us, cheeks bright, calling ahead that a messenger had just arrived: a princess – Elizabeth – had been born.

'No prince!' wailed Mary.

Skid laughed: the birth of any healthy baby being, in her view, I suspect, a cause for celebration. 'Not this time, no.' She was struggling to catch her breath, screwing up her eyes against the sun, fending off children and dogs but then capitulating to the crawler, Bobo, and hoisting him into her arms. 'Soon, though, I'm sure.'

'Or so hopes the queen,' a knife-edge to Katherine's muttered aside, startling me. Surely this new queen had no fears? She was the right queen: that was what was important.

That was what we'd been told. All she had to do was be the right queen; and she was, because the king said so and no one could know more about queens than a king. Besides, he'd already made one mistake, so he'd be unlikely to make another. The queen just needed to be the queen, didn't she, and eventually God would grant her a baby prince.

Skid was keen to make something of the news – back in the house, unbeknown to us, the baby would've been dismissed as a bastard half-Boleyn – and we were her ideal audience. 'Think of her nursery!' She nuzzled Bobo's neck. 'Imagine all those riches for that little tiny girl . . .' Prompting speculation among us about the densely carved cradle and its silk-lavish embroidered canopy, its swan-down pillows and fur coverlets. We imagined a room furnished with solid gold jugs and bowls, and, stealthy in a corner, a jewel-studded clock. From the velvet-hushed windows there would be a river-view; and underfoot, a wool-warm floor. This princess would have her own astrologer, we decided, and her own confectioner, and a dozen white horses caparisoned in purple. 'Won't the christening be marvellous,' enthused Skid, reminding us that the king and archbishop would be there, and dukes and duchesses, and lords and ladies, telling us that the nave-long train of the baby's gown would rattle with pearls while bells roared from the Tower. 'She'll be married one day soon to some very important king,' she said, and we contemplated her stationed somewhere across the sea, her skin as luminous and fragranced as English summer rain.

When the speculation had run its course, Skid dutifully praised our harvest (Girls, you have worked hard!
Yes, Mary, that's an impressive haul you have there!), and
tried, even, to interest her babies (Oh, look, Maribel!
Mmmm, don't these look delicious!), before trudging off
back towards the house, unrelinquished by Bobo,
lumbered with Mary, and pursued by the dogs, who were
anxious not to miss anything, their pace picking up as
Maribel – left with her brother and stepsister – began
screaming her indignation.

Jo Bulmer lugged her basket beneath a new tree. 'So, no
prince: that'll be a curse from the old queen.'

Wearied by the job in hand, none of us responded. I
glanced at Katherine: it was her cousin, after all, whom Jo
Bulmer had just deemed cursed. Katherine's gaze was
upturned, running along apple-ribboned branches.

'I mean, it's all very well, marrying for love,' Jo Bulmer
said, although actually she sounded disapproving. 'It's very
laudable, I'm sure.' 'Laudable' being, presumably, one of
her mother's words. 'But not –' on to tiptoe, grabbing an
apple – 'if you're *king*,' plonking down on to her heels,
'because if you're *king* –' she chucked the apple upwards,
to have it slap back into her palm – 'you have to be above
all that, don't you. For the sake of your country.' Having
deposited the apple in her basket, she straightened with
a sigh. 'Anyway, "marrying for love" – I don't think we
should be dignifying it with that, because, in this case, it
was rather more basic than that.' She looked pleased with
herself for this particular judgement, which I suspected

to have come from her mother, not least because it was beyond me.

Katherine yawned. 'It always is, isn't it?'

Batting away a wasp, Jo didn't acknowledge that Katherine had spoken. I hadn't understood Katherine; but neither, I was pleased to see, had she.

That autumn, a music teacher was finally appointed, the son of a neighbour. 'Young Mr Manox,' according to the duchess, who'd accompanied him into the day room to give a personal introduction. She had a twinkle in her eye. He'd have been young and fresh-faced to her, but to us he was old enough to be interesting. Probably around twenty. Tawny-blond, tousled. Head dipped and hands clasped, a picture of deference but for the smile. And oh what a smile: a big, bashful beauty of a smile.

When the duchess left him alone with us, he addressed us not as everyone else did, as 'girls', but as 'ladies'; and he sat among us, squeezing on to the bench across the table from mine. First of all, he asked us our names.

'Miss Bulmer.' Jo smiled, politely.

Next to her, inexpressively, Alice said, 'Miss Restwold.'

Maggie's turn: 'Maggie,' she said.

'Maggie!' He was gratified.

'Jo,' corrected Jo, quickly.

He laughed, warmly, and gave her a nod of his head, a little bow. '*Jo.*'

'Alice.'

'*Alice*,' and the same, and then so on until we'd finished and he could express his consternation at two of us having the same name.

Jo laid a hand on Katherine's arm. 'This is Kate.' Actually, only to Jo was she Kate.

He turned to me. 'She's a Kate and you're a Cat.' He said it as if it were fact, which threw me. Had he misunderstood? Should I correct him? Because I was no Cat. And, anyway, if she were to be Kate, I didn't need to be Cat, did I? I could stay as I was: Catheryn.

'Cat . . .' I dithered.

'*Cat*,' and there was the smile again.

Henry, he asked us to call him. He asked us what we each knew of music: what we'd heard, what we'd liked; which instruments, what kinds of voices, what kinds of songs, which Mass settings. He told us that our understanding and love of music mattered at least as much to him as any technique he could teach us. The first of our daily two-hour lessons – on the lutes – was over all too soon, and we departed the room invigorated.

How did we repay him? Reaching the courtyard, Jo issued the rallying cry, 'So, do we reckon he's married?' and instantly it was as if nothing else had been on my mind. Katherine raised her eyebrows in mute endorsement of the question. Dottie's jaw dropped, literally, and Alice's habitual frown deepened. Little Maggie said, grimly, 'Well, I just hope she's nice.' And so there it was, voiced: the unspoken consensus that of course he was married or at least spoken for, because how could he *not* be – a young man as lovely as he? The question, then, was, *What's she like?* The presumption, that she should answer to us.

Mary's was the lone voice in opposition: an indignant, possessive, 'Leave him alone! Let him be!'

And I'd have liked to have heeded her, to have been as detached as I usually was, as dismissive, because I knew that speculation about his private life – his love life, no less – was no way to thank him for the attention he'd given us. Yet it was all the more thrilling for it: compelling, in its contrast with how well we'd behaved in his presence.

There followed three days of us being on tenterhooks whenever we were with him, listening for any mention – half-mention, even – of the lady; then, afterwards, each of us publicly lamenting the lack of any hard information whilst privately thankful, probably, because the speculation could romp onwards unhindered.

'Bet she loves his eyelashes,' I remember beginning, one afternoon, churning butter in the dairyhouse. 'Bet those lovely long lashes were what she noticed first.' Thinking, *This isn't like me*, but then wondering if I hadn't had myself wrong because it'd come so easily. Skid had gone off with Mary, who'd claimed to feel sick, leaving us free to indulge in some speculation, and there I was, starting us off.

'Can't *stop* noticing them,' Katherine offered from across the bench. 'Can't stop herself. Always trying to get him at just the right angle, to get herself a good view of them.'

I shook my head. 'Having to hide it, though – doesn't want to make him self-conscious.' Those girlish lashes.

Katherine wouldn't have it: 'If that's what she thinks, she has him all wrong, because he's very proud of them.'

'D'you think she's pretty?' Alice wanted to know, giving her hands a thorough wiping on her apron.

The question, for Katherine, was, '*How* pretty?' Or, 'Pretty, how? I mean, blonde-pretty, or mysterious-dark-pretty?'

'Little-pretty?' I wondered. 'Or willowy-pretty?'

Maggie, taking pans to the wash-house for their scalding, paused in the doorway. 'D'you think she's smiley or pouty?'

'Well, she's certainly pouting now,' I said. 'She hasn't got a lot to smile about, has she: now that he's with *us*.'

Jo, tamping butter into pots, finally caught on and came up with, 'He might've been *her* teacher, back in the past.'

'But her parents forbade their love.' Maggie grinned.

'And now she won't eat.' Katherine, smirking. 'She's just lying there in her room, wasting away.'

'Which is silly,' I said, 'if you think about it, because she'll need to be strong enough to climb down from the window when he comes for her.'

Katherine was quite clear: 'He won't come for her, not after all that pouting and the fussiness with her food.'

'And all she has to sustain her is a posy that he gave her when he left,' I said, having to add, 'Not to *eat*, I don't mean to eat. She *pressed* it.'

'Presses it now to her heart.' Jo was pleased with herself.

'Her bosom,' corrected Katherine, which got a laugh.

After three days, though, Jo brought our speculation to a brutal end with, 'Henry, are you married?' It came in response to one of his ever-hopeful *Any questions?* thus proclaiming itself loud and clear as an abuse of his good-natured openness. During the excruciating hiatus, he mustered up a smile to cover his bewilderment and, perhaps, to spare her, make light of her misjudgement. Perhaps he decided it'd be better to answer the question in order to make nothing of it, to get rid of it and move on. Perhaps, upon the briefest reflection, he decided it was inevitable, even understandable. In any case, 'No,' he told us. 'Not married.'

But, 'You have a sweetheart?' Her arms were folded: levelling with him, was clearly how she was thinking of it. As if this were an equal exchange. This second question was, surely, even more intrusive.

Crucial, though: she wasn't wrong about that.

He signalled his helplessness with an exasperated sigh of a laugh. If he answered this one, where would it end?

Mary yelped, 'Leave him alone!' which only made matters worse.

He held his silence, though.

Which, of course, we all took as confirmation, because that was what we wanted.

On our way into dinner, later that morning, we continued.

'D'you think she hates us, for having him?'

'D'you think she makes him talk about us? Or does she forbid it?'

'She'd have to seem interested in us.'

'But she'll hate that!'

'Good.'

'But maybe she *is* interested in us. I mean, *I* would be, if it was me. "Know thine enemy" and all that.'

'She *must* hate us. He'll be humming the songs we've been singing with him: he won't be able to help it.'

'Oh, she'll hate *that*.'

'Yes, but if she thinks she can stop him, she's wrong. You can't go around telling a man to stop humming. That'd be a mistake. He really wouldn't like it.'

'And anyway, he *likes* our singing. He likes *us*. He *wants* to hum our songs.'

'D'you think she's writing to him?'

'How often? Every day?'

'Yes, but is *he* writing to *her*?'

Whenever Henry Manox presented us with a song or piece which could possibly be construed to feature love as its subject, the room would be threaded with meaningful glances. It didn't have to be about romance; we were quite happy to misappropriate religious devotion. It might simply feature springtime, and perhaps only in the title. Clear evidence nonetheless, in our view, of our teacher's lovesickness.

Did he know what we were up to? He gave no indication that he did, treating us with respect such as we'd never known, granting us his full attention and being scrupulously fair with it.

Then one day a chance remark had us realise that there was something of his life about which we could legitimately badger him: his time in London, before he'd come to us. It had become clear, from the odd comment, that he was missing the city. But what he missed – what he spoke of – surprised me. To me, who'd never been there, London was a place of festivities. Everyone spoke of the dragon-bearing processions of St George's Day, the flaring torches and thousands of glass lanterns of the Watch on Midsummer Day: the press of the crowd, the streets impassable, curfew flouted, and thieves and drunkenness and dancing. Henry Manox, though, spoke of buying a cheese roll from a strolling vendor, and sitting to eat it on some steps in a garden square in the sun. Of skating on the Thames, the fog like snow in the air. Walking in drizzle along the bank at Southwark on Sundays with a friend and his dog. Visiting the tailor and teasing his apprentice, indulging his cat. Haggling over gut at the market and heading home to re-string but being waylaid by friends and spending the afternoon instead at a tavern, swapping scrawled sheets of music. A simple life – but, then, mine was so very much more so. In the year since I'd arrived, my sole outing beyond the village church had been down lanes that were strewn with bracken drying for spreading on the fields, before a strictly supervised hour or two at the local Michaelmas Fair. I could only wonder how it would be to choose the tailor on whom to bestow my custom and have him grateful and eager to please me.

During those weeks, that autumn, there were times when I'd lose myself in imagined riverside strolls under sky-broad smudges of cloud, the dog trotting ahead, carried away, and the distant river-traffic passing imperceptibly. In my imaginings, I'd end up walking too far and fear myself too tired to walk back, but of course I'd do it anyway and do it easily although, when I'd finally stopped and settled in a tavern, the blood inside my legs would be nudging onwards. The friend accompanying me on these walks was Henry Manox and in my daydreams this was something we did most Sundays; it was something we liked to do.

Then one day, while Henry was demonstrating a finger-position on the lute, he did a double take. That was all – a double take – and it was only by chance that I witnessed it. I'd been peering at his fingertips on the lute's strings and had just happened to glance up in the instant when his words and attention parted company. He was thinking, I saw, but not, now, about what he was saying. Shooting my gaze along the line of his, I came to Katherine. Somehow – I hadn't seen how – Katherine had got him to look at her to the exclusion of the rest of us.

A day later, I saw how she'd done it. I saw her give him a look which I knew – just knew – was the one she would've given him. I'd never before seen such a look from her. With the rest of us – whenever she looked at any of us – there was the suggestion of squinting, of deflecting glare, despite it being her own eyes that glinted. There was something sideways about her look, regardless of the angle it was coming from. Whereas this – the look I caught her giving our teacher – was wide-eyed. Not helpless – no helpless-ness in it – but, on the contrary, expectant: a frank expression of interest, but not, I sensed, in what he was saying. I drew my own glance away and around the room. My companions seemed oblivious. Dottie, chewing a nail, was staring at the wall. Mary was scrutinising the persistent sore patch on one of her fingers. Alice blinked emphatically and suppressed a yawn. Maggie was frowning at Henry in her effort to follow what he was saying and Jo looked about to take issue with him.

What was Katherine doing? No, I knew what she was doing – she was getting him to look at her – but *why*? Surreptitiously, I checked again, and then again and again, whenever I could, but glimpsed nothing else untoward. After the lesson, though, on our way to dinner, Jo complained, 'He was useless today, wasn't he,' and no one disagreed. He had indeed been useless. He'd seemed distracted. 'What on earth was up with him? No letter from *her*, lately: could be that.'

'No letter from her ever again, I hope,' growled Maggie, which elicited a wicked smile from Dottie and something similar even from Alice. I glanced at Katherine. No reaction. Either she hadn't heard, or she was declining to join in.

That night, when Katherine took off her hood, she said, 'Do you think he's seen her bare-headed?' *He, her* . . . I'd only just begun to follow when she added, 'When does a man first see his lady bare-headed?' She spoke gravely. 'When does that happen?'

Jo launched in with, 'I dread it. I'm happier with all this garb on, I can tell you.'

Sensible Alice, sounding bored, said, 'There's nothing wrong with your hair, Jo; I don't know why you go on about it.'

Folding her lappets, Katherine wondered, 'What about being naked?'

An intake of breath from Dottie. 'Oh, Kate, *don't*.'

Katherine turned to her. 'But he has to see you naked sometime, your husband.'

'Mine won't,' Dottie whispered.

Alice objected, 'He *doesn't* have to. That's what nightshirts are for.'

Katherine rose, to hang up the hood. 'They want to see you naked,' she said, matter-of-fact. 'And it's what you want, when you're married.'

Jo puffed, 'Katie Howard! I really don't know where you get your ideas from.'

Maggie was cheerful: 'I'm never marrying. I'm for the Sisters.'

Jo took Maggie's hood from her, took it with her own to the pegs. 'You're too valuable for that, Missie Morton. Your father isn't going to waste you on the nuns.'

Katherine said, 'Does she have a good figure?'

She.

She gazed down over herself, palms pressed to her hips as if to lay herself out to better view, and turning from side to side as if looking for something. No one responded; everyone as clueless as I was, no doubt, as to what a good figure might be.

A couple of days later, on our way into the day room, a pomander detached from Alice's girdle and fell to the floor; the resulting hold-up had us all crowded in the doorway. Henry hadn't seen what had happened, he was turned away from us, delving into his bag. Katherine didn't pause behind Alice and Dottie but squeezed through behind our tutor's back, resting a hand on his shoulder. That little hand of hers, the lightest of touches. He turned instinctively to a questioning tilt of her head – *What? I can't touch you in passing?* – which he hurried to placate with a smile of his own. Within a heartbeat it was all over; and I might never have seen it, had I not been immediately behind Kate and on the lookout.

Later that same morning, when we were taking our places at the table for dinner, she whispered, 'I bet Henry's a good kisser.' I alone was close enough to hear but Grace was about to be said, so I couldn't have responded even if I'd known how.

The duchess's was such a staid and thrifty household that her hosting of the wake for the local church's dedication day, the first Sunday in October, came as a surprise. Even more surprising was how lively the evening was: the hired musicians were particularly good and the duchess probably could've done much, had she wished, to reign them in. Towards the end of the evening, with the duchess's permission, Henry Manox approached each of us in turn for a dance. He started small, beginning with Maggie, who rose gamely to the occasion, flushed with exertion as Henry shepherded her through the steps. Next, Mary, who was resolute in her refusal so that he could only retreat, but barely concealing his relief. Dottie, offered his hand, needed no persuading, her front teeth clamped over her lower lip and winking their shine as she bobbed and skipped. Alice avoided any enthusiasm in favour of competence and, at the end of it, looked moderately pleased with herself. Then it was my turn, but self-consciousness had me making a poor show of it, my gaze fixed on my feet. Last but one came Jo, who trod on his toe, and then, laughing, he hobbled exaggeratedly over to Katherine. She was very graceful: the high-held head, and the lightness of the touch of her hand to his. She danced not for the audience – as each of us had done, in our individual ways – but, I saw, for her own pleasure. She took it seriously, her pleasure, and so did Henry Manox, honouring it, stopping his jesting to mirror it.

The following morning, as we were leaving our lesson, Katherine stopped beside our teacher and packed for him: sheets of music into his bag, and his lute into its case. She did it briskly, absently, her finishing flourish a grim little smile, *There*. As if it'd been a chore for her, but it wouldn't have been done unless she'd stepped in. As if it were customary for her to do it. As if there were an understanding between them – already an understanding – although his startled expression gave lie to that. Alice noticed, I saw, but she was expressionless, so I didn't know what – if anything – she made of it. Mary had already thumped out of the room. Dottie was busy with Maggie and Jo was interrupting her: *And, Little Miss, you'd better . . .*

The day after that, Katherine walked from the lesson at Henry Manox's side. We'd always gone clattering from the day room, freed, streaming ahead of him, but this time she hung back and took the place at his side. She did so with the same nonchalance as she'd packed his bag. Almost a show of reluctance. He slowed to her pace – had to, or he'd have left her behind. And so she claimed him.

Thereafter, whenever he entered the room, he'd smile at her – her alone, before relaxing into a broader, easier smile for the rest us. The smile for her was quick and guarded, like a signal. Whenever she left, she'd reach for his arm in passing: a touch pitched between a pat and a squeeze, a furthering of her claim on him.

In class, the two of them were subdued, dignified, as if their special relationship was a responsibility nobly borne. Around them, our singing lost its carefree ebullience.

Back in our room, our talk – of him and his lady – stopped so abruptly, completely and itself unremarked upon that it might never have happened. Indeed, days passed before I even noticed its absence. We'd given him up. Katherine's taking of him had occurred in front of our eyes and we'd fallen in step with it. As if we'd been toying with him until a time had come for handing him over to someone, and Katherine had stepped up. She'd been the one of us who'd known what to do with him.

I was happy to let him go, because he wasn't whom I'd thought he was. He was just a man who'd had his head turned by Katherine Howard. I still daydreamed of strolls along the Thames, but the friend at my side wasn't Henry Manox: he was, instead, no one I knew; a man I had yet to meet.

We began leaving them to it, going on ahead from our lesson; Jo striding away to look as if she were leading us, as if it were her idea. When we gathered in Hall a quarter of an hour later, Katherine would be there, slipped back among us as if she'd never been gone.

Then, though, came an occasion when we found ourselves covering for her. One morning, the duchess intercepted us – 'Ah!' – in the courtyard. 'Good morning, girls.' She was frowning, clearly failing to see whom she'd come to find. The only one of us who was missing was Katherine. We barely dared move enough to curtsey; barely breathed. 'Where is Katherine?' No one – not even Jo – was able to think fast enough. There was no reason we should have been worried: Katherine could've been anywhere, she could've simply gone to the jakes. But my heartbeat was so loud to me that I feared it detectable. We stood there dumbly, each expecting another to speak, until the duchess interrogated this suspicious silence of ours with her own. 'When she chooses to reappear,' she said, finally, 'please tell her that her Uncle William is here and her presence is required in the office.'

No one spoke until she'd gone into a stairwell. Then Mary crowed, 'That does it.'

Jo slammed her down: '*Mary.*'

But Mary had a point. We were carrying Katherine's absence and could be held to account for it. Katherine might not be destined for much, but it was for the duchess to ensure that she was destined for more than the likes of Mr Henry Manox. If we jeopardised that, we'd incur her displeasure. And we were in her household only on her sufferance. I said, 'If the duchess finds out –'

'She won't,' decreed Jo, marching ahead, not looking back.

I tried again: 'But if she –'

'She *won't.*' She whirled and glared at me. '*Will* she.'

About a week later, there was a knock at the door of our room one evening just after we'd retired for bed. Skid, we assumed; no one else would come to our door at that time. Alice was quick to call, 'Come in!' but the response was slow, the door opening a mere crack.

Maggie voiced her cheerful impatience. 'Come on in!'

There in the doorway – but only just, only gingerly – was Henry Manox, to be greeted with a collective, horrified intake of breath. Dottie was already in her nightshirt. Maggie and Jo were down to their petticoats, and I was unpinning Mary's kirtle. We were all bareheaded, and Dottie's silky hair was loose. He caught no one's eye, offering a smile that was more of a wince. Then he looked at Katherine, who was reclining on her mattress. Hood off and hair loose, she was otherwise still fully dressed: she dawdled, last thing; she liked to take her time.

'Kate?' he offered it like a reminder, but nervously.

She stared back, and what seemed like a long time passed before she answered: 'Not now.' If he was waiting for her to say *when*, he was disappointed. Eventually, he blinked, which was when I realised he hadn't yet done so. Then came the wincing smile again, but for her this time and even more pained. Still nothing, in response. She was staring him down. I lowered my own gaze, not wanting to see it but detecting that he dipped his head as he backed from the doorway in a kind of bowing out.

A couple of days afterwards, I was in the little ramshackle banqueting house, drowsy in the last of the day's sun, when I glimpsed the pair of them below in the far corner of the flower garden. It felt odd and uncomfortable to be watching them, but it would've been odder to turn away and face the wall. Katherine was ahead of him; she'd come to a halt by the gate and turned to him. She was standing her ground, I realised, and he was teetering on the brink of stepping into the space that had opened up between them, afraid of pushing her further into retreat. Although I couldn't hear it, I could see that she had plenty to say: she was speaking at length and emphatically with rhythmic nods and a jut of her jaw, and this alone – her speaking at length – was enough to captivate me. He was taking it with shakes of his head – trying to shake it off, to deny or dismiss it – and the occasional truncated interjection, throwing his hands around, offering them up, open and splayed. Imploring her. Then, to my horror, he gestured towards my little banqueting house, and she did as he bade, turned and looked over, apparently giving it reluctant – if only momentary – consideration. Clearly neither of them saw me; I'd have been hidden by the oblique fall of the light. I wouldn't be able to leave without them seeing me, though. What would I do if they clattered in downstairs? Would I – should I, could I – declare myself? But then they'd guess that I'd been watching them. To my enormous relief, Kate turned back towards the gate and walked away from him. Released from the stand-off, he leapt after her but she whirled around to catch him at it and once more he halted, his shame and resentment all too obvious. She spoke again, briefly, then continued on her way, banging through the gate. He lingered, kicking at the grass, at nothing.

I couldn't leave until he did. Luckily, he did so within a few minutes. That, though, was the last I ever saw of him. He didn't turn up to tutor us the following day. No one ever gave us a satisfactory explanation for his sudden departure – just that he'd 'moved on' – and while the other girls speculated and mourned him, Katherine said nothing and neither did I.

November 6th

Francis and I were woken before first light by a series of raps on the door. Francis stumbled from the bed, snatched at the door and had a brief, subdued exchange with someone on the staircase. I didn't hear what was said. Returning, having closed the door, he whispered to me: 'More questions.' My scalp crawled, icy. His whisper and his haste with his clothes made it clear that whomever he'd spoken with was waiting for him. Leaving, he ducked to my side of the bed and dropped a kiss on to the top of my head.

I couldn't bear to stay in that room without him, and I knew that I had to give some kind of warning to Kate, so, despite the early hour and the risk of disturbing Alice, of incurring her ever-ready disapproval, I went back to my own room to brave waking Thomasine for her help with a wash and a change of clothes. Then – still early, Alice still resolutely shut-eyed – I made my way over to Kate's apartment.

I was barely through the doorway of the Presence Chamber when Maggie bolted over, wide-eyed and pinch-faced, to break the news that Kate was with Archbishop Cranmer; he'd sent his secretary for her.

The *archbishop*? And, '*Now*?' Before seven.

She hadn't even been dressed, Maggie burbled; Anne Basset, who'd been on sleep-in duty, had had to do her best, alone and fast, to help her dress. Anne was nowhere in evidence, now: Maggie was on her own in the room, except for a couple of duster-brandishing chamberers. No one else in the queen's retinue was ever up for six o'clock prayers, but Maggie looked awake enough to have been to Lauds at three.

'Is Anne with her?'

'No.' Maggie sounded scared. 'The man said she should go alone.'

'And she *did*?' Kate, queen, who took orders from no one. She'd have gone without a backwards glance, though, it occurred to me, because the oddness of the request – Cranmer, before seven in the morning – would've had her thinking there was bad news of the king. It was Maggie's assumption, too, I realised; and had I not known that something else was going on, it would also have been mine.

'What did he say?' – the man who'd come for her.

Maggie bit her lip, apologetic. 'I didn't hear, he was very quiet.' And she whispered, 'What d'you think's happened?'

I wanted to tell her, I really did: my old friend, Maggie. I would've loved to pour all my uncertainties down into those deep blue eyes of hers. If Kate had never come to the duchess's, Maggie would've been my mainstay. How simple life might've been, and how good I might've been. What, though, could I tell her? It made no sense. If this had anything to do with Francis's questioning about Kate's past, why on earth would the archbishop be involved? The investigation was Wriothesley's project. And the archbishop, of all people, wouldn't be interested in the romances of a girl-queen back in the days before she was queen. He had no interest in her, whatsoever. He was a man of ideas – reformist ideas, moreover – and Kate, for all that she was queen, was just a girl, and a traditional girl at that. They were, of course, perfectly respectful in each other's company, but Kate made no secret among us of her scorn for him – needing precious little encouragement to mimic his studious, doleful expression – and I doubted he felt much more charitable towards her, with her ever-expanding wardrobe and constant partying. Kate would've much preferred his rival, Bishop Gardiner, to be archbishop, not only because Bishop Gardiner was a good old-fashioned Catholic but because, as she said, *He's got balls*. Bishop Gardiner was unpleasant but in a way that was open to teasing – or from Kate, anyway. No one could ever tease the fair-minded, even-handed Archbishop Cranmer.

Likewise, though, I told myself, it was impossible to imagine the archbishop giving anyone a hard time – or anything but a deeply understanding time. If he was indeed required to persuade her to unburden herself to him, he'd probably called her early so that she could be back before most of her ladies arrived for duties and no one would ever be any the wiser. Kate wouldn't come to any harm in the care of that mild-mannered man. On the contrary, he was probably the safest person of all for her to be with. If this was indeed about her youthful excesses, he'd be doing his utmost best to look understanding and, instead of worrying, I should be smirking at the prospect of his discomfort. So, I told Maggie that I couldn't think why he'd have called her, and perhaps even half-believed it. We took ourselves to a corner of the room and settled down with our embroidery while we waited for news.

Only a little later, Alice arrived. She asked us where Kate was, but clearly suspected nothing.

Maggie let her in on it: 'We don't know.'

'You don't know?' Alice was baffled.

'She's with the archbishop,' I corrected, 'but —' girding myself against the half-truth — 'we've no idea why.'

Alice's frown deepened. '*Cranmer?*'

'Well, he was archbishop, last I heard.'

Putting me in my place with a long look, she turned her attention to the sewing basket, rummaging for her own needlework.

'I imagine it's nothing,' I offered, conciliatorily but cringing at my dishonesty.

She flashed me a frown, her scepticism quite plain, but said nothing and I appreciated her caution.

'We hope so,' Maggie chirped.

Well, we'll see, won't we, said Alice's look.

The ladies began arriving for the day: Lady Margaret, first, trailed by Anne Basset who'd evidently gone to find her. Coming in, they both looked tense but, spotting the three of us, instantly adopted bland expressions. Neither passed comment on the queen's glaring absence, Lady Margaret going to busy herself with the writing of a letter and Anne Basset embarking on virginals practice: the tedious and, soon, maddening repetition of particular phrases. Any minute now, I kept thinking, it would be Kate who came through that door, with Francis following, and it'd all be over, it would all have been cleared up. *Any minute now.*

More ladies turned up, often in pairs, sometimes with flurries of little dogs at their feet. In they sailed, those ladies, their good cheer and ease startling me anew, each and every time. They'd be fussing over each other and the dogs, smoothing raindrops from their hoods and releasing dogs from leads when Lady Margaret succeeded in catching their eye and instantly they were cowed, glancing around to see it for themselves: no queen. I pitied them, in a way, because they knew nothing: only that something was amiss. Even to think of the king's death was treason, so they'd be guarding hard against that. Whereas me: at least I had no concerns in that respect. I might not know much, but I knew that much.

The ladies who'd served under previous queens seemed to have an idea of what to do under the circumstances, immersing themselves in the most subdued of pursuits: needlework, book-reading, letter-writing. No board or card games, nor any music except Anne Basset's. Perhaps Lady Margaret permitted it of her because she'd been the one to suffer the shock of the archbishop's man coming for the queen. Lady Margaret, Anne Basset, the Lizzies Fitzgerald and Seymour, the Parr sisters: these ladies were old hands and they knew, it struck me, how to await bad news. They were practised at it. They'd served under previous queens, and knew not to ask questions nor give anything away of any unease or suspicion. As for the ladies who, by contrast, owed their position simply to being Howards: well, until that morning, I'd rather envied their kinship to the queen, but seeing them huddled together – her sister and cousin, her stepmother and aunt – I realised that they were as out of place as we three maids were, and as dependent on Kate for their safety.

The old hands resented the Howard-ladies. They were too well bred to show it, but the disapproval was always there. Understandable, in a way, because they'd been born to the potential of a position in the queen's household but their kin had had to work hard to secure each actual place – petitioning, bartering and buttering up, calling in favours and promising others – whereas the Howard-ladies had simply come along with Kate, instantly elevated from a period of disgrace for which the family had as yet paid no dues.

As for we maids, Alice and Maggie and me: we'd neither been born to a life in the service of the queen, nor earned it. We'd been personally favoured by Kate, and she'd continued to shower us with favours. Any time that she was free to spend as she wished, she'd spend with us. At the dining table, she had the three of us occupy those sought-after places that were closest to her, and there we'd sit, dressed in her cast-offs: hoods, cauls, shawls, furs, gloves, sleeves, and the kirtles and gowns that had been capable of being adapted to fit us, most of them barely if ever worn, many of them having come to her as gifts and been passed directly on to us.

With no group, that morning, as on any other, was Jane Rochford: not a family member nor girlhood friend, but not quite accepted either by her fellow old hands. While we waited for Kate, she reclined on cushions, absently stroking Lizzie Seymour's little dog. I recalled the rumour that her well-placed and fictitious hint of her husband's intimate rela-tionship with his sister, Queen Anne Boleyn, had secured his execution. In the four years since then, no man had come along to relieve her of her widowhood and she remained, unique among us, neither maid nor married lady.

At nine, Lady Margaret led us, as usual, to prayers. She looked drawn, but that was nothing new. At eleven, dinner was delivered up from Kate's private kitchen, the centre-piece a roast swan which, dressed for a queen, eyed us accus-ingly. No one dared make a start on it, turning instead to the side dishes, although soon those delicacies had subsided into their sauces and grown puckered skins. Eventually, the swan was taken away, untouched.

Kate's unexplained absence had cast a spell whereby no mention was made of it, but no one, I knew, would be linking Francis's disappearance to hers. If she wasn't here, then neither would he be: in the minds of everyone else, there'd be nothing mysterious or sinister in Francis's prolonged non-attendance, and I was grateful for that. Soon, this would be cleared up and the ladies need never know anything of his and Kate's shared past.

I'd been indoors all morning and, despite the warmth of the braziers clinging to me like a fever, I wouldn't leave the room: I was going to stay until Kate and Francis returned. Francis would know to find me there. The afternoon hung drizzling at the windows and, on the riverbank, a wind bullied the trees. By mid afternoon, I simply couldn't believe that there were any more questions for anyone to ask of either Francis or Kate, or any other way to ask them. Perhaps the pair of them, having been released, had gone for a bracing walk together to clear their heads? Perhaps they'd even met up with Henry Manox and – who knew? – were at this moment laughing hysterically together, swapping stories and strenuously making light of their individual humiliations at the hands of their interrogators.

Supper was served at five and while some of the ladies – glad of the distraction – now ate hungrily, I didn't even join Alice and Maggie in going to the table. At six, evening prayers were conducted as usual in the queen's closet and, as usual, we all had to be seen to attend. Lady Margaret left the door open, I noticed: listening for any arrival back in the Presence Chamber. Nothing, though. But then, at last, a little after the strike of eight, the door opened and in came Kate, bursting free of the men who escorted her. No Francis behind her, but he'd have gone to his room. Kate's eyes were lowered but she failed to hide that they were tear-swollen. She'd have hated it to be seen – even I, her oldest friend, had never seen her cry – and I felt desperately for her. We all scrambled to our feet, dizzied after the day's inactivity, and Lady Margaret started forwards but Kate looked instead to me and my heart shrank because I was certain, then, that her absence had been related to Francis's and that there was no good news. The knowing, accusing look made it all too clear. With a switch of her gaze to the far door, she indicated that I was to follow her.

Ahead of me, she stormed into her private day room. It was unlit – Lady Margaret had neglected to have it prepared – and she retreated a step or two, dismayed and disoriented. I grabbed a candle and rushed to her, but by then she'd taken the plunge and was already across the room, shadowy. I dashed behind her, across the golden room and through the airlock – that confusion of doors – into her bedroom, where she stood at the window. Putting the candle down on to a chest, I pushed shut the door then leaned back against it, only too aware of everyone's intense curiosity piling up on the other side. The candlelight bounced, precarious, and the air was so cold as to feel adversarial. My heart seemed to be trying to bump me from my body.

The enormous bed had been stripped – presumably by the lone, put-upon Anne Basset, in the morning – and Lady Margaret hadn't had it re-made. Kate left the window and came to sit on the edge of the bare mattress. If she'd had any doubts, my silence confirmed for her that I'd known she was being investigated.

'Why didn't you tell me?'

Faced with her fury, the last of my resilience dissolved and tears burned into my eyes. 'Would it have made any difference?'

'I'd've been forewarned.' She was incredulous: a forewarning would've done, it would've been something.

'I know,' I wailed, 'and I'm sorry, but Wriothesley said it'd be worse for Francis if he told anyone.' And God knows it was bad enough already.

'Francis told *you*,' she accused.

But that was different and she knew it. 'You'd've gone to someone with it, you know you would.' She'd have gone protesting to someone and Francis would've been made to pay for his lack of discretion. Surely she understood that Francis was so much more vulnerable than she was? The king's men didn't have to follow any protocol with Francis: they could do whatever they liked to him. 'And anyway —' this came as little more than a whimper — 'I thought it'd blow over. I thought they'd resolve it.' Feebly, I dared to ask: 'Have they?'

Because it was just possible that she'd allow it, that she'd sigh and say, *Well, luckily for you, it so happens . . .*

But she didn't. She slid her eyes from mine in what looked like disgust.

Despair floored me: *why* couldn't it be sorted out? There was no pre-contract between Francis and Kate: it was as simple as that. Why would no one accept it? 'What's *happening*, Kate?'

Her eyes slid back to mine, deadened. 'Cranmer says the

king has asked him to look into the matter.' Said expressionlessly, to make clear she was quoting.

The king: the words seized my heart and knocked the air from my chest. So, it really was as bad as it could possibly be: Francis was in trouble with the king. 'But *what* "matter"?' I had to know: what matter, *exactly*?

'The "matter" –' she shouted at me – 'of who I was fucking before I became queen.'

I hated that she saw me flinch.

She looked away again, wearied. 'Well, that's the gist of it, of what Cranmer's saying. I don't know that it's true, of course.' She was right: it might not be true. Cranmer might be bluffing.

'The king might not know anything, yet.'

This, though, I realised, was wishful thinking. Cranmer and Wriothesley would never risk bringing the queen in behind the king's back for such questioning.

She came back at me, chin jutting. 'I tell you this: they're going to have to answer to him for having me in there all day, alone, and asking me those questions. When he finds out how Cranmer's been going about this, he'll be livid.'

'Will he?' Again, some hope: the hope that he'd see this as outrageous scandalmongering. He adored her and would soon put a stop to it. He'd be man enough to forgive her girlish carryings-on; perhaps even to clap Francis on the back.

'Of *course* he will!' She slipped off the bed and paced, frantic and furious, stirring the meagre candlelight, threatening it. 'He'll be outraged! I'm the queen! I'm his queen!

No one – *no one* – can get me alone like that and ask me –' She smothered herself, one hand over the other, wild-eyed, then uncovered her mouth to hiss, 'Jesus, Cat, you would never believe it,' an inhalation rasped like a sob. 'You wouldn't bloody believe it: the *questions*. And from *Cranmer*. Cranmer! Of all men. *Why Cranmer?* Oh God,' she flailed. 'I feel sick, I feel sick just thinking about it.'

I didn't want to hear about the questions; they were questions about what she and Francis had done together. I grabbed her hands, clasped them.

'He hates me,' she whispered into my face, her own unevenly illuminated, scary. 'Cranmer: he hates me.'

I shook my head. I doubted the archbishop hated anyone.

'He does,' she insisted, fearful. 'He's always seen me as a stupid little girl and now he thinks I'm worse. God, no: he *knows* I'm worse.'

'Stop it,' I said; I didn't know what else to say.

'The questions.' She was staring into my eyes but it was as if she didn't see me. 'You wouldn't believe the questions. What and how and when and where and with whom –'

'So, deny it,' I countered, 'deny it all.'

'I can't,' she yelled, dropping my hands – throwing them down – and whirling away, too close to the candle's flame. Turning back, a little more composed: 'Not all of it. Manox's stories tally with Francis's, Cranmer says.' Wriothesley questioning Francis and Henry Manox, the archbishop questioning the queen. 'So, it's two against one.' And then she was quoting: '"You like to be on top", "You like a finger –"'

'*Stop it.*' I didn't want to hear it.

She blazed at me, accusatory, folding her arms, gathering herself: 'Your boyfriend has been talking.'

'They're *making* him talk.'

'Well, I wish I could shut him up.' And she was off again: '"You don't like your nipples being licked, you use your hand as well as —"'

'*Listen!*' I had to stop her, and make her see sense: 'You have to tell Cranmer there was no pre-contract.'

She looked puzzled. 'I have.' Then half-laughed, as if I'd said something preposterous. 'Of course I have! You can be sure I'm sticking to it — no pre-contract — whatever rubbish Francis is telling them.'

That stung. 'He's saying there was no pre-contract.'

She made a dismissive sound, disbelieving, and it was all I could do not to slap her. 'No, *you* listen.' She stepped up close to me. 'There was no pre-contract, or all this —' an arm behind her, in the air '— is nothing, and I'm not queen. And *you:* you'll be back home, getting married off to . . . to someone.'

Not Francis. A reminder that I was only here and living this life because of her, that I'd only have the future that I longed for if she had hers as queen.

She retreated to the bed and briefly lowered her face into her hands. 'The king didn't *ask* if I was a virgin when I married him.' Believing himself in love and keen, presumably, to believe his luck. Nor did any of his men think to ask, though. They didn't think to doubt little Katherine Howard, seventeen years old and raised in a good old-fashioned Catholic household.

I pressed back against the door again, made myself exhale. 'He'll forgive you.' I desperately hoped he would; I did think he might. But Francis: would he forgive Francis? Francis hadn't broken any law, but that was nothing against the wrath of the king.

'He'll have to,' she said, dryly.

'He loves you.'

'All the more reason for him not to forgive me. Cat –' she appealed, *You don't understand* – 'I was his little virgin.'

I did understand, perfectly.

'I acted the little virgin on my wedding night.' Suddenly, she beseeched me, 'Stay, Cat. Please. Stay with me, here, tonight.' When I didn't respond, her look turned searching and she read in my eyes the reason for my hesitation: I needed to go and find Francis. She was safe, here; she was safe enough, and now I could go and find Francis.

She bit her lip, lowered her gaze, withholding something. 'What?'

Still she hesitated. Then, 'He's not here.' She said it quietly, looking up, wide-eyed. 'I thought you knew.'

'Knew what?' Blood was pulsing in my ears.

'Cat,' she broke it to me, 'he's been taken to the Tower.'

'Tower?' Which tower?

'This morning,' she whispered, her unblinking eyes ghastly in the half-light. 'I'm sorry, I thought you knew.'

'The *Tower*?' My legs had begun trembling fast and hard: a quite spectacular trembling. 'Are you *sure*?'

'Cranmer said.'

And Cranmer, so far, as far as we knew, hadn't lied.

'But –' I needed air – 'he was *here*. They were questioning him *here*.' Why would he need to be taken to the Tower? A flash of a vision: Francis being manhandled, a mere slip of a lad, a blond boy in linen and silk. I demanded, 'Can't you – ?' *do something*.

She pressed her fingertips to her lips, pressed them white, and her eyes reddened. She whispered something; I failed to catch it.

'What?'

'I'm to stay in my rooms.'

'*What?*' My trembling was distracting me; I lurched, grabbed hold of a bedpost. 'But who – ?'

She shook her head. What did that mean? Didn't she know? Or was she refusing to talk about it? 'But you're the *queen*.' A surge of fury. 'Aren't you*?*' *What kind of queen are you, confined to your rooms?* Then, clutching that bedpost, I took a deep breath and inched around to sit beside her. Because there really was nowhere else to go. And so there we sat, side by side, confounded. 'Cranmer said?'

She sniffed, and nodded.

'What – exactly – did he say?'

'He *said* –' her tearfulness was giving her a nasal tone – 'I must keep to my rooms.'

And me? Was I, too, confined to her rooms? Because of her, because I was hers? Francis in the Tower and me trapped here, hours and hours away from him. Was there anything I could do?

But, 'Can he . . .? Cranmer: can he . . . command . . .?'

She shrugged, and stated the obvious: 'Well, he did.'

'But where did he think you'd *go*?' I probably shouldn't have said it: driving home her helplessness. Worse, 'What are we going to *do*?'

She rose to it, though. 'We'll wait,' she said, decisive. 'Wait for it to be over. Which it will be, soon. Because there's nothing for them to find.'

Yes. Well, yes, of course: I had to remind myself that there'd been no pre-contract, and that was a fact; that was *the* fact. What on earth had I been thinking? I should trust to the truth. I closed my eyes to concentrate on calming down, which was when I remembered that there *was* something. There was something else, much more dangerous than a mere long-ago dalliance. It was so obvious that I couldn't voice it: it would be absurd, in a way, to have to voice it. I needed to, though, because it might well come to light and she needed to be thinking about that, and fast. 'But what about –'

She turned to me, expectant. I'd hoped she'd have known what I was referring to, but clearly she didn't, or chose not to.

I'd have to say it. *Say it*: 'Thomas.'

No change in those widened eyes of hers, not a flicker, nothing. 'But they're not looking for Thomas,' she said, kindly, patiently, as if I needed help to understand.

'No,' I agreed, playing along, playing for time, fighting my frustration. How could I make her see? Why did she refuse to see? 'But what if they . . . come across him?'

'"Come across him"?' She was perplexed, almost amused. 'But how would that happen? There's only you who knows. I mean, and —' she gestured towards the door, *Jane Rochford*.

'And Francis,' I said.

'— and they're not going to say anything, are they.' Something like a little laugh, at the very idea.

I tried: 'Francis —'

Francis, in the Tower. I couldn't say it, I just couldn't, but actually I didn't have to; I saw her catch on. 'Cat,' she was emphatic, 'Francis would never betray me.'

But hadn't he already? Put like that — 'betrayed' — hadn't he already? *You like a finger . . .*

She read my look. 'Not about Thomas,' she specified. 'Messing about, years ago,' she spoke dismissively, 'that's one thing, and anyway they already knew it, and then they found Henry Manox, too, so Francis had no choice: he had to own up. But *this* . . .'

Oh, you don't have to tell me: *this* is deadly.

She shook her head, definite that she was beyond danger.

'But,' I was going to have to say it, 'he's in the Tower.' Don't make me say this, I seethed inside even as I'd said it. Don't make me say any more. It was illegal to use nefarious means of extracting information from prisoners, but it happened, everyone knew it happened: sometimes, it happened.

She raised her chin as she shook her head again. 'No, he wouldn't ever betray me.'

So, I did have to spell it out, and I hated her for it: 'We don't know *what*, under the circumstances, he might do.'

'*I* know.' Rueful, as if — gallingly — she pitied me for

failing to appreciate their bond. Then, with a catch in her voice, she said, 'Oh, and thank God for Thomas,' and I saw she was crying – really crying, big tears. 'I tell you, Cat,' she swiped at the tears with the back of a hand, 'I'd die if I didn't have him. I would, I'd die. He's all I've got.'

Surely she didn't believe that.

'I love him, Cat, I love him so much.'

It was nonsense and I couldn't bear to hear it. She didn't know what love was.

'He's the only reason I get up in the mornings. If I didn't have him, I'd just be wife to . . .' She sniffed hard. 'I'm so scared he'll go and marry someone else and won't be there for me when –'

I slapped a hand over her mouth. *Enough.* Treason, to talk of the death of the king, even to contemplate it. How could she be so reckless? She could get us all killed! She stared at me, horrified by what I'd done, not at what she'd said. I took my hand away. 'You can't talk like that.'

She flared, 'There's no one here!'

'But you can't even *think* like that!' *Don't you understand?*

She didn't, I saw: she didn't understand. And I didn't think I could make her understand.

We let it go, neither of us saying another word, and there followed a lengthy, miserable silence broken only by her sniffs. Eventually, with a shudder, she said, 'Let's get into bed.'

We looked at it forlornly awaiting its evening ritual – the arrival of the ladies, their checking under the mattress for daggers and the covering of the mattress with its canvas cover and laundered sheets, before the kisses of Lady Margaret wherever she'd touched it and her making the sign of the cross. All of which had always had Kate struggling to keep a straight face. Neither of us was laughing now. The ladies hadn't come, this evening, and it was unlikely they would. Kate heaved herself up with a sigh and, from a chest, took two clean, lavishly embroidered nightshirts. There were no sheets – no one having fetched any that day from the Wardrobe of the Bed – but the bedcoverings, the blankets and furs, would more than do.

I wondered, though, if she shouldn't be showing her face back in the Presence Chamber; shouldn't she be trying to keep up appearances? Not running in here and shutting the door. What would they – out there – be making of this? I dreaded to think. Wasn't it dangerous for her to be cutting herself adrift?

'Shouldn't you – ?' I nodded towards the door.

She merely rolled her eyes.

Some of them would eventually come to us, though, wouldn't they: some of them, surely, would turn up to wait on their queen? Lady Margaret, if no one else, although I recoiled from the prospect: Lady Margaret, whose lover had died in the Tower; Lady Margaret with her patches of reddened, broken skin. But, anyway, she wouldn't just leave us, abandon us here, even if it was what we wanted. If nothing else, she'd be aware that no fire had been laid.

I didn't believe that Kate didn't care. That roll of her eyes was bravado and this was not the time for it. She couldn't be oblivious to the shame of having run in here with red eyes after a whole day's detention. The ladies would have to be faced, sometime. Or would they? Perhaps when we next walked into the Presence Chamber, they'd all have gone. I had no idea what was happening. Anything, it seemed to me, could happen.

We began undressing, releasing the catches at each other's napes; lengths of precious stones crunching down into our cupped hands. Having eased the jewelled frames from our heads and lifted them and their silky veils away, we untied our crossed-over plaits and teased free our hair. Then came the unpinning of the bodices of our gowns, kirtles and petticoats: picking through the back-fastening and side-fastening layers that we could reach for ourselves, before turning for help with the others. Working down the rows, we slid pins from fabric and collected them in our teeth. Weary and distracted, we pricked ourselves on some, overlooked some and had to backtrack, dropped some but left them on the carpets. As each layer of clothing came loose, we raised it from the other's shoulders, holding them for each other to step free, taking the dead weight of it in our arms and laying it over one of the chests. Her scarlet petticoat was so soft that I almost crawled into it and wrapped myself up in it to sleep.

Then I lay in that fur-heaped bed thinking of Francis, wondering where *he* lay, whether he had covers over him. I willed him to feel, through the air and across the miles, how my every thought was of him; and then, in my mind, I reached him, not with the bearhug that I might've anticipated but the lightest, the softest of touches, a ticking of my fingertips down over his ribs, a dab to the scantily protected bone of his nose. As if those touches held a strength that his captors could never have. As if they were all that were needed to safeguard him.

Also Francis Dereham by many persuasions procured me to his vicious purpose and obtained first to lie upon my bed with his doublet and hose and after within the bed and finally he lay with me naked, and used me in such sort as a man doth his wife many and sundry times . . .

Jo Bulmer left the duchess's to get married when she turned fourteen. She came back from a visit home with the big news. 'It's happening!' she called to us, thundering the length of the gallery behind us as we headed to evening prayers. 'It's all arranged!' We turned to see her breathless, flushed, bright-eyed. 'I'm getting married!'

And suddenly she had us: all a-flutter, gathered around her, gawping and gasping. Even Mary.

Privately, though, my reaction was relief: at last, we were going to be rid of her.

'Who?' Dottie, radiant with excitement, was the first of us to be asking, 'Who is he?'

Jo cited a name – not one I'd ever heard – before rattling off the pertinent details, his various properties: estate here, estate there; manor houses here, there and everywhere. This was who he was: owner of all that property. And that's who she'd be – mistress of it all.

'Anything in London?' Dottie again, hopeful.

'No,' no London residence, 'but I'll persuade him,' she laughed, which in turn made us laugh because we could well imagine her mode of persuasion and indeed she came clean, 'I'll *insist*.' With an arch of an eyebrow, she laughed harder: me, the wife. It was almost touching to see her so hopeful.

'When's it happening?' piped Maggie, on tiptoe. 'When's the wedding?'

'Next month!' A verbal flourish of triumph, because anyone could be betrothed but this was actually happening and in no time.

Squeals from Maggie and Dottie, amid which Alice sounded caution: 'But you won't be living with him,' she checked. Not for a few years yet, she meant.

Jo turned to her, eyes wide for emphasis. 'But that's just it! – I *will*.' And then she looked around to garner the admiration and good-hearted envy that she was due, because anyone could get married at our age, but to be mistress of a household: that was really something.

Not that I'd have wanted it for myself. I was thanking my lucky stars that it wasn't me. It might well have suited Jo Bulmer but I wouldn't have wanted it: to be taken from the duchess's, from my friends, to assume sole charge of a houseful of servants.

'Will you share his bed?' This came from Kate, and there

she stood, hands loosely clasped, head inclined, a picture of polite interest.

Share his bed. Bed was where married couples made babies: that much, we knew. Marriage beds were blessed with babies. As for how those babies were made: the house was full of dogs and we lived close to a farmyard, so we couldn't help but know how it was for animals. Not that we ever discussed it: just averted our eyes and contrived knowing smiles at comments made by the labourers or the pages. Sometimes their comments held suggestion of malign intent on behalf of the dog or stallion, as if the animal were enjoying what it was driven to do, which, to me – having witnessed the exertion and desperation – was puzzling. Not as puzzling, though, as the occasional remark implying that the bitch or mare had been looking forward to it.

From what little we'd glimpsed of animals mating, it was hard to imagine what married couples were doing to get babies. Skid was almost always pregnant but she and Mr Scully wouldn't be behaving like dogs. Whatever it was that the Scullies were doing, I knew it would have to be done. Their godly duty was to make babies, and the Scullies were godly people. No doubt it was done under cover of darkness, slowly, with the utmost consideration for Skid. No doubt they kept firmly in mind the end result: the gift from God, the baby.

I was surprised that Kate had dared mention the bed-aspect of marriage, and Jo was similarly taken aback. We all mirrored her grimace, apart from Alice, who couldn't shift the expression of concern, and Kate, with that look of mild interest.

'Four children?' Jo checked with us. 'Four, d'you think? Is four enough? Four times, then,' she proclaimed, to our nervous hilarity. 'I'm deciding now: four times is all we're doing it.' *Wife*: she'd tell him, she'd make herself absolutely clear.

Kate knew more about such matters than she'd let on, as I was soon to find out. One afternoon later that week, the two of us found ourselves alone in each other's company. Mary was visiting home, Jo was having a fitting with the tailor, Dottie and Maggie were ill – nothing particularly serious but requiring Skid's ministrations – and Alice, having had it and recovered, was accompanying the duchess on a visit to a bereaved neighbour. Only Kate and I were in the duchess's day room. While I attempted to stitch whitework stars – splayed, knobbly blobs – around a pillowcase, Kate was creating a blackwork border of a fern-leaf motif on a bedcoverlet for the baby that her sister Isabel was expecting. In her time, Isabel had lived at the duchess's. We chatted for a while about Izzy and the coming baby, her first. When we'd said all there was to say, we settled into a companionable-enough silence, which, eventually, Kate broke with, 'After Henry'd gone –' The pause was ostensibly for a troublesome stitch, which she made a show of scrutinising, but it also enabled me to catch up. I did have to think: *Henry?* Did she mean Henry

Manox? As far as I was aware, no one had mentioned him since he'd gone. I'd forgotten him.

'After Henry'd gone,' she resumed, 'I thought I was going to have a baby.'

This must've been the very last thing I'd been expecting her to say. I wondered if she *had* said it – if I'd heard correctly. But, then, it wasn't something about which I was likely to make a mistake. We all knew what you had to do to have a baby, though, unless you were the Virgin Mary. You had to do whatever it was that married couples did, and Kate and Henry Manox hadn't been married. Had she been thinking she'd be having a virgin birth? Despite my utter confusion, I was careful to sit with my head bowed over my stitching as if this were an everyday revelation. Wary of jeopardising it, I was careful to take it exactly as it was being given.

He'd forced her, I realised: that must be what she was telling me. Henry Manox had sprung himself upon her. Staying outwardly composed, I flared with fury on her behalf. She was so small and demure across the room from me: I simply couldn't believe she could've been subjected to such an act. And Henry Manox! – he hadn't seemed the type. But, then, what did I know of men? Perhaps they were more like dogs and bulls than I had realised. It occurred to me that there'd been a discordant note of admiration in those comments made by the labourers and the pages, as if they'd do what the ram was up to if given half the chance. And I'd seen Henry Manox pursuing her, that time in the garden: I'd seen his impatience and his persistence.

'No one knew,' she was saying, focused on a fern-leaf. 'No one knows.'

She'd told no one, until now, until me. But why now and why me? We weren't friends, but nor did we enjoy indifference. Did that make us enemies? Rivals?

'Three months,' she was saying, 'of no monthlies.'

'Three months?' *No one knew* – for three whole months? A lady's monthlies stopped when she was expecting a baby: that, I knew. So, for three whole months Kate had lived with the fear that a baby was on the way. I was trying to recall the months – which three? – that had seemed unexceptional to me but in fact had been extraordinary. She'd passed them off as ordinary when, right under my nose, they'd been anything but. How had she done it? I'd never credited her with anything much, but suddenly I was impressed.

And I couldn't help but ask, 'Weren't you scared?'

She looked up, and her answer was an exasperated half-laugh: *What do you think?* Then, 'But we hadn't actually . . .' She stopped short with a pointed look.

Oh, so they *hadn't*. But –

'I just didn't know, though, did I?' And she was back, diligent, at the sewing. 'Because: three months? Nothing for three months? I wondered if perhaps – well, you know – while we were . . .' She glanced back up but then her eyes slid sideways on a half-smile and dipped away. Something private, then: something to do with their romance. 'Well, perhaps one time, when we were in that little summer-house, there'd been some stuff on his fingers and then, you know, when his fingers went inside me . . .'

She frowned down at a stitch, as if it were guilty of inso-
lence.

My banqueting house? And fingers, inside her? I had no
idea what she was talking about. Where would his fingers
be inside? Her mouth? There was an inside, I knew, that
was specifically to do with babies, but that was no place
for anyone's fingers and certainly not when kissing. Was that
what she meant? But how on earth would he have done
that? Wouldn't she have noticed? And 'stuff'? *What* stuff?
Just any old stuff – dirt? – or some specific stuff? It sounded
bizarre, distressing. *And in my banqueting house.* 'I thought
he was so nice,' I blurted.

'Me, too,' she smirked. 'And he was.'

I almost laughed in disbelief. 'But he made you –'

Dropping the sewing into her lap, she levelled with me.
'He never made me do anything.' It was important, clearly,
for her to establish that; unusually, her eyes held mine. 'If
anything –' she shrugged, releasing me – 'it was the other
way round, because he was always so scared of Aggs.'

Aggs: the duchess, Agnes. That was how Kate referred to
her, to amuse us – that dignified old lady, *Aggs* – and here
she was, doing so even though there was nothing in the
least amusing about what she was telling me.

Unable to follow, I leapt ahead: 'But didn't you try to
tell him, to track him down and tell him, that there might
be a baby?'

She'd returned to her methodical stitching. 'No.'

'But wouldn't he have come back to marry you?' If there
had been a baby on the way, they'd have needed to be married.

She huffed, derisive. 'You think my family would've let me marry Henry Manox?'

But how could they not – if he was the father of the baby? They would've had to get married.

'I'm a Howard –' but she loaded the words with scepticism and weariness – 'which means I'm worth more than Henry Manox. Anyway –' the flash of an upwards glance – 'I didn't want to marry him. I'd never wanted to marry him.' And I heard from the tone – nothing defensive in it – that she was telling the truth.

I was perplexed. Kissing in the banqueting house and the business of the fingers, yet she hadn't wanted to marry him? 'But if there *had* been a baby, and you *hadn't* married him, what would've happened?'

She didn't even bother to look up. 'I'd've been delivered of the baby and sent to a nunnery for the rest of my days.'

What? Did she mean there were girls in nunneries who'd had babies? And did the nuns think those babies were from virgin births? I had so many questions, but no idea where or how to start, so there we were, stitching onwards in silence. Something, though, thrummed loud and clear inside me: *Don't you ever go through anything like that again on your own.* That was what I wanted to say. *You tell me, next time.* I didn't say it, but that was only because I knew, somehow, that it was already understood.

It was a surprise, Jo Bulmer being the first of us to be getting married, and perhaps even a little awkward because we'd all assumed that Kate would be first. Kate had always said that as soon as a Howard girl was fourteen, she was considered ready for marrying off. The delay in her own case was due to the sudden uncertainty of the Howard family's prospects, of which we'd known nothing before Jo Bulmer had arrived back from a second marriage-preparation trip home. She kept the news until we retired to our room; then, 'Listen, girls,' as soon as the door was closing behind us, 'listen: the queen's in the Tower.'

That stopped us in our tracks.

'How can she be?' Little Maggie spoke for all of us: it was impossible, because the queen was the queen, so who on earth was there above her to be able to send her to the Tower?

Mary was more blunt. 'Don't be wicked!'

Tiresome, more like: yet again, I suspected, Jo Bulmer was repeating some nonsense of her mother's.

Pointedly, she turned from Mary to address the rest of us: 'The king put her there.'

Mary wasn't having it: 'But he loves her!'

Back then, we didn't even know how much: not for years would we learn how he'd exiled his long-faithful, much-loved first wife for her and damned himself and his country.

'She has *displeased* him.' Jo Bulmer whirled to counter Mary with her own considerable displeasure. The emphasis was to make clear to all of us that she was repeating what she'd been told; for once, she was making no attempt to claim it as her own.

'How?' Alice wanted to know. What could the queen have done? Stolen from him? Plotted to kill him?

Jo Bulmer floundered but didn't try to hide it from us. 'That,' she admitted, 'I don't know.' An expression of uncertainty from her was such a rarity that this could only be the truth. 'Either my mother doesn't know,' she elaborated, 'or she won't tell me.' Rueful, she stepped to Kate to lay a hand on her arm. 'I'm sorry, Kate,' and she sounded genuinely so, 'but she *is*: she *is* in the Tower.'

Kate shrugged, quickly, as if to say *Nothing to do with me.* Which was when I remembered that this relatively new queen was her cousin. Of course: that was why we'd heard nothing of this, because we – in a Howard household – were too close for comfort. The duchess had no business with this new, religion-reforming queen, but unfortunately she was family nonetheless. The best the duchess could do now would be to maintain a dignified silence, and she'd have anticipated that a houseful of girl-bright speculation would be distinctly unhelpful.

'And,' Jo Bulmer said, grimly, 'there's going to be a trial.'

A trial?

Kate raised her eyes, guardedly watchful.

A trial. This was serious, then. No lovers' tiff. No shoving of the queen into the Tower to teach her a lesson. She'd done something seriously wrong, which was going be made public at a trial. Who, though, would conduct such a spectacle? Who would dare to stand there, voicing allegations and questioning her?

Jo Bulmer answered before anyone could ask; to Kate, she said, 'Your uncle's in charge of it.'

Kate lowered her gaze. Surely it'd fool no one, her uncle's

attempt to salvage what he could of the king's favour for the Howards? Surely everyone – even the king – would see such naked self-interest for what it was? I pictured the duke addressing the jury of peers, strutting and choleric, nursing his cough, peering rheumy-eyed from balding furs, his distaste for the world unconcealed.

Jo Bulmer conjectured, 'People did used to say she was a witch –'

'Witches aren't true!' Mary was outraged; and simultaneously from Alice a derisive, 'Oh, Jo, for goodness' sake.'

'"People",' I quoted back at Jo Bulmer. 'Not courtiers, not the king.' Because perhaps there were people in the depths of the countryside who believed or half-believed in witches, but no one else did. That could be no explanation for what was happening to the queen.

She was indignant: 'I'm just saying!'

'Well, *don't*.' She was always 'just saying' and I was sick of having to listen to it.

'All I *mean* is, people did used to say she turned him from his wife.'

Kate was the one who brought it to a close, and as only she could do: turning from us with a world-weary, 'You don't need witchcraft for that.'

The following morning, at the first opportunity, Mary confronted Skid, darting across the courtyard to her as if breaking free of us, lips a-quiver to give the impression that we'd been thwarting her quest for the truth. 'Is the queen in the Tower?' Poor Skid hadn't even had the chance to empty her chamber pot; she had to stand there with it, toddlers whining around her knees while Oddbod, instead of placating them, cradled Beezer, the household's prime ratter. I could hardly bear to see Skid put so mercilessly on the spot, but I did notice how she took time to consider her response. 'I don't know, lovey,' was what she decided upon, and it came as little more than a whisper. 'I don't know anything about all that.' *All that*: an admission, surely, that something was up; and lots of it, too. Her gaze studiously avoided ours; she dealt solely with Mary, heading her off with, 'When there *is* any news, I will tell you,' and a hand on her shoulder, a squeeze, to close the encounter: *Enough, now.* Mary resented it, of course, and stormed off, which gave the rest of us the advantage of looking admirably calm. I, for one, though, was beginning to lose patience with how little we were being told, always having to make do instead with half-rumour from Jo Bulmer.

Later that same day, though, I did learn the truth of the matter, although at the time I could make scant sense of it. We girls had been sent to the flower and fruit gardens to help weed. Mrs Jenkins, the farrier's wife, earned extra for her family by being responsible for weeding, and she had Mary and Maggie busy among the lilies, Dottie and Alice amid the irises, and Kate, Jo and me in the strawberries. When Jo suffered a nettle-sting and rushed into the meadow in search of a dock leaf, Kate took the opportunity to whisper, 'I know what they're saying the queen did.' She hadn't paused in her weeding, hadn't so much as raised her eyes, and she'd barely been audible.

I was careful to do exactly as she did: keep weeding.

'I asked Aggs,' she confided.

How – when – had she done that? I was surprised that she'd dared. But, then, this matter – whatever it was – concerned her family and her future, so perhaps it was expected, perhaps even admirable in the duchess's eyes, that she'd take an active interest in her prospects. The duchess had avoided divulging anything of it to us, but perhaps she'd been more forthcoming to a family member.

'It was men.'

'Men?' Men mustered against the king, I took her to mean: insurrection. That was how I understood 'men', in those days: as in, 'the duke's men'.

The queen's men.

I'd misunderstood her, though, which she spotted. 'No –' was all she said, sliding me a look which, to my surprise, I understood. *Men*: romance with men. I was sure that was what she was implying with her look, but I was just as sure that it was impossible. Because the queen was married to the king, who was the most that any man could be. She already had the most to which any woman could aspire: what on earth would she need of lesser men? 'But –'

A slight shake of her head: there was something I'd failed to grasp. '*Lots* of men.'

And again I understood even as I didn't: although I was definitely on the right track, this had nothing to do with romance because a lady could only love one man – romantically – at a time.

'Lots of them,' Kate hissed. 'That's what they're saying.

Behind the king's back, for ages, but now she's been discovered.' She searched methodically around leafy clumps. 'Even the king's best friend. Even her own brother.'

I assumed she'd be going on to say more: *Even her own brother says* . . .

But nothing.

Even her own brother.

I sat back on my heels and looked at her, drawing her eyes up to mine; and at that, she lost her composure, broke it with an uncertain gasp, attempting to laugh it off but falling short. 'God, can you *imagine*?' Still the forced humour. 'I mean: *my* brothers! – ugh!' and a little shudder to try to make light of it.

I couldn't respond in kind, I just couldn't: it was too much. 'D'you think it's true?'

She shrugged, but there was nothing carefree in it: a savage chuck of her shoulders. The truth was irrelevant, she seemed to be indicating. I was going to press her, but suddenly Jo Bulmer was bustling back towards us.

For the rest of the afternoon, I agonised: was it something that could happen to a woman, to be driven to men like that? If what Kate said was true, people were believing it of our queen. The great and the good, no less, were believing it, with sufficient confidence to stage a trial. I couldn't help but recall those bitches I'd seen subjected to the assaults of dogs: why would a lady ever lay herself open to anything like that? Perhaps the queen was, in her own way, like the mumbling, wild-haired madwoman we'd once glimpsed at the Michaelmas Fair, slashing at herself with a knife. But Kate had said that the queen had been uncovered, which suggested that for a while she'd kept it secret and I was puzzled because that was nothing like the madwoman with the knife. The queen's madness was such that it had been unknown for a time even to her own husband, which, it seemed to me, was no madness at all.

By the time that an ashen-faced Skid informed us, a week later, that the queen had been executed, her fate didn't seem inexplicable to me. Grisly and shocking, yes, but not inexplicable because – this was how I understood it, back then – there'd been something terribly wrong with her. Something within her had broken, she'd been wild and malign, almost inhuman: much as a witch might be, if only witches did exist. That was how I understood it back then, when I didn't understand it at all.

On the day of Queen Anne's beheading came more bad news for the Howards: the king's betrothal to Jane Seymour. The Seymours were everything that the Howards weren't: they were newcomers and reformists, they were forward-looking and on the up. And that wasn't the half of it, that summer, for the Howards. The duke had managed to get his only daughter married to the king's teenage son – illegitimate, but adored and favoured – only for her to be widowed within the year. Then the duke's hothead son had an all-too-public spat with the Seymours, becoming obsessed with the new queen's sister-in-law and refusing to take no – both hers and her husband's – for an answer. Last, and worst of all, the duke's young half-brother, the duchess's handsome son, was imprisoned in the Tower for having fallen in love with that prime piece of royalty, the king's niece, Lady Margaret Douglas; and there, within a month, he died of a fever.

All that we girls knew was that he'd died. The duchess took herself off to the family's Norfolk home to mourn. We didn't know it, but the family was seriously adrift from royal favour and would have to lie very low indeed. Around that time, my mother sent for me and I had a week at home. No doubt wary of alarming me, she avoided all mention of Howard-problems and I remained none the wiser. There was no talk, either, of marriage for me – my parents would've been acutely aware of the disadvantages of trying to make plans for me, associated as I was with the family, before any turning of the tide of royal favour.

It wasn't unusual for me to go home – each year I had several trips back – but I was finding it harder every time. I missed my friends' company, their chatter, and sleeping alone had me feeling oddly conspicuous. Then there was my mother's misconception of daily life at the duchess's – her belief in demure, beautifully dressed young ladies under-going scholarly instruction – with, I sensed, her dread of being enlightened to the contrary.

That week, I made myself busy around the house and garden, eager to show my mother what I *had* learned at the duchess's (the duchess's dairy produced quite a range of cheeses, her herbery was renowned for its medicines, and I'd become by then a more skilled confectioner than my mother), but, in truth, just as keen to hide what I *hadn't*, avoiding any situations in which she might ask me to read or write at length or to translate something from Latin or Greek. It was exhausting to keep up the pretence that the duchess's household was all that she'd hoped it would be; and there was a sense in which I envied Kate, who had no mother to go home to.

That autumn, the duke redeemed himself in the king's eyes to some extent when he was despatched north to suppress the growing rebellion against religious reforms. Having been defeated by a clutch of wayward, lovelorn young Howards, the duke could be a lot more impressive in a military campaign. No matter that he and the rebels were on the same – Catholic – side; he didn't hold with insurrection, judged it impractical. In the end, he secured his victory with matey assurances of a royal pardon, which he'd have known very well hadn't a hope in Hell of being granted.

Back at the duchess's, we girls had been made aware that the new queen – Jane – was expecting a baby. When news of the prince's birth reached Horsham, it came accompanied by a smidgeon of hope for the Howards: the duke was to be a godfather. Nevertheless, as the duchess ushered us into the obligatory celebratory Mass, she'd have been gritting her teeth because the rival Seymours now looked to have it well and truly made. Only a week later, though, came word that the queen had died. For we girls, this was the stuff of legend: the new queen – meek and mild and much loved by the king – had succeeded where the others had failed, delivering the longed-for prince, only to die as she did so. Skid informed us that the duke was in charge of the obsequies. He'd have had some homework to do as to how to proceed, because at no time in the king's long reign had there been the death of a queen who'd not already been exiled or executed.

The year I turned sixteen, there was still no talk at home of marriage for me. My parents were biding their time because, for as long as there was a vacancy for a queen, everything was up for grabs. With any forthcoming royal marriage, there'd be new allegiances to consider. I had no complaints: I was in no rush.

It was when I returned from one of my trips home around that time that Kate asked me about my mother. We'd endured morning prayers and would be going to Mass, but first, as usual, there was sweeping to be done and Kate and I found ourselves at the same end of the gallery. Brandishing my broom, I made a sarcastic remark about the joys of being back, which was when Kate asked, 'Is your mother nice?' She'd glanced up to deliver the question and there was nothing in the glance that I could detect, no clue as to why she was asking or what exactly she wanted to know. If I'd been asked the question about anyone but my mother, I could've answered instantly. But my mother? And, anyway, did she mean nice in general, or nice to me? Being nice in general would involve being polite, I supposed, and my mother was certainly that. Kate's question, though, I sensed, had concerned *me*. But it wasn't my mother's job, surely, to be nice to me. She had a job to do for me and she did it, she did it assiduously, but the job was to hope for the best for me and do the best for me. It was Skid's job, surely, to be nice to me, which she was: obliging and generous and reassuring. In any case, 'nice' wasn't a Kate-like word. Was this a trap? At the very least there was an expectation and if I answered incorrectly, my mother would be found wanting. I'd be letting her down. Only when Kate prompted, 'What's she like?' did I realise that I was wrong to be harbouring suspicions. She had in fact spoken easily: it really was just a simple question. 'Is she kind?' she asked. It was possible, I realised, that Kate had little or no ex-perience of what a mother could be; just this notion, perhaps, that a mother should be kind.

Instead of answering, I found myself wanting to know, 'Do you remember *your* mother?' I knew that her mother was dead – as was Alice's, and Dottie's – but knew no more, no details.

With one of her half-smiles, she announced, 'Jocasta Culpeper,' as if needing to hear the name. Then she was back to her sweeping. 'No.' Brisk, but cheerful enough. 'I was three.' *When she died.*

A pang to think of Bobo, Lilyflower and Pie, those of Skid's babies who were three or younger: how painfully they'd miss their mother if the worst were to happen.

'I do remember a lady, though,' she said, 'and I think perhaps it was her. There's *some* reason I remember this lady. Lifting up a girl, she was, the lady: that's what I remember.'

She shrugged. 'That's all I remember. I think it was Izzy that she was lifting, although I've no idea why I think that.'

'Does Izzy remember her?'

'Yes.' Kate resumed the sweeping. 'She says she was nice.'

At the beginning of 1539 the duchess made a bid for a return to royal favour by moving her household to the Howard residence in Lambeth, opposite the king's principal palace of Whitehall. Probably the duke had impressed upon his stepmother – respected matriarch of England's foremost family – that while the king was actively seeking a new bride, it would do no harm to make her considerable presence felt close to the seat of power. A new queen would mean places for new ladies in positions of influence at court, and there were several eligible Howard girls languishing on various branches of the family. A couple of years had lapsed since the various disgraces. The duke probably judged that it was time for the Howards to make a move, to try to regain some ground – and there was certainly no more central ground than that Lambeth residence. The move would make clear to their rivals that they intended to get back to business.

The Lambeth residence – Norfolk House – was more palace than house. Behind the red-brick, two-storey gate-house were paved courtyards rather than the rutted mud and matted straw of Horsham. The house was brick-built and glazed, draught-proof and water-tight – there was water inside, in places, but, incredibly, it was on tap. Even more incredibly: also indoors, tucked away here and there, were single-occupancy water-closets. Every room of the house was clear of musty, dusty rushes, the floor painted instead to look like marble. The Hall opened on to a garden of yew-bordered rose beds, and the gallery running from Hall to Oratory was no bare-boarded thoroughfare like Horsham's but a long, furnished room displaying Howard treasures: vivid portraits and gleaming tapestries, Venetian glasses, intricate clocks and compasses. The Oratory was as grand, I imagined, as a cathedral. And the stables were packed with the duke's horses. Being a town house, so close to London, there was space only for a garden and orchard: no outhouses or farm. So, laundry was collected, and most of our food delivered. Meat and fish came fresh from the London markets, whereas at Horsham we'd lived half the year out of briny barrels. The river delivered visitors, too, not the farmhands and wheel-wrights of Horsham but noblemen and ambassadors, their oarsmen liveried and their vessels fluttering canopies and banners. They disembarked on to a sweep of stone steps guarded by mythical creatures flourishing gilded teeth and claws.

Only Dottie didn't come, her parents keeping her closer to home with a placement in the Carews' Sussex house-hold. We never saw her again, never even heard from her. The rest of us embraced the drastic change in our circum-stances, smartened ourselves up. No more worsted. It was time, too, because all of us but Maggie would be turning seventeen, that year. We really were ladies, now, and needed to look the part. My parents were good enough to send funds for me to be fitted for a couple of new gowns: one winter, one summer. It was the duke who had to stump up for his niece: good quality gowns but nothing too fancy, certainly not as fancy as she'd have liked.

With no laundry to do and little food preparation, nor any tutoring – we were deemed old enough, after the move, not to need it – we girls found ourselves with more time on our hands, a fair proportion of which, in those first few weeks, despite the stinging chill, I spent on the steps by the river. The river-traffic was glorious. Even the smallest wherry had an air of self-importance as it sped along; even the dungboats hauling London's waste to distant fields. And the water itself: muscular, contemptuously strewing eddies. Sometimes, if I was lucky, I'd see the great royal barge, towed and flanked by a flotilla from where the drummers' oar-driving rhythm came scattered across the water, snatching up my own heartbeat.

The duke enjoyed the privilege of a suite in whichever palace the king was occupying, but even the most gener-ously proportioned suite accommodated no more than himself and a couple of servants, so whenever he was in or near London he stationed his retinue at the Lambeth house, as did his London-lodging half-brother, Lord William. They were forever turning up, trailing various attending men. We'd hear them clattering up to the gatehouse on horse-back, frostnails on the flagstones, or bounding up the river-side steps, the courtyards ringing with chill-banishing claps of leather gloves, with jangling spurs and buckles. Wherever we turned were men with razor-raw faces.

Our first glimpse of Francis Dereham came towards the end of our first week, one evening at supper. Despite his youth – he looked, at most, a couple of years older than us – he was important enough to be sitting beside the duke. We'd soon learn that he was a new gentleman pensioner of the duke's: the son of a family friend, taken on as a retainer, taken under the duke's wing in the expectation that over the years he'd become one of his closest assistants, one of a handful of right-hand men. He stood out from those other men, given away by his too-new clothing and by being fine-boned and fresh-faced, quick to smile. There was the hair, too: like a dandelion-seedhead.

He stood out, and he was Kate's: she laid claim to him when she first lay eyes on him. I glimpsed her do it at supper that first evening: the widening of her eyes and tightening of focus which was always the sign of her embarking on a campaign of watchful pursuit – of falconer, or tenant farmer, clockmaker's apprentice, apothecary, caterer's assistant – around the duchess's house and grounds. To my knowledge, that was as far as it'd gone since Henry Manox, probably because no man or boy had dared take it any further.

That evening, when we were back in our room, there was a rap at one of our windows: unmistakably the sound of a thrown pebble. Alice, who was nearest, made the move: opening the window, leaning out, immediately drawing herself back in and re-fastening it. 'Boys,' she reported, returning to unpinning the side-seam of her bodice.

'*Boys?*' Mary was scandalised.

'*Which* boys?' Maggie, puzzled.

Me, too: puzzled. Pages? Stable boys?

'Those two,' Alice replied, absorbed in the pins, 'of the duke's.'

To my surprise, I knew instantly: the boy with dandelion-seedhead hair, and the companion sitting beside him at supper. No one else asked for clarification, either – they, too, all seemed to know. I glanced at Kate, but she didn't meet my eye. Removing her hood, she asked Alice, 'What did they want?'

Alice was momentarily taken aback – what did it matter what they wanted? Whatever it was, they wouldn't be getting it – and barely responded. 'I didn't –' *ask? listen?*

Maggie re-opened the window and, below, something was said.

'They have almonds,' she relayed back.

'For us?' I asked, stupidly.

'Well, so they said.'

'Get them up here, then.' Kate sounded bored: bored already by the delay.

Predictably, Mary protested, 'No!'

'One of us could nip down there and take the almonds off them,' suggested Maggie.

Kate tutted. 'Just tell them to get up here,' but instantly did so herself, flinging open the window with a put-upon lunge and whistling into the darkness as if for a pair of dogs.

We were all stunned into silence, except Mary. 'What did you do *that* for?' When Kate offered no response, she declared, 'Well, *I'm going*,' and, despite being in her nightshirt, slammed from the room to who knew where. Maggie dithered as to whether she too should go – then, panic rising, made a run for it, her hair wild.

Alice, who'd only just managed to free herself from her gown, snapped, 'Get me back into this,' to neither Kate nor me in particular, and neither of us made any move to help her. I decided not to bother with mine: my kirtle would have to do, and I didn't mind too much that my head was uncovered. We were, after all, still officially girls, still maidens: it was perfectly acceptable for us to be hoodless. The duchess required us to wear our hoods around the house but we weren't around the house: we were in our own room. And, anyway, I'd have looked silly if I crammed it on, as Alice was now doing with hers.

When the knock came, Kate didn't hesitate, reaching decisively for the door before standing back with her arms folded, adopting an expectant air, requiring them to account for themselves. Duly, they looked self-consciousness as they shuffled in, their exuberance checked. The one who didn't have the fluffy hair – the stockier of the pair – took the lead, head bowed, deferential. The fluffy-haired, fresh-faced one, following, had none of his caution, the ice having been broken, the way paved for him: he sauntered in, slope-shouldered and grinning.

They came into the middle of our room. 'Ladies,' the stockier one greeted us, nervously, and they both bowed and announced themselves: Ed Waldegrave, the leader; Francis Dereham, his friend. We three said our names, then Kate gestured impatiently towards a mattress (Mary's, as it happened): *Come on, then, let's see what you have for us.* They knelt on it and we gathered around.

As we crunched on the almonds, the talk was of supper: the quantity and quality of it (both found wanting); the seating arrangements (also unsatisfactory, apparently); and then, from Ed, 'Do you ever get any decent music around here?'

'Never,' said Kate, deadly serious and absolutely correct but still somehow making it sound as if they were sharing a joke.

Ed did most of the talking, that evening. He was the conversation-maker: engaging, garrulous, keen to ingratiate himself. Francis chipped in, often to bring him up on something: he was sharper-eyed, keener-eared, and less concerned with keeping the peace, although he didn't stint with that unguarded smile of his. They stayed for perhaps as long as an hour.

Over the following couple of weeks they came many times to spend their evenings in our room. That time of year, mid-winter, after the Christmas festivities, there was so little else to do. They came calling with sweeteners – apples, or dried fruits – which they'd filched from the kitchens, and, just as importantly, with firewood, the origins of which remained a mystery. So, our evenings were transformed: we were sugar-stoked, toasty, and thoroughly entertained. Mary didn't like it, of course – but, then, she didn't like anything, and she didn't present much of a problem, choosing to keep company more often with the duchess and the Scullies.

As those evenings became routine, we grew more comfortable in one another's company and the boys began to stay later, the courtyard clock striking ten or eleven before they said their goodbyes. Mary would've returned, by then: sleeping fully clothed – pointedly – on her mattress. Maggie might've fallen asleep, too, but she'd have done it differently, more easily, settling deeper into her blankets like a puppy.

Into our room came the tang of the Thames, the sweetness of horse-sweat and saddle-wax, and the hint of different ales brewed in other grand households and palaces. The boys got around and it was from them that we learned something of the enormous changes that had been going on in our country. We heard that the king had refused to defer to the pope as God's representative on earth, claiming that the pope was merely another bishop – the Bishop of Rome – and declaring himself head of the church in England just as he was the head of everything else. The boys said he was taking for himself all the riches in England that had belonged to the church and thereby ultimately to the pope; his men sending monks and nuns from pope-faithful abbeys and priories so that the buildings and land could be sold for cash to nobles and, even, lesser men. They explained the king's reasoning: where in the Bible is there mention of any pope? The same question, though, could be asked of so much else: where in the Bible is there mention of purgatory? Where are saints, and the sacraments? And people were indeed asking those questions, the boys told us,

Francis rolling his eyes in exasperation, *Does it matter?* The Archbishop of Canterbury had more questions than most, they said, a pressing one of which concerned the forbidding of priests from being married despite there being no mention in the Bible of celibate clergy. 'Nothing to do with him having a secret wife and child of his own, of course,' Ed said.

We squealed, delighted, scandalised: 'He *doesn't!*'

'Oh, he does,' Ed assured us. 'Everyone knows, but nobody knows if the king knows, so no one dares breathe a word of it.'

Archbishop Cranmer was also keen for us to be able to worship in English, apparently: the Bible should be available in our own language, he was saying, for us to read. 'No thanks,' was Kate's considered opinion, and I felt she had a point. Bad enough to have to go to prayers several times a day, let alone tackle the Bible. The duke's view, the boys told us, was that the changes were uncalled-for, with the exception of cold-shouldering the pope, who was a foreigner when – in the duke's view – God was an Englishman. There was no need, declared the duke, for any further reforms, and many agreed with him. Not, though, unfortunately, the archbishop – whom the duke considered pitifully bookish – nor the king's other main man: his fixer, his lawyer, Thomas Cromwell. Bully-boy, blacksmith's boy: Master Cromwell was a man of no breeding, according to the duke. Everything awful that had happened during the last few years – the deposing of queens, the sacking of abbeys and desecration of churches – was just business to Master Cromwell. The man was jumped-up, the duke said, and needed cutting down.

The boys were an invaluable source of gossip on the Howard family itself. From them we learned that Lord William was so frequently at the duchess's because he was hassling her for advances on his inheritance, and it was they who told us the full story of the fate of the duchess's other son: his love affair with the king's niece, his incarceration in the Tower and his death there from a fever.

On the subject of the duke, the boys excelled themselves. Tommy-boy, they called him, or Tommo, Tom-Tom, Tombo: anything that came to mind and, despite their obvious affection, the irreverence cut him down to size. They told us that he lived in fear of the duchess, that his mistress had grown sick of him ('Oh God, you should see how she looks at him!'), his estranged wife made no bones about wishing him dead and his widowed daughter, Lady Mary, complained to anyone who'd listen that he'd distribute food to hundreds of paupers at his gates to demonstrate his benevolence while keeping her penniless.

We loved it, the idea of the duke – the strutting duke – beleaguered by his women. And that was just the women. His too-clever son gave him far greater cause for concern. And if life at home was bad enough for the duke, it was barely any better at court. He might well have been England's most senior nobleman, but – the boys informed us, cheerfully – no one liked him. The only other nobleman of comparable rank, the Duke of Suffolk, could be said to be just as old-fashioned, but he was strapping and urbane, and, anyway, he'd been the king's boyhood friend. The king had enjoyed years of pranks and high spirits with Suffolk, years of joshing and hunting, none of which could ever have happened with the weaselly, watchful old Duke of Norfolk. Neither duke, though, it had to be said, had anything in common with the men on the rise: Thomas Cromwell, Archbishop Cranmer and the senior Seymour brother were grafters, they were serious men of learning.

The duke could bow and scrape all he liked – and he did, the boys said, he did – but somehow he never got it quite right: not in the king's eyes nor anyone else's. Not that the king didn't find uses for him: he entrusted the duke with the jobs that no one else would or could do. He knew that the duke would do them, and do them properly. Oh, he'd go away grumbling, but he'd give it his best shot and face the consequences. Dealing with difficult queens, difficult bishops: he'd do it for his king because the king's word, the king's honour, the king's authority was all that mattered to a Howard. And so, fiercely Catholic though the duke was, he hadn't baulked at betraying his fellow Catholics – those mercy-pleading Pilgrims of Grace – nor shirked from hanging stubborn bishops from the gates of their abbeys at Kirkwall, Whalley, Jervaulx and Fountains.

But he's not a bad bloke, the boys would insist, coming over sentimental: he treats us fine, he's fair. And what was clearly, for them, the ultimate accolade: *You know where you are, with him.*

Even back then, I didn't take it as the recommendation that it was intended to be.

Over the weeks, we girls — with the exception of Mary — grew relaxed enough in the boys' presence to discard not only our hoods but our gowns, which left us sitting around in our soft kirtles — no less covered, of course, but more comfortable. Ed, I noticed, didn't ever quite meet Kate's eyes; everyone else's, but never hers. He'd stop just short of looking directly at her, even as he kept talking, fast and funny. Which left Francis free to do so, and this — I saw — he did. Ed was all mouth; Francis, all eyes: his particular gift, those big riverwater-coloured eyes, and they were solely for her.

At some point, she must've reciprocated, she must've given him the look although I didn't actually see her do it. I'd known that she'd do it sometime, because he was hers: I knew it, and I'm sure everyone else did. And, anyway, why would we mind? We had Ed, with his stories. Our evenings were Ed's show. Francis's comments, although sharp enough, were infrequent and brief; he was a mere debunker, detractor.

One evening, I saw that Kate was resting against Francis's shoulder. Until then, I hadn't even noticed that they'd been sitting side by side. I marvelled at how they'd got them-selves to that point: what understanding had passed between them, how they'd reached it, how it had been broached. As far as I knew, they'd done it wordlessly. I was certain that was something I'd never learn to do: this language of no words was one that I'd never learn to speak. Not that I minded. It wasn't for me, I felt.

Over the following few evenings, her resting against him became a laying of her head on his shoulder, and then, some evenings later, a leaning back on him. And then there she was, lounging back on him, between his knees, her eyes either half-closed or closed, as were his. They'd withdrawn from us, and we'd let them go. What choice, though, had we had? Sometimes he'd tease her hair with his fingertips, sometimes lay his lips down on to the top of her head, all of it as natural-looking as a flutter of breeze.

Then, one evening, when Ed rose to leave, Francis – eyes closed – didn't move. Nothing unusual in that, but normally Ed would chivvy him: *Come on, Sunshine*, then a prod of his toes or a small, slack kick. This time, though, instead, he made a face – an expression of affection – to convey that he couldn't quite bear to disturb his enviably peaceful friend. Then he was off, backing away through the doorway with a fingertip to his lips to keep us hushed. It was so unexpected that we were too slow to object. Mary was already asleep, anyway; Maggie, too. When the door had closed, Alice frowned and I shrugged back at her. Kate and Francis did look to be asleep: comfortably so, enviably so. Untouchably so. Waking them would take some doing, by the look of it, and it was late, I was tired. Easier to leave them be. The fire was low: the room would soon turn chilly and then – uncovered as they were – they'd wake and he'd leave. It was merely a matter of time, so why force it?

Besides, Ed hadn't forced it, and he knew the ways of the world.

By unspoken agreement Alice and I undressed as far as we decently could – kirtles off and down to our shifts – before extinguishing the wicks. Under my blankets, I listened for Francis to stir and leave. What had promised to be easy only moments ago proved a strain as I listened on and on into the darkness and silence, there being no distractions. After what felt like ages, I did hear a stirring on her mattress, but then it turned into a protracted business, their waking: a stirring, a settling back down again, a further stirring, then nothing again. Eventually I gave up on them – must've done – to be carried away by sleep. When I surfaced in the morning, he was gone. No harm done.

A couple of evenings later, it happened again; and a couple of evenings on from that, again. And then, before the week had ended, it had become something they sometimes did; by the end of the following week, something they did more often than not. We tolerated it. Those boys shouldn't have been in our room anyway, but they were; and now Francis stayed a little later than Ed. That was all it was.

Earlier in those evenings, Francis had begun to go further with his kisses: no longer on to the top of her head but lower, on to her ears or neck, and not absently as before, but lingering. Sometimes the pair of them would be joining in with the rest of us when suddenly Kate would turn to Francis and for a while they'd be kissing and we'd avert our eyes. That's what they were doing, too, later, in the darkness: that was the sound that I could now distinguish, a clicking of the moisture in their opened, joined mouths, not dissimilar in its stealth from the creaking of a floor-board.

During those evenings, Ed continued to entertain Alice, Maggie and me, keeping us informed of the varying fortunes of the Howards. The duke was winning some, losing some. He and his supporters had triumphed with their Act of Six Articles, enshrining the old beliefs, although they'd had to concede an English Bible in every church. Ed reported the duke's disgust: *So now every Missus Mop can have a quick flick through before debating the finer points of theology with her priest.* In retaliation, Cromwell was spring-cleaning at court, sweeping out the old and bringing in new men, his own men, as well as masterminding a new law – or 'abomin-ation', to use the duke's term for it – whereby merit was to be favoured in the new Privy Council over rank. 'Well, he would,' said Ed, 'wouldn't he.'

Meanwhile, he told us, the king continued his search for a new queen. He'd been considering French princesses because Cromwell said he should: a link with France – against Spain – would be prudent. He'd been drawn to the idea of Mary of Guise, before her retort: *For a big woman, I have a slender neck.* He'd been taken with a portrait of Christina of Denmark, until her quip: *Had I been born with two heads, I'd've been happy to consider it.* Now the quest was turning to the Low Countries, which, we all agreed, sounded desperate.

If, at times, Kate and Francis chose not to partake in the gossip-mongering, it was their loss. It looked boring, by comparison, their nosing into each other's faces.

Later, in bed, they'd pause sometimes in their kissing and I detected that, despite the darkness, they were looking into each other's eyes. I could actually hear the silence: it had a distinct, audible quality. Other times, I heard them moving around under her blanket: the sounds longer, the length of a body. They were putting a lot of effort into keeping quiet: their caution rang in the silence. By hearing them, I knew, I was failing them.

One day, when Kate and I were taking the dogs for their riverside run-around, she told me, 'Ed likes you.'

Odd, surely, for her to feel that she had to say so. 'Well, I should hope he does.' Certainly I hadn't detected anything to the contrary. And me, too: I was very fond of him.

'No –' she was amused – 'I *mean*, he *likes* you. "Likes" you.'

Oh. But that kind of 'liking' was for someone who'd be comfortable resting back on someone else. Not for me. Flustered, I threw it back: 'Don't be stupid.'

Even though I didn't look at her, I detected her smirk. 'Francis told me.'

Ed and Francis had discussed me?

'So,' she was asking, 'what are you going to do?'

She and Francis had discussed me? When? What else had he said?

'Are you going to sit beside him?'

I didn't want to do that. Not that I didn't like Ed, but I didn't want anything to change. What Kate was telling me, though, was that it already had. All those enjoyable evenings I'd spent in his company, I'd assumed that we'd been looking out together at the world, but now here was Kate claiming that in fact he'd been looking at me.

Well, he'd misunderstood me: I had no interest in romance. Back when I'd given up on Stephen the kitchen-clerk, I'd given up on romance in general. And then when marriage had become a real prospect for all of us girls, it occurred to me, we'd stopped all the marriage-talk. For me, at that time in my life, God was my private preoccupation: not matters of doctrine, not forms of worship, but my personal relationship with God: what He knew of me, whether He listened to me, whether He cared.

I'd deflected Kate with my blustering but, despite myself, I was intrigued. Ed was a bright, bold presence – square-jawed, broken-nosed, and wind-tanned; his new-looking hosiery, I'd glimpsed, already worn thin on the heels and balls of his feet. By contrast, I felt shamefully insubstantial. No match for him. He handled horses, I poked about with a needle and thread and plucked at lute strings. The most strenuous activity I undertook at the duchess's was the punching of a pestle into a mortar.

That evening, I kept my distance, guarded it: mine.

I wondered, though: was he looking at me? I didn't catch him at it. What did he think he could see in me? Nothing that I'd intended to show him, that was for sure. I suspected that Kate was inventing his interest in me because she wanted company. She was with Francis and she wanted one of us to be with Ed. Simple as that. Strength in numbers. And it would have to be me because it wasn't going to be Mary, or earnest Alice or little Maggie.

A couple of days later, at dinner in Hall, Ed smiled at me: directly at me, and me alone. There it was, and a propos of nothing: a smile that was dazzling, unequivocal, and mine. What should I do with it? Instinct had me responding in kind although my own, on the hop, was embarrassingly lame. After that, I lowered my gaze and kept it lowered, all the while wondering what I should do. I saw now that Kate was right and I did hold something of his – his attention, his interest. It'd been bestowed upon me. So, what should I do with it?

Over the next few days, I pondered: he saw something in me, or thought that he did, but what was it? I recalled what my mother had told me: *You're no one's fool.* I wasn't sure if I believed her, but no one else had ever made any claims about me so it was all I had to go on. And she'd said it grudgingly, so I didn't think she'd have made it up. She'd said it as if it were a rare quality, but one of which she was wary. It hadn't sounded like something that would make me loveable. Was that what he had seen, though? Was that what he liked? For all my wondering, sometimes I let myself imagine leaning back on him and feeling his ready laughter rumble up my backbone. That'd be something, I realised: to be up close to all that life.

One morning, when we were helping to lay the tables in Hall, Kate teased me: 'You've not sat next to Ed, yet.'

I hadn't, no. Admittedly, the prospect was intriguing. I *could* sit next to him. I could do it, and only I could do it. Kate might go on about it all she liked and he might be hoping I'd do so, but it was my choice, I realised. Only I could make it happen.

She took it upon herself to assure me, 'He'd be a gentleman, he wouldn't do anything you didn't want him to do.'

Well, it hadn't occurred to me that he would. He never dozed off in our room as Francis did. That would never happen: he was too correct, too reliable. There would only be my leaning back on him: that was as far as it would go. There'd just be that rumbling up my spine. If I didn't turn to face him, he couldn't kiss me. What would it be like, to kiss like that – as Kate and Francis did? How on earth did they manage to breathe?

A couple more evenings passed before I did end up sitting next to him, in our room. It was nothing, though, I told myself: someone had to be sitting next to him and, on this occasion, that someone just happened to be me. And actually I was nowhere near him; it was just that there was no one between us on the mattress. My heart, though, was overly pink: that was how it felt – skinned and palpating. As I'd settled down, he'd smiled at me: a smile separately and definitely for me. Not, though – to my relief – a knowing smile. On the contrary, grateful and trusting. I didn't respond, and avoided Kate's eyes despite her trying to catch mine. I sat it out, that evening: that was how it felt.

The following afternoon, as we all converged on Hall for the baptismal feast of the latest Scully baby, Ed walked alongside me. His eyes – his smile – sought mine, swooped below my gaze to scoop it up. Or tried to, but I refused to play, stared ahead through the doorway into Hall. We were walking side by side but were otherwise just like everyone else. The space between us, though, made itself felt.

From then on, it became something he'd always do when we came across one another – girls, boys – although there was never anything much to it: just this gentle, unassuming walking alongside me. Our jumbled-up steps seemed to take on a merriness all of their own, though; they seemed to be playing with each other. And did I imagine it, or did the others withdraw a little to leave us to it? We were surrounded by their absence, and buoyed up by it.

By now, we always sat on the same mattress in our room in the evenings. Not close together, but with no one between us. And so that was what it was, what it had become: a walking side by side, a sitting side by side. Never as much as a walking or sitting *together*. But whenever we walked, I noticed, our pace slowed despite the cold, our footfalls became closer, became measured: making some-thing of the time together.

Then one afternoon he came into the herb room, where Alice and I were making up some Arabian white ointment. He'd come to see me, he said, and indeed that was precisely what he did, that and no more; just pulled up a stool, then sat down to watch me. As an explanation, he offered, 'I'm waiting for the duke to –' but then didn't bother to finish. I didn't stop my work with the pestle. We didn't talk and it was uncomfortable but perhaps not wholly in a bad way.

When he'd gone – *Well, I reckon ol' Tommo'll be just about ready for me, now* – Alice took the unusual step of venturing comment: 'You really like him, don't you.' Incredibly, she looked pleased for me, and I didn't want to brush her off, but, as far as I saw it, I liked him because he was likeable. My liking him didn't seem to have anything much to do with me: it was simply how it should be, and how it was. How, really, could it be otherwise? I ended up saying, 'He's all right,' although, in retrospect, I doubt she was fooled.

The truth was that I'd begun to ponder: would my parents allow me to marry Ed? How would that be, to be married to Ed? He'd be employed in the duke's service; we'd do nicely. I envisioned us living in a fair-sized London house, with well-stocked stables. God willing, there'd be children, and then we'd send them to grow up in Kate's household: they'd have a Howard-sponsored upbringing, as I'd had. It could work very well. I wondered what he was hoping for, from life, and what his family was planning for him. He seemed to love his life as it was; but, like it or not, there'd be changes coming, as there would for me, and I suppose I was wondering if perhaps we could do each other a favour.

Meanwhile, Francis's staying late in our room continued. Not every night, but often. Mary continued to complain, which only encouraged Alice, Maggie and me to affect a lack of concern because none of us wanted to side with her. Once, when she complained, 'This sinning is happening in my room!' Alice countered with, 'It's *our* room,' as if that were an answer and the last word.

I wondered if one day – one night – I'd be doing that, with Ed. What if I was tired, though? On those late winter Lenten evenings I was so often deeply weary, longing for repose under my blankets. What if I wanted him to leave me alone? How would I get him to go? But if I wanted him to stay, how would I deal with Mary?

He'd be warm, though: that would be something.

One day a letter came from Jo Bulmer. She wrote regularly, but never told us much. There probably wasn't much to tell: no doubt she was busy with her household, but not much of it would've been newsworthy. While we sewed, Skid read the latest letter to us, appropriately doleful when relating how Jo had had a fever, but suitably cheerful on the subject of a new gown being made. Later, when we were leaving the room, Kate caught my eye and directed it to the letter on the floor beside Skid's stool. Smirking, she whispered, 'D'you think she's done it four times, yet?' I'd forgotten that particular declaration of Jo's: *Four times is all we're doing it*. Risible, Kate was implying: the notion that there'd be four times, or anything in the region of four times, or even any limit at all. On her way through the doorway ahead of me, she added, conversationally, 'My brothers say that men think about it all the time.'

Her brothers had said such a thing in her earshot?

She slid me a glance and stressed, '*All* the time.'

Mr Wolfe slunk Lenten-stupefied across our path in the direction of the kitchens, and he didn't look to me as if he were thinking of sex; but then he glanced at us and suddenly I was less sure.

'Then they dream of it.' Clearly, she found that amusing. 'Every night.' I mustered a smile as she added, jauntily, 'I'm not saying that I don't dream of it sometimes – of course I do – but not *every night*.'

I kept the smile there on my face but I was wondering: dream of what, exactly? Of what, exactly, do those dreams consist? The only dreams I could ever recall were of being chased, being trapped, being too late.

Her head tilted as if making the politest of enquiries. 'Has Ed made a move on you, yet?'

My skin prickled. 'Move?'

She gazed away, the cloud-crammed sky reflected on her eyes. 'Didn't think so. For all the talk, he's quite shy, isn't he.' She sounded fond of him. The eyes came back to mine. 'If he did make a move, you wouldn't turn him down, would you? If he held your hand, I mean, or took your arm?'

I didn't know what to say; I didn't know.

Ahead, Mr Wolfe halted, turned and backtracked – 'Afternoon, ladies' – which allowed me to get away with a shrug.

'He's a good lad, is Ed,' she concluded, cheerfully. 'He's lovely.'

But not as lovely as Francis, I realised. It'd always been Francis, for her, from the very start, from first sight, and understandably so. Ed was all very well – funny and charming but failsafe, he was solid in every sense – but Francis was something else, with those eyes and that flaxen hair and how everything of him – the blood, the very pulse – seemed barely held in check, so that even if your finger-tips skimmed the surface of him, you'd burn.

Not long afterwards came the first fine day of spring, the scent of sap tangible in the air, almost indecent. Strolling back across the courtyard from evening prayers, Kate suggested to Francis, 'Let's go for a walk,' then surprised me with, 'Coming?' Ed and I had been walking alongside them; it was easier to continue in step than to decline, and anyway the loveliness of the day seemed to call for it, as did the tantalising prospect of Lent soon being behind us.

We ended up on the riverside steps, looking over the brimming river, watching it flex inside its shiny, supple skin. To my horror, though, Kate and Francis turned to each other and began kissing. I glimpsed Francis's hand on the swelling of her bodice that was her breast, and recalled how she'd stood in our room back at the old house in Horsham and, looking down her body, made reference to a 'good figure'. I was furious that I'd allowed myself – allowed *us*, Ed and me – to be drawn here and left high and dry. I couldn't look at them and I couldn't look at Ed, but then he managed to catch my eye and his look was such a frank admission of defeat in the face of the awkwardness of the situation that I found I was laughing. It was blissful to be laughing about it, and I was so grateful to him; he always knew what to do; he could do anything, I told myself, he really could, he was so good with everyone and in any situation. Intoxicated by relief, we talked more than usual. Settling on a step, shone down upon by a couple of big, blowsy evening stars, we talked about our families: our parents, and his siblings. There seemed to be, between us, an assumption that what Kate and Francis were doing – kissing – wasn't for us; but as a half-hour passed, I wondered where that assumption had come from. I considered if I should challenge him: *How do you know?*

Try me, I wanted to say.

That night, Francis stayed in our room. I listened, actively listened. Well, why shouldn't I? The pair of them didn't care, did they; if they did, they wouldn't be doing it. Right there, alongside me. So, just for a while, I listened. What *was* it that they were doing? Definitely something: there was industry in it, that was for sure.

The following evening, in our room, was when Ed first took my hand. Done before I realised: my hand taken up into his. Not much of a move, in the end, after all. His hand was calloused from rein-holding and I relished it: the roughness, the chafe of his skin against my own. When he took his leave, he raised my hand to his lips, and, simultaneously, his eyes to mine.

Over the weeks of that spring, I came to love that look in his eyes; I loved, too, how his eyes came to me first and last across rooms and courtyards. The very fact of his existence surprised and delighted me. And to think how nearly I'd overlooked him. Not having overlooked him, in the end, seemed to me an extraordinary stroke of luck and was enough to humble me.

I loved the obstinacy of the dirt under his fingernails, the grain of golden down on the backs of his hands, and how he chucked those hands through his boyish hair. I loved his unlikely fondness for rosemary – sprigs of which he'd carry as a kind of comforter – and his child-like fascination for bats. To me, back then – having been shut away with the same companions year after year – his quirks were little short of miraculous.

There were no more moves from him: instead, on Easter Monday, on our way back from the Oratory, he pulled me into a stairwell and tendered a request: 'May I kiss you?'

I'd been worrying about further moves, anxious that I'd be wrongfooted and reflex would have me draw away from him. So, what came from me in reply to his earnest request was a laugh of relief, which he took as capitulation. And then there we were, kissing, and from the first touch of our lips it was as if we'd always been doing it, as if there'd been none of that walking and talking, but just this.

And from then on, in the new world that dawned with the end of Lent, we were kissers of each other: that was what we were and what we did. There was nothing else and nothing better than kissing, and every kiss was like a pledge: *Let nothing come between us.*

Nothing did. It was wonderful how everything around us accommodated our endless kissing. Days and evenings became infinitely expandable, yielding time for it before and after tasks and meals and Mass. Until then, the days had felt, to me, imposed: an endless succession had presented themselves and required me to live through them. Likewise, Norfolk House had been made up of rooms that demanded something of me – that I eat, sleep, sew, pray – but now those places were mere stop-gaps on the way to spaces in which we could kiss: staircases and walkways, porches and gateways, all of them conveniently casting their own cover of shadow. We spent a lot of time with one or other of us pressed back against a lime-washed wall or painted linen-fold, coming away with our shoulderblades glowing or gilt-sparkly.

Back in our room, though, in the evenings, Ed was the same as ever: more than ready to make conversation, to give his all to everyone else, and I was proud of him for that. Actually, I was fairly proud of myself. We were no Kate and Francis: we were able to turn to each other without shutting Alice and Maggie out. We might even have been better company than before: bolstered. But I did rest back on Ed, as Kate did on Francis; I did detect his laughter rumbling in my backbone before it reached anyone else's ears. That was my privilege.

Every evening there'd come the time when he'd announce his leaving – 'Right-o' – with a quick kiss to the top of my head and I'd follow him to the door, step the other side of it with him and there we'd kiss for a while, him running his hands over my face, shoulders and waist, as if to take an impression of me away with him.

One April afternoon, Kate and I had been left in the gallery to look through fabric samples, the tailor having gone to take refreshments with Skid and the duchess. We were keen to enter into the clothes-acquisitional spirit of Easter although in fact we weren't in a position to buy anything. Mary and Maggie had no interest and had gone off elsewhere, and Alice was ill in bed because of her monthly. Examining some black broadcloth, Kate remarked suddenly, 'It's awkward, isn't it, when you're kissing a boy and it's digging into you.'

Despite my surprise, I did know what she was referring to. It was a fact of nature, was my view. A foible. I didn't want to think too closely about it – or, indeed, at all. We girls had our problems – monthlies – and boys had their own: that was how I saw it.

Re-folding the length of broadcloth, she said, 'They *need* to do it, don't they.' And, before I could respond: 'Francis wants me to do it with him.'

The floor seemed to lurch beneath me.

She glanced at me, expectant.

I simply couldn't imagine her and Francis having that conversation. When? How? Ed and I would never have any such discussion. At the back of my mind, though, was an unease: had Francis talked this over with Ed?

'And it *is* tough on him, expecting him to wait.' She placed the folded broadcloth back on the pile. 'And it's not as if we won't be getting married anyway.'

That was the first I'd heard of it, although it didn't come as any surprise. I'd assumed it was the aim; no one could be around the pair of them for long without coming to that conclusion.

'So, in a way,' she shrugged, 'why not now?'

'Because you'll get pregnant.' If nothing else, there was that: the fat fly in the ointment. I wasn't totally naïve: I knew some people did it before they were married – between their marriages, too, and outside their marriages – but I also knew what stopped those who didn't.

'Not if we're careful,' she said. 'Izzy –' her sister – 'used a lemon.' She slammed the side of one hand into the palm of the other, a chopping motion. 'Half a lemon, the rind of it, the dried rind.'

I must've looked perplexed – I didn't know much about lemons but I knew they weren't for that – because she went on to explain, 'You put it up.'

Up?

Bringing her fingertips together: 'You squash it to get it up there and then –' fingertips springing apart, making a cup of her hand – 'it catches all the –' *you know*. But then she said it anyway: 'The stuff.'

Stuff, again.

Up; I did get it, then, but instantly wished I hadn't.

'Later, you take it down.' And when I didn't respond, 'Well, anyway, Izzy says it's either the lemon or you let them do it up your backside.'

I was going to laugh, until I realised she was serious.

'And you know –' she sighed, ran her fingertips over a sample of pinked velvet, 'I do really want to do it, I really want to feel him inside me.' A slip of her gaze into mine. 'Don't you think that'd be amazing?'

I'd honestly never given it a thought. Because all that was for later, wasn't it? Later in life. Married life.

'You can't get closer than that, can you. You'd think it'd hurt, wouldn't you, but, according to Izzy, it doesn't. Think about it,' she urged, 'think about when you're being kissed, how you open up. You can feel it, can't you: how you're widening. Well, a bit more of that and you'd be ready, wouldn't you.'

Think about it. Well, after that conversation, I couldn't help but think about it; I didn't mean to, I didn't want to, but I didn't seem able to stop. It was always her and Francis, though, that I found myself thinking of – imagining that I was her and Francis was whom I was kissing. I could see, now, that he wanted to do it: I could *see* it, I only had to glance at him to see it because he shone with a kind of readiness. Whereas Ed: Ed had never been like that. Solid Ed. Or so I thought, but, actually, it was around this time – or was it my imagination? – that something did change, and exhausted though he was from hunting all day every day in the duke's retinue, he'd grind against me in stair-wells and breathe exasperation into my ear. It was as if just by having listened to Kate, I'd started something that couldn't be stopped.

It was around this time, too, that a change came over Alice, of all people. One evening, after the usual card games with Skid and Oddbod, she didn't return with us to our room, she suddenly wasn't there with us; and then, when she did come in, perhaps an hour later, there was a different rhythm to her, to her footsteps and her taking off her hood, her settling on to her mattress. What was different was the existence of a rhythm, coming with her as if she'd been propelled. Wherever she'd been, something had been going on: she'd been somewhere and she'd been doing something, which was rare enough in our little lives but perhaps particularly in hers.

'Where've you been?' was Maggie's harmless enquiry.

'Chapel.'

Well, that was ridiculous: hers wasn't the demeanour of

someone who'd just come from chapel. Anyway, the question had elicited a frown and although Alice was forever frowning, this one was different from usual, a whiplash.

Tentatively, Maggie touched the bottom of Alice's gown. 'But your gown's wet.' It hadn't been raining; it hadn't rained for days. Likely she'd been on the riverside steps – but what had she been doing there, and why had she claimed to have been in chapel? That frown, though, had made clear that she wouldn't welcome further questioning.

More and more often, she wasn't around at bedtime and then, when she did walk in, late, she looked as if she were walking *out* on us: brisk and dismissive. I worried that she'd had enough of what was going on in our room – the kissing – and, frankly, who could blame her? It wasn't only on evenings, though, I noticed, that she was absenting herself. Previously so punctual, she began turning up at Hall in the mere nick of time, squeezing on to the bench as Grace was about to be said.

Then one day a Howard-liveried man was waiting for her when we left Hall, and a word in her ear had her following him away. By the time she returned, we girls were in the Spicery, the quarterly inventory having been entrusted to us.

Looking up from a jar of pungent dust, Kate was uncharacteristically direct: 'Where've you been?'

In the corner of my eye, I detected Mary, with a handful of cloves, squaring up to object on Alice's behalf, just for the sake of it.

But Alice was already answering, 'Oh –' then suddenly

not answering after all, shaking the question off as if she'd decided she could get away with it.

Well, she was wrong about that. Kate replaced the stopper in the jar, replaced the jar on the shelf and then faced her down, folding her arms and tilting her head. Alice frowned, took a breath as if embarking on a complicated explanation but then let it go and said instead, 'Seeing Lord William.'

Not such an odd answer, actually, because we all knew that she'd recently had some doings with Lord William.

A month or so beforehand, she and I had been returning from a Skid-errand at the laundry when Lord William had come hopping into the courtyard, supported by a pair of his men. We'd slowed up, unsure how to behave: we were mere girls of the household, and here, clearly indisposed, was the duchess's son.

'It's my ankle,' he'd blurted, crossly.

'His lordship fell,' snapped one of the men, 'on the steps,' the riverside steps. Not a plea for help; rather, an explanation to put a stop to our gawping and see us on our way. Lord William's pride had taken at least as hard a knock as his ankle; he was shaken and hadn't yet righted himself. Nevertheless, Alice was there before I knew it – perhaps even before *she* knew it – kneeling at his feet and only then asking a perfunctory, 'May I?' She acted with such authority that he gave himself over to her without another word, only a nod at one of his men to get down there and remove his boot.

I was flabbergasted, glancing around for someone to come to our aid, but there was no one, no help forthcoming: it was just us and them, and this odd little encounter would have to go to its conclusion. The wool-clad ducal foot was presented to Alice and she examined it, unselfconsciously uttering commands: *Can you push against me? There? Does that – ? How about there? A little harder? That's right, against my palm.*

He grumbled and exclaimed but his breathing was coming under control.

I stood there, useless but attentive, focusing on the foot to avoid looking the wretched Lord William in the face. Eventually Alice gestured for the attending man to replace the boot. 'It's a twist, my lord,' she confirmed, standing up, 'not a break.' Then, 'My advice is to keep it raised. We'll go and get some cold cloths to wrap it in.'

Would we?

'Where,' she asked the attending men, 'shall we bring them?'

The duchess's day room, we were told.

Lord William was still awkward, but also grateful. 'Thank you,' he said to her, unsmiling, grave; and called after her, 'thank you.'

We didn't catch each other's eye until we were out of their sight. I was surprised to find that I was shaking. 'How do you know about ankles?'

'Five brothers,' was the answer.

'That's a lot of ankles.'

'Ten,' she confirmed, with no glimmer of humour.

As good as her word, she did take those cool cloths to the day room where, to my relief, they were taken from us at the door. And that, I'd assumed, was the end of it, except for her taking delivery, days later, of a token of Lord William's gratitude – a drawstring purse embroidered with foxgloves – and enlisting Skid's help to write back with her own thanks.

Was she now saying that something had been going on ever since?

'Lord William?' Kate queried. 'What did he want with you?'

'Just –'

'Just what?'

'To talk,' and, to my surprise, she unleashed on Kate a defiant glare: *Satisfied?*

Far from it. 'Talk?' As if that were preposterous, which, I suppose, it was: Howard men weren't known for their conversation, and certainly not with girls. 'What about?'

Evasive, again: a shrug.

Kate persisted: 'He wants to talk to *you*?'

Uncalled for, and I cringed, busied myself with a jar of nutmegs.

Alice, though, shrugged it off, at which point Kate had the sense to leave it.

Whatever was going on, it continued apace, Alice often gone. Hard to imagine from the look of him, but Lord William obviously had a fair bit to say. He'd picked well: Alice was no talker, which, by default, must've made her a listener of a kind. Kate continued to be cynical, but behind Alice's back. *Off for a good bout of talk*, she'd say; *Off for a talking-to*. I couldn't fathom her displeasure. Was it because this involved her own uncle? Step-uncle, though, and anyway they had no relationship whatsoever – I'd never witnessed them exchange so much as a glance. Frankly, Lord William was embarrassing: that rattled-looking, pinch-mouthed man. So, I didn't think her gripe came from any sense of trespass. Was it, then, because Alice – plain, boring, unassuming Alice – had been singled out? Was that somehow an affront to Kate?

Once, disparaging, she put it to me: 'Do men *ever* just talk?'

Well, certainly she and Francis didn't seem to; but I'd not have said she appeared to miss it.

Ed was a talker – even if there was nothing to say, he always managed to come up with something and to make it entertaining, too – but, of course, he didn't *just* talk. He kissed, too. Whereas Lord William: he couldn't do anything but talk to Alice, because he was married and she was in the care of his mother.

Once, Kate said to me, 'He's probably trying to get her to lend him some money,' which, I have to admit, did make me laugh.

Sometimes, she'd veer to being defensive on Alice's behalf: *He really shouldn't be behaving like this towards her; she's worth more than this, she deserves more than being strung along.* I wondered, though: what was 'this' that she deserved more than? And was she really being strung along? Then she'd be back to finding Alice at fault: *He'll be behaving like this with all his women-servants, so if she thinks she's going to get something out of this, she's mistaken.*

I didn't think that Alice was planning on getting anything out of it. I didn't know her well, despite all the years that we'd lived alongside each other, but I did know that much, and Kate's diatribes had the effect of making me feel sorry not for Alice but for Kate.

One day when we leaving the Oratory after Mass, Kate whispered to me, 'Come to the kitchens.'

Kitchens? But didn't we usually steer clear of the kitchens? Go too close and there was the danger of being enlisted: the dreaded call of cook or steward – *Ah!* – and a tray handed over (*Could you . . .? To Mrs Scully?*) or a basketful of something needing to be trimmed or topped and tailed. In the kitchens, a person – any person, even passing – was no more than a pair of hands.

There was a shine to her eyes. 'Lemon-hunting.'

It took me a moment. Then I laughed.

She laughed, too, but, 'I'm serious,' and her fingers closed on my forearm.

I tried and failed to shake her off. 'You *can't*,' although I wasn't clear myself whether I was referring simply to stealing from the kitchens.

She raised her eyebrows: *Just watch me.*

Which was exactly what everyone was doing, I felt, as we made our way there. Two girls heading for the kitchens? Two girls, one full of purpose, leading with that determined chin of hers; the other, skulking. Oh, a lemon, definitely: half each. There were sidelong glances from the duke's men,

I was sure of it. *So, leave her,* I told myself, *drop away behind her.* Trooping along in her wake, though, I persuaded myself that when the time came, she'd grapple with the half-lemon, find it impossible – unwieldy – and give up. No harm done, and then that would be that. If she wanted to mess about with fruit, who was I to stop her? *Be it on your own head.* Or, indeed, wherever.

When we stopped at one of the lesser-used doors to the kitchens, I looked to her to know where fresh lemons would be kept. We'd had no dealings with lemons, we'd never been let loose on imported fruit. Reading my look, she shrugged, wide-eyed, clearly enjoying being clueless, the challenge of it, then took a guess, the obvious one: 'Fruit store?'

Down the stairs and third door along from the wine cellar.

Inside the fruit store, apples on racks soured the darkness like tiny severed heads.

'Stand guard,' she hissed, then urged herself amid the racks and along the shelves, 'Lemons, lemons, lemons . . .' before, 'Oranges!' with a trace of a laugh in it.

Come on, I willed her, *come on.*

And after what felt like ages: '*Lemons!*'

'Quick,' I sent back behind me.

'All right, all right.' She emerged and shoved me, unnecessarily, in the direction of the stairs.

Not until we were outside and across the yard did she open her hand to reveal it to me: such an imperfect-looking little thing, lumpy-skinned. She glossed it with her thumbpad. 'They were in sawdust,' she said, 'in a box.'

Inexplicably, I shivered.

'Do you think it's the right size?' She was serious. 'There were six or seven in there and they were all different sizes; I just went for a middle-sized one —'

And suddenly we were laughing at the absurdity of the discussion. Catching my breath, I asked her, 'Are you really, really going to do this?'

She didn't respond, and her silence said loud and clear, *Are we going to have to go through all that again?*

She'd already told me that not only had her sister had sex with her husband before their marriage, but there'd been a handful of boys and men before him. And the same had been true, she'd insisted, of some of Izzy's companions at the duchess's, and of friends Izzy had made since her marriage. Kate had even named the ladies to me, to substantiate her claims. She said that men might well want their spinster-brides to be virgins, but they knew and accepted that they often weren't. And of course they knew it, she said, because — think about it — who are those spinsters doing it with? Men know very well what girls are up to, she'd said, because they're up to it with them. Some of them, she'd claimed, even liked the idea of it: they liked a lady with a bit of experience. That was how it'd been for her sister's husband: it'd quite excited him, he'd liked her to tell him all about what she'd done, he'd liked to think about it and she'd even ended up making bits up for him.

Now she closed her hand over the lemon.

I was worried. 'What if it doesn't work?'

We set off back towards our room. 'It can't *not*, can it?

It just −' and again she cupped her free hand as when she'd first told me − 'catches everything.' Then, genuinely, '*Could it not work, d'you think?*'

Don't ask me. And something else had been puzzling me: 'How do you get it back down again?' At a push, I could accept that it could be got up there − but down?

'Well, it must be possible,' she said, 'because Izzy did it and she didn't say it was difficult.' One of her half-smiles: '*What −*'

'− *goes up* . . . I know, I know.'

'I mean, it's not endless, up there, is it? It's not some cavern.'

How did she know? I had absolutely no idea what was 'up there'.

'Unless −' a sideways glint − 'you're the endlessly baby-laying Skid, that is. I doubt there's a fruit on God's earth that can help Skid.'

Later, when everyone else was busy filing into Hall for dinner, I kept watch as Kate slipped into the duchess's day room and secreted the two halves of rind on a jutting stone high up in the fireplace so that it could dry out. 'It'll just bring us closer, Francis and me,' she said to me as we began our dash to Hall, 'and how can that be bad? It's just the next stage for us. And if I do get pregnant, then so what? Just happens sooner than it might've done. It'll serve to focus the duke's mind.'

That'd be a huge favour, though, from the duke − to allow her to marry as she wished − and I doubted that any forcing of his hand was the way to win him over.

From its hidey-hole there, it haunted me, that eviscerated, toughening lemon. I suspected that boys and girls had always met up after dark and hung around together – if not in their rooms then in stairwells or stables or orchards – and while the duchess wouldn't be best pleased if she came to know of it, the worst we'd suffer would be a thorough ticking off. Boys in our room of an evening was one thing, though; intimacies involving half a lemon were something else. Even if Kate was right and men knew and accepted that not every spinster-bride was a virgin, there was a façade to be kept and, knowing about the lemon, I was behind that façade. And the duchess wouldn't want me there. That wasn't my place.

From then onwards, I tried not to listen at night, I tried so hard – as if it were me rather than the pair of them who should be lying dead still and stealthy. I didn't seriously think they'd do it there, in our room, on the mattress next to mine – but in the darkness, late, their leave-taking definitely became more protracted.

A week later, on May Day, when the household gathered in and around the arbour that had been built from lopped boughs in the garden for the festivities, there was a touch of Kate's fingertips to my arm and her breath in my ear: 'We're going to slip off, this evening.' *We*: her and Francis. She was business-like as she let me in on it: no smile. Serious business, this: time for the lemon. *Don't you ever go through anything like that again on your own* . . . Well, here I was, being told; but, then, she'd be needing someone – one of us – to know, to be able, if necessary, to cover for her.

Slip off where?

I didn't ask, but she told me anyway: 'Our room, while everyone's busy.' The household was being treated to a masque, after the feast, and, after that, dancing: for once, we were all going to be very busy until late. 'I want a bed, Cat,' she made clear. 'I want it to be special.'

'Yes,' I heard myself agreeing with her. 'Of course.' Then, 'What should I say?' *When anyone asks.*

She shrugged. 'You can say whatever you like.'

That evening, they saved their disappearing act for the dance and then, suddenly, there it was, done: I looked around the crowded Hall for them and they'd gone. I both knew what was happening and didn't know, which was the oddest feeling. Maggie was first of the others to notice Kate's absence, perhaps a quarter of an hour later: 'Where's Kate?' Then, 'Oh –' a glance around, 'Francis, too,' *Silly me.* She was assuming, though, I knew, that they were outside some-where, kissing amid heart-shaped lilac leaves under a sky crackling with starlight. Then Skid came across the dance floor: 'Where's Kate?' Concerned that she was missing the fun. She didn't know to look for Francis, for his absence.

'Headache,' I said, hoping hard that Kate didn't burst back into Hall in glowing health.

Skid was pained on her behalf – 'Oh dear!' – and my heart gave little kicks of protest: *Liar*, it said; *Liar, liar, liar.*

Ed and I danced together many times, that evening, but there was, I felt, an awkwardness between us. Neither of us knew for certain that the other knew what was happening between Kate and Francis. I didn't like how Ed looked uncomfortable. Francis, in his place, I suspected, wouldn't have looked like that; he'd have carried it off with aplomb.

I wondered if Kate and Francis would reappear but they didn't and, by the end of the evening, I was dreading the scene into which we girls would stumble when we reached our room. What we found there, though, was Kate alone on her mattress, asleep or at least feigning sleep. We disturbed her by turning up, but she turned away with a harsh sigh of exasperation which the others didn't heed. They were over-excited and over-tired. I was mindful of her, though. Her presence there posed so many questions, but even if I'd known what to ask her, and even if she'd answered me, I didn't know that I'd have understood.

The following day, nothing was mentioned; she gave no indication of anything having happened. Perhaps it hadn't. Either way, she seemed to want to keep it to herself, and fair enough; and I was relieved, in a way, because nothing was expected of me. I'd find out sooner or later, I knew, and I was in no rush. Then again, I couldn't quite relax: I was forever watching my back, fearing that I'd turn around and there she'd be, springing some revelation on me.

She and Francis made three further discreet disappearances, that week; it was a busy time for the household and they made the most of it, slipping away under cover of the various picnics and river-trips. She didn't bother to warn me any more: I'd turn to say something to her but she wouldn't be there, and it was like falling off a step, a tiny misjudgement that reverberated through me. I understood that I'd been called upon – wordlessly – to cover for her, should the need arise, and I didn't resent it; if anything, I was flattered. I was the one, I felt, who enabled those disappearances to happen.

As for Ed and me: that May week when we should've been in high, playful spirits, we were merely going through the motions. We didn't spend any time together, anyway, except in the company of others. There was so much company, that week, that we'd have had to make a conscious effort to avoid it and, notably, neither of us did.

Towards the end of the week, when we girls were freshening the flower arrangements in the Hall and Kate and I had drifted together to the top table, she paused emphatically – sprig of blossom aloft – to give me a very deliberate look. Softened, though: none of the usual deflective glare and tilted chin, and her eyes were widened rather than narrowed. She'd paused as if she'd been called to account, which she hadn't: I'd said nothing. It became clear, though, that for all this pose of hers, this apparent teetering on the brink, I was the one who was going to have to actually raise the subject. Tentatively, I whispered, 'Are you all right?' She'd know what that meant, but she could take it however she wished. She gave me a grateful little smile, '*Very* all right, thank you,' before treating me to a very different kind of smile, a real one, the biggest I'd ever seen from her, the shock and thrill of it flaring beneath my breastbone. 'D'you know,' she confided, 'I think I'm going to need a whole lemon tree of my own.'

I was shocked anew, but so pleasurably that a laugh bubbled up; and then there we were, flowers laid aside on the table, both laughing.

'An *orchard*,' I whispered back.

'An *estate*.' But then she drew in her lower lip and I knew that something different was coming. A question: 'Cat, listen – could I be harming myself? I mean, is it possible –' she was clearly anxious – 'to do it too much? Could you –' a shrug, *I don't know* – 'wear yourself away?' Understandably, she grimaced at the prospect.

I had absolutely no idea, but she certainly had me worried. 'Well . . .' *I don't know*, 'does it feel like you're . . . being . . . worn away?' Could I even ask that? Well, I just had. And anyway, she was the one who'd started it.

She considered: 'No, actually.' Then a rush, 'Oh God, no, no, not at all,' concluding, 'I think I must be made for it.'

At that point, Skid reappeared in the far, bough-wreathed doorway, flanked by her corpulent husband and lean, hungry-eyed Mr Wolfe; and there, surveying the tables, they held a brief, earnest discussion. We waited until they'd gone before Kate resumed, 'What about you and Ed? When will you start doing it?'

I didn't know how to answer that. The answer was that I didn't want to do it with Ed.

A table away, Mary sneezed and, reminded of her presence and of – more distantly – Alice and Maggie, we turned cautious again. Then, from Kate, 'Are you worried it'll hurt? I know Ed's a big bloke, but it doesn't work that way. Izzy said the biggest she ever had –' she straightened up a handful of irises – 'well, my father's master of the horse was really quite a small man, but Izzy said he had far the biggest.'

Which had me laughing again.

'What?' She, too, though. '*What?*'

'*You.*' Was there no end to her knowledge and the seriousness with which she took it all?

Discarding some wilted primroses, she said, 'But you could *not*, of course. You could refuse.'

Unbeknown to her, I was in no position to refuse anything because nothing had been asked of me. Good news, though, that – if and when the time came – refusal would be an option.

'Some ladies do,' and suddenly she sounded keen to give them the respect they were due. 'Honor Baynton did: Izzy told me. Honor was always very definite –' and she raised her own hand – '"Not until the ring's on my finger."' She dried her hands on her apron. 'I mean, there are other things to do, aren't there.'

It took me a moment to realise that she was referring to bed: other things to do in bed, not other things to do with one's time in general such as flower-arranging. I hoped she just meant kissing. *Please don't mention the back passage again.*

She lifted an impressively flower-filled pitcher for taking over to the buffet. 'Izzy always said that once men get their way, that's all they ever want to do. I wouldn't say that was completely true of Francis, but I do know what she means.' She smiled across at Alice, raised the pitcher to her: *See?* Then, to me, speaking sideways as she turned away, 'I mean, ideally you'd just have them lick you all the time, wouldn't you,' and then, even more baffling, 'just as long as you didn't have to do it back very often.'

All this talk of hers had made me realise that, although I liked Ed's company, I wanted no more from him: no ring on the finger and certainly no licking. Once I'd acknowledged it, the kissing, even, became a bore, a chore. I couldn't explain it to myself, such a profound change, but it was a fact. Ed knew it, too. The way that he looked at me, with questions in his eyes that I didn't want to answer. I didn't feel obliged or beholden to him. I knew very well that I owed him nothing. And all the conversation that I'd always so much enjoyed: I was beginning to realise that I'd heard it all before – if not word for word, then in kind, and I didn't want to have to sit there listening to more of it for years to come.

So, one day I made up my mind and asked him to meet me later, before supper, on the riverside steps. It was a creamy evening and when he arrived we stood side by side for a while to savour it, spotting a heron hunched in flight, before I braved myself to break it to him that I needed to be on my own. I didn't know how else to put it. He didn't look at me. 'I'll leave you alone,' he sighed. 'I'll back off. Have as much time as you need.'

So, unfortunately, I had to spell it out for him: 'For good,' I clarified, doing my best to sound suitably apologetic.

He didn't like that. 'That's ridiculous,' he said, frowning at me. 'Because how can you know? Take a break,' he said: 'I've offered you that.'

Offered: that rankled, and only hardened my resolve.

'I do know,' I said.

'You don't,' he countered. 'How can you?' He was angry, but what had me flinch was the note of disgust. A chasm had opened between what he'd thought or hoped I was, and what he now saw I was. Stupidly – *stupidly* – I'd assumed he'd be understanding. I'd assumed that he'd rise to it, for my sake. And the shock of it: he'd always been kind and fun, but here suddenly was someone else quite different. I'd been stupid not to see it. I was having a narrow escape, it seemed. Suddenly it was imperative that I go for it, that escape.

Then he came at me with, 'What's this *about*?' Suspicious, accusatory.

I didn't follow: it was about what I'd said it was about.

'Is there something you're scared of?' Unpleasant, insin-uating, and I guessed what he was referring to. Unbeknown to me, he'd had plans for us – we were going to be doing what Kate and Francis were doing – and he didn't like that I wasn't going to go along with them. I didn't rise to that; did my best to ignore it and merely reiterated: 'Ed, I want to be on my own.' I didn't care about explaining it, I didn't care what he understood of it, because, clearly, *he* didn't care; he simply wanted something of me and was annoyed that he'd now be denied it.

From then onwards he kept out of my way, which was easy because the hunting season was at its peak and he was out with the duke all day every day and, in the evenings, like all the men, he was exhausted. He'd have had to make a special effort to come and find me, and he didn't.

I was thankful for being left alone but I didn't experience the relief that I'd anticipated, probably because I was dogged by a sense of having been cheated. I had no grounds, I was being unfair, because I'd never asked anything of him, nor even expected anything, so how could he have failed me? What I couldn't shake, though, was the feeling that he hadn't been *true*. Perhaps it was that he hadn't been all that he could've been, that there was a fundamental laziness to him.

The very opposite struck me as being the case with Francis, who always appeared so wonderfully gallant towards Kate. I left it for Kate to come to me about what had happened between Ed and me; I couldn't face trying to explain it. A whole week passed before she noticed, or, more likely, before Ed admitted it – something of it, some version – to Francis, and Francis passed the news on to her. We were in the herb room, tying up bunches of herbs for hanging to dry, when she broached it with me. Mary had been drawn away by some Scully children playing in the courtyard; Maggie was at Sext, and Alice had gone to fetch more twine for us. Kate asked, 'Has something happened between you and Ed?'

'It's over,' I said, quickly and lightly, as if it were nothing much, which, unfortunately, had something of the truth to it.

'Oh.'

I felt obliged to offer something more, and anyway I wanted to deflect any further questions. 'I just didn't –' But then it occurred to me I had no intention of explaining myself to her, even if I could. So I shrugged, letting it go.

'Really over?'

I confirmed it.

Where did that leave us? Well, it left us: there was a lengthy pause. Then, 'Are you . . . all right about it?' A direct – if imprecise – question, which was something unusual from her.

'Yes,' was all I had to say, and, 'Thank you.'

She placed a thyme-scented hand on my shoulder, momentarily, and I appreciated it.

That summer, Kate and Francis became public about their romance: there was less subterfuge until, it seemed to me, there was none. Often they held hands in Hall, sometimes even exchanged little kisses. He teased her as *Wifey*, *Wifelet*, in earshot of all and sundry. Eventually, there couldn't have been anyone who was unaware that Kate was spoken for. Not even, surely, the duchess.

Midsummer, Mary was called home for good – for no particular reason of which we were aware – and Alice transferred to Lord William's household. The first we heard of Alice's impending move was from Skid, one evening: a mere passing remark, '... when you get to Lord William's . . .' but which had Alice darting a furtive glance at Kate.

Kate made her wait until the very end of the day for the inevitable interrogation, ambushing her with it when she was down to her shift.

'Off to Lord William's, are you?'

Alice jumped as if she'd been pinched. 'Nurserymaid,' she

said, so fast that she had to backtrack, to make clearer: 'I'm going to be a nurserymaid.' And she began combing her hair, hard.

Pointedly, Kate said nothing; just glittered at her, for so long that Alice not only had to look away but, eventually, move away, down on to her mattress and under her blanket. Only then did Kate mutter, 'Oh, I bet you are.'

And later, through the darkness, from Kate's mattress: '*Laundry*maid,' full of disdain.

'Nursery,' I whispered back, having first listened and judged Alice to have fallen asleep. 'Nurserymaid,' I corrected.

She was dismissive: 'Usual Howard-family practice.'

I didn't understand.

'The duke,' she prompted, 'and Bess Holland.'

I knew from Ed and Francis that the duke lived with Bess Holland, who wasn't his wife, for whom he had put aside his wife, but where did laundry come into it?

'That's his wife's complaint,' Kate explained: '"my laundrymaid", although really she was their steward's wife.'

I rose on to an elbow, amazed. 'You think Lord William is going to put aside his wife for Alice?'

She breathed a laugh at my naïveté. 'No. He can't afford to. Needs to keep in their favour. They're the ones with the money. They fund that household.'

After Alice had gone, I began spending a lot more time with Kate and Francis because Maggie, I now noticed, was so often in the Oratory. Whenever Kate and Francis weren't making themselves scarce, they seemed happy enough for me to hang around them. Ed's absence seemed to make no odds; in fact, it was the three of us in a way that, when Ed had been around, it'd never been the four of us.

It was a long, hot summer and we laid low, doing the bare minimum and drifting through the days. The sun was solid in the sky for weeks on end and we turned careless beneath it, Kate becoming freckled: *My ladylike complexion gone to blazes*. Kate's freckles and Francis's smiles are what I remember of that summer: Francis had always been perfectly pleasant to me, but those smiles of his for me were new. I'd never considered him to be lacking in confidence – far from it – but that summer he gained a certain ease around me. I liked, too, how he conducted himself around Kate. Up close to the pair of them, I could see what was in his eyes whenever he looked at her, and it wasn't what I'd assumed and was accustomed to seeing in the eyes of others: there was no adoration or awe. More often than not, it was an affectionate mock-exasperation, and sometimes not even wholly mock. That was how he regarded her whenever she turned up with a fussy alteration to her dress or whenever she made one of her asides. And she took it; she seemed to expect it from him, perhaps even courted it. I realised that he knew as well as I did that she didn't take herself half as seriously as everyone else assumed she did.

Can I remember what we three talked about, during all those long, heavy days? I don't think we did talk, on the whole. It was too hot, even, for talking. Living through those weeks was like dragging one's fingertips through silt: engrossing and pleasurable, yet nothing much at all. We co-existed comfortably, and there was something in those days of the earliest times that we'd spent together – although those times had been evenings, of course, and cold, and there'd been a crowd of us, and we'd done nothing but talk. But still, there was something, I felt, of that time: the sheer, easy pleasure taken in others' company.

Only one occasion stands clear in my memory: a river pageant. In retrospect, I doubt the duchess had any interest in waterborne horseplay, especially not a mock-joust between the king's barge and a rival one designated – disparagingly, would've been her view – as belonging to 'the Bishop of Rome'. But we'd have had to be seen to be appreciative of the king's fun, so a canopy had been hauled out of storage and hastily erected over the riverside steps. Beneath it, on cushions, we sweltered as sunlight struck at us from every surface: the oiled hulls and the sails, the flat of each oar held above a flounce of silvered droplets, and the river-ripples; the boil-washed linen of the spectators, their buffed buttons and badges, their embroidered silks and gemstones and the pearly vein of every feather in every cap. Dutifully, we craned to watch the two barges parry among a flotilla of smaller vessels, some of which were carrying musicians – the efforts of whom we couldn't hear – and others whose purpose was a mystery until 'the Bishop of Rome' was capsized by the king's barge and its occupants swam to them for rescue. On the opposite bank, a little further downstream and at an angle and thus only faintly discernible – from the flickering of a canopy, its pulsing in the breeze – were the king and his party and I was amazed that we were so close to the monarch: close enough, almost, to see him. Never did I think that we'd ever come any closer.

One day that autumn, though, Kate rushed with it to the gallery, where I'd gone to idle on the virginals when the duchess had sent for her. Whirling in, slamming the door and dropping back against it, she clearly had big news: she was brimful of it, her breath held, cheeks burning, eyes popping.

'What?' Whatever it was, this news would be of someone else because nothing ever happened to *us*.

'I'm off to the new queen's household.' Delivered with a hitch of her eyebrows, a tilt of her chin.

My heart faltered. Big news, indeed: much more so than a forthcoming marriage, which was the biggest news that I could ever hope to announce. Not entirely unexpected, though, I reflected, as she began gabbling about the new clothes she'd need. I shouldn't have been surprised. She was a Howard, after all; I'd forgotten she was a Howard. Bottom of the pile of Howards but, as far as the duke was concerned, if there was an opportunity at court, any eligible Howard would do. His little niece could be dusted off. And *she* probably hadn't forgotten who she was and what she was due because, for all her excitement, she looked as if this were news for which she'd been waiting: she looked ready for it. And that surprised me. Perhaps all our time here, and in particular this last lovely summer, had been a mere interlude for her, a bit of fun: time off from the often irksome but potentially profitable business of being a Howard. Perhaps she'd been biding her time, it occurred to me, and only playing at being one of us.

Us.

Francis. Did Francis know? I had to interrupt her – '. . . at least three gowns . . .' – to ask.

'Not yet,' she confirmed, carefully expressionless, before continuing: '. . . and three's the very least because . . .'

I wondered what he'd make of it, how he'd take it. What would this mean for the pair of them? Could they keep their romance going, with her at court? I turned to the window, it had a river-view and across the water was the palace wall: miles of it, immensely tall. She stepped up behind me, the scratch of a glass-studded pomander audible on the damask of her gown.

'See?' she reassured me. 'It's only over there –' The king's most favoured palace, where she'd most often be. 'I'll be back over here all the time.'

I asked her, 'Aren't you scared?' Because *I* would be. That vast palace . . . the new queen, a foreigner . . . We knew so little of anything, here. We'd been running wild, here: in so many ways our lives were scarcely different from how they'd been back in Sussex. Because, wherever it was, the duchess's household was a backwater, even bang opposite the biggest palace in Christendom. What did we girls know, really, about anything? About anything other than stitching and table-laying. But I was forgetting: Kate was a Howard, a nobody-Howard but still a Howard. Perhaps that made the crucial difference, perhaps she couldn't help but know more than

I did: either born knowing more about life in palaces, or at least learning it in the cradle. My unanswered question – *Aren't you scared?* – turned into a statement, instead, of my own inadequacy. But then she did answer. 'No,' she said, and what was odd was the wistful tone in which she said it: 'I don't think I'm scared of anything.'

When I next saw her and Francis together – later that day – it was obvious that he'd had the news broken to him. However she'd done it, he'd taken it as a blow: he was physically diminished, his head low and a lack of focus in his eyes. Perhaps I'd been naïve, but I'd been trusting to her to find a way to break the news that could've been taken better. Hoping, too, though, that he'd have found a way to be pleased for her; or, at the very least, to be able to look it. She looked no less cross with him than he did with her. There they stood, together yet not together, side by side but the space between them obvious and ominous.

From then onwards, what I'd regarded as my little alliance with Francis – the exchanged glances, the mock-exasperation – began to suffer. His exasperation, once so charmingly mock, turned real enough, and no doubt he regarded it as his alone. I'd not have disputed it – it was, after all, his lover who was leaving – but I was disappointed that he didn't confide in me. Over the following weeks, he withdrew from me as he did from her, as if I were merely an extension of her. What I'd come to consider as a friendship of a kind – albeit a small, quiet kind – must have been, I realised, an illusion. The glances that he'd appeared to exchange with me had probably, actually, been for her benefit.

Only once did I make the mistake of addressing our mutual loss. Kate had been whisked away at the end of dinner for one of her pep talks with the duke. Leaving the Hall on my own, I came across Francis just outside the door, looking at a loss in the courtyard under the blue-dimpled moon that haunted the afternoon sky. Joining him, I said, 'She'll only be across the water,' but heard it for the embarrassing and infuriating platitude that it was, because she'd be in a different world and we both knew it. Worse, it was a world to which she'd always belonged, in which she'd always had one foot even if we'd been guileless enough to allow her to blind us to it. She was returning home, in a sense, and it was faintly shaming for both of us that we'd ever assumed that she was really ours.

Myself, I was finding Kate's impending departure a more troubling prospect than I'd anticipated. I was disoriented by the depth of my feeling. We were so very different, I reminded myself; we had nothing in common. There'd been the one good summer, and, before that, there'd been a year or so when circumstances had drawn us together, when Jo Bulmer had left, and Dottie, too, and Kate and I had just happened to be the two who'd had romances. But that was all.

She was *just a girl,* I told myself: a girl who wanted nothing more than to turn heads. Why, then, faced with the loss of her, did I feel so bereft?

'Just a girl' was, funnily enough, how she'd described the new queen to me. 'She's no princess, you know,' she'd said, one day while we were embroidering. 'She's just a girl; a duke's daughter.' She'd have known what I'd be thinking: 'Yes,' half-smiling down over a row of little Tudor roses that she'd created in red silk, 'just like me.'

But this duke's daughter wasn't homegrown, as Kate was; this duke's daughter was coming from somewhere important – or important to Thomas Cromwell, was what her uncle had told her – at a time when both France and Spain were proving troublesome. This forthcoming marriage had the purpose of making an alliance.

'With where?'

'Cleves.'

'Cleves?'

'One of the Low Countries.'

Small countries, more like, against the might of France and Spain. I'd never heard of any Cleves, but, then, I suppose, I hadn't heard of many places. I did know, though, that the Low Countries were Protestant. We, in England, were Catholics: our king was a Catholic – he might well refer to the pope as the Bishop of Rome and himself instead as the head of the Church of England, but the Church of England was Catholic and he'd decreed that Protestants were heretics. I asked Kate how we could have a heretic for a queen.

'Well, yes, that's what my uncle says.' She grimaced: 'At length, and not so delicately. But she's promised she won't practise her faith here; she'll be Catholic when she's here.'

'So,' I dropped my embroidery into my lap, 'she's been chosen because she's from a Protestant country – against France and Spain – but when she gets here, she's to stop being a Protestant?'

'Apparently. And –' Kate winced – 'she only speaks Dutch.'

Dutch? I'd never heard of it.

'A kind of German. The king speaks a lot of languages, but Dutch isn't one of them. No one speaks Dutch.' Then, 'My uncle says the king's nervous about choosing a wife from a portrait. I mean, the others all do it – all the other kings – but ours never has.' She shot me an amused look. 'Likes the personal touch, does ours; a bit of a romantic. Stays close to home in matters of the heart.' She smirked: 'Marries his widowed sister-in-law and his friends' daughters.' Then, 'I hope she's a laugh, anyway, this latest one.'

I was doubtful: 'Are queens ever "a laugh"?'

'Well –' she raised her eyebrows, 'they can dance, can't they? Dancing's what I'm after, when I'm there.' She set her handiwork aside, and stretched expansively. 'Not needle-work. I mean –' gesturing towards the embroidery, dismissive – 'I can do that *here*, can't I.'

The weeks went by with Kate and Francis still often at each other's side, but it'd become a deliberate stance, the joy gone from it. And how they held hands – he'd reach for hers and she'd allow it, let hers lay there in his, lifeless. I dreaded to think how they might be conducting them-selves in private. I knew what she was doing, I just knew it – she was trying to get away from him without a confrontation. She was seeing it out until she was off, away, and then, I suspected, she wouldn't look back. He probably suspected it, too, but I knew she'd be denying it to him, or at least refusing to confirm it for him, so what else could he do? Except be there at her side, as usual, and take her hand in his, and, probably, in the evenings, while Maggie was at prayers and I made sure to linger in Skid and Oddbod's company, take her to bed.

The royal wedding was planned for Christmas Day but gales delayed the duke's daughter's channel-crossing. She stayed for two weeks in Calais, news of her reaching our household from Lord William who'd been sent ahead in the welcoming party. Word from Lord William was that she'd grown up without ever learning to dance or play cards, but she was a willing student. Similarly, she'd been denied the pleasures of good food but was now more than making up for it. One evening, she'd even invited her new friend the Lord Admiral to her rooms for supper, apparently unaware that this was improper conduct for a betrothed lady. He hadn't known what to do, Lord William reported back: to go would be to risk the king's displeasure, but, on the other hand, he didn't want to refuse a kind invitation from a lady of whom he'd grown fond. In the end, he'd braved it. Hearing this tale, Kate raised her eyebrows. 'I have high hopes that my needles are going to stay in their box.'

Finally, on St Stephen's Day, the queen-to-be set sail for Deal; then from Deal she headed for Dover, before suffering more atrocious weather on the day's ride to Canterbury, where she dried off and warmed up in the king-appropriated, extensively refurbished abbey. Next stop was Sittingbourne; then Rochester, where the duke was in charge of the welcoming party. One of his accom-

panying horsemen was Francis, and it was Francis whom
the duke despatched back to us with the news. No one
official would miss Francis: he could dash home to the
Howards with a forewarning.

As soon as he'd had his audience with the duchess, he
came crashing in on Kate and me in the gallery, where we
were practising dance steps. Clearly, it'd been some ride: he
was mud-caked and the smell of him came into the room
as a whole separate entity.

'Big trouble,' he announced, obviously shattered but with
barely suppressed glee.

Kate and I demanded, '*What?*'

Kate's future, as she saw it, depended on this royal match
proceeding without a hitch.

'The new queen.' He swiped the moist, still-red tip of
his nose with the back of his hand.

'*What?*' We'd both said it, but Kate stepped up close to
him and I winced in anticipation of her grabbing his shoulders to shake it from him.

'The king. Doesn't want her.' All of a sudden, his excitement had vanished and he looked defeated.

Kate voiced our confusion: 'He's met her?' The king was
only supposed to meet her when she reached her destin-
ation of Greenwich.

Francis nodded. 'Went ahead, couldn't wait.' He began
pacing and I sensed that he wanted to sit down but there
was nowhere and anyway he'd have been too filthy. 'Turns
up in Rochester, sneaks into her room in disguise and
doesn't like what he sees.'

Kate bridled. 'He'll get over it.' I could almost hear her telling herself, *No great emergency*.

Francis rounded on her to insist, 'No, I do mean that he really, really didn't like what he saw.'

I interrupted: 'But he'd seen a portrait, hadn't he?'

A contemptuous look from the pair of them put me right: painters paint over imperfections.

Kate challenged him, 'Well, what's he going to do?' Meaning, what *can* he do?

'He's ridden off to Greenwich, calling a Council meeting.' He stopped by a window, appeared to be looking into the distance but although I couldn't quite see his eyes, I knew they were glazed. 'The duke says he's furious, frantic. Just kept saying *No*; came out of that room saying *No, no, no*.'

She said it again: 'But what's he going to do?'

Francis shrugged and there was a sharpness to it, Advent fasting having taken a toll on him.

Could the king – I could hardly think it – send the Dutch lady back? All that pomp and ceremony and procession and then having to go home: how on earth would that poor lady feel?

Kate wanted to know: 'Is she really *that bad*?'

Another shrug: he didn't know, did he; he hadn't seen her. He turned around to offer, 'She's plain, is what I've heard.'

'Plain,' I disparaged, meaning that it couldn't be so bad, especially when there was everything else at stake.

Kate muttered, 'But there's plain and there's *plain*-plain, isn't there.'

Francis said, 'She's tall, I know, and . . .' he was searching for a word, '. . . angular. And dark.' He looked away from Kate, who was comely and pale, to address me instead. 'Well, this I do know: when we got to Rochester, Lady Browne called for the duke –' Lady Browne, who was to be head of the queen's ladies – 'and she said to him, "Look, this won't do, we're heading for a disaster, there's been a mistake because this is just some girl." That was what she said: "just some girl".'

We took a moment to consider: a lack of polish, then, was the problem; she was raw, somehow, perhaps.

'So then the duke goes haring round to Lord William, wanting to know why he hadn't said anything when he'd first seen her in Calais and there might've still been time to call a halt, and Lord William said –' Francis puffed an incredulous laugh – 'you know what he said? He said that the only time he was close enough for a good look at her, they were firing off all these celebratory rounds and he couldn't see her for all the smoke.'

Despite everything, we all smirked.

Then Kate snapped, 'Lord William wouldn't have known, anyway,' and shot me a look. *Alice*, the look said: *Think how plain Alice is, and he doesn't see that.*

Nevertheless, the royal wedding went ahead: not on the first day of Christmas but the last, Twelfthtide, in the Chapel Royal at Greenwich. Years later, I heard that when the king had challenged Cromwell with a desperate *What's to be done?* Cromwell's shamefaced reply was *Nothing.* The man who'd separated England from Rome couldn't come up with a

convincing excuse to send back that gauche, goodwilled
Dutch duke's daughter.

When, some weeks later, she came from Greenwich to
Whitehall, her attendants returned to Cleves and her English
ladies reported for duty. Kate was to be in attendance for
only two weeks in every four, the pressure for places and
lack of accommodation at the palace meaning that maids-
in-waiting would follow the same schedule as the proper
ladies-in-waiting who regularly returned home to their own
families.

Those first two weeks when I was left alone at the duchess's,
I spent more time than usual in the company of Skid and
her children, and accompanied Maggie more often to the
Oratory although there, in the midst of so many people,
was where I felt most alone. As for Francis: he all but disappeared from the duchess's household. Only from an occasional glimpse of him as he crossed the courtyard to or
from his staircase did I know that he was still officially in
residence. Presumably he was being more dutiful towards
the duke than he'd previously been, and perhaps, as a consequence, he was invited to dine in the duke's company,
because I never even spotted him in Hall.

Then, on St Bride's Day, in the second week of Kate's
absence, I did come across him. I'd been indoors all day
and, late afternoon, headed for the river in the hope of
clearing my head and working up an appetite for the coming
feast. The day had already given up the ghost, rolling over

into dusk and sinking fast, giving up the pretence of anything other than darkness, and the air was clogged with woodsmoke and recently fallen rain. I'd not expected to find anyone lingering around the steps at such an hour on such a bleak day but there was a figure squatting on a step, hunched into a cloak, hood up, crouched below lions whose grandeur was redundant in the murk. I don't know how I knew it was Francis, but I did. With an alarming whiplash of one arm, he skimmed a stone across the black, breeze-furred water and away it raced into the darkness with no one but him to track it. I halted – fearing that to distract him would be to break some kind of spell – and began to retreat, picking up each numb-soled step that I'd made and laying it down in reverse to take me back around the corner of the gatehouse. Somehow, though, he detected me, and swivelled to give me an approximation of a smile, his face scoured by the cold. 'Hello!'

I bounced the greeting back with a little too much enthusiasm, compounding my awkwardness with, 'I was just –' Just what, though? *Passing, going, on my way.* Standing there and not, in fact, going anywhere.

His nod – forlorn, resigned – seemed to say, *You, too, then.* So then, of course, I couldn't. Nor, though, could I just stand there, so I stepped closer, which slackened my hold over him, permitted him to return to the river, to skim another stone. Again came the considerable force and flex of his arm, which had me taking a step backwards even though I was nowhere near. Near enough, though, to sense how he was taken up by it: the leap of his heart into his throat and the snap of his focus on to that bouncing, dashing stone. Then came a small sound – no more than a breath – of satisfaction. 'Oh, I'm good at this,' but he was joking because he wasn't one to care in the least about stone-skimming and would be likely to make fun of anyone who did. 'What are you good at?' It was an entirely pleasant enquiry, judging from his expression and tone, yet it had me wary and again I took an unintentional step backwards. Which gave him what he was looking for. 'Ah!' – all smiles, still – 'Good at leaving.' *Like your friend* was unsaid, but I heard it in the silence and didn't appreciate it. He was being unfair. I was nothing like her. *Stupid boy*, was what came to mind: stupid enough to have fallen for Katherine Howard. *Don't take it out on me.*

He'd turned back to the water and was once again taking aim. 'Don't go.' He lobbed the pebble. 'I've missed you.' No plea, just an observation.

'Well, I haven't been anywhere,' I objected, folding my arms hard against the penetrating chill. Chance would've been a fine thing.

'Would you, though?' and he glanced around at me, interested.

I didn't follow.

'Would you want to go there?' A dismissive nod at the opposite bank, the palace. A proper question, I detected; the nod might've been dismissive but he was after a proper answer.

'I've no place there,' and he knew it.

He looked amused. 'But would you *want* it?'

The best behaviour and best clothes, Lady This and Lady That. '*God* no.' I couldn't help but laugh, tipping back my head and breathing deep to relish the sour river air.

He laughed, too, and flung a stone, setting this one on a path of long, confident strides over the water.

Quickly, I dared: 'She *had* to, Francis.' As a Howard, Kate had a job to do: the job of promoting family interests. I hadn't liked saying it – my heart snatched at my breaths in panic – but it was the truth and we should both accept it.

Rising from the step, he gave me a long look but I couldn't tell what conclusion, if any, he came to and he said nothing as we walked back to the courtyard together, our footfalls ringing hollow on the freezing flagstones, before going our separate ways.

The following day, Candlemas, my longing for like-minded company had me slip from the beeswax-scented haze in the Oratory towards the riverside steps even though it was too much to hope that he'd be there. But there he was. My heart spied him before I did and dealt me a lightning strike. Recovering myself, I went down those steps to join him and, that afternoon, he taught me how to skim stones so that, come suppertime, I was better at it than he was.

From that day onwards, we were the pair who'd been left behind: that was the part we played. Stuck there at the duchess's when Kate had moved on, we were sticking together. Terrible twins, making much of our separateness, together, from everyone else: turning up late for everything – Mass, meals – and sitting apart from everyone, or, better still, staying down by the river.

We were friends, of our own accord; we didn't need Kate to help us. He was quite different from her, which surprised and pleased me. Free from her, he had a lot more to say, all of which was funnier and more affecting than I'd anticipated. Whereas Kate focused on what others tried to hide or overlook, Francis was expansive and inventive: *What if . . .?* He never overdid it, though: unlike Kate, he never assumed that I wanted his company; he always approached me cautiously, courteously.

Then Kate was back before I knew it. I'd been waiting for her, or certainly I'd started the fortnight that way but had lost sight of her impending return because she took me by surprise. One afternoon, I dropped by our room for a pair of gloves and there in front of the window were clothes which I didn't recognise and which didn't belong in the girls' dormitory at the duchess's, clothes which looked to have a life of their own as they stood stiff with stitching and with enough fur as lining and trimmings to give them hackles and an underbelly. Those clothes were turning towards me and inside them was Kate. Around her neck was a crucifix so large and heavily jewelled that I half-expected it to clank. Howard jewellery, no doubt, which had been lain aside for dressing up any Howard girl making it into a queen's household. The crucifix's rubies made her look paler than ever but her eyes still glittered as she greeted me: 'Hello, you.'

They were only clothes, I reminded myself, and it was only small, colourless Kate inside them, but later, when we went to supper, I saw awe on others' faces. In their eyes,

Kate was really special, now: *properly* special, a lady of the queen's household. And under their stupefied gazes, she walked slower than ever. In just fourteen days, she'd become regal in her bearing.

That first evening, I watched Francis watching her, and saw how he tried to hide it. His helplessness frightened me, I despaired to see him so reduced: my funny friend Francis turned mute when she walked into a room. *Don't get taken in*, I willed him. *See her for what she is: nothing much, a little girl in a lovely dress.* Who was I, though, really, to talk? Me, who loved her, too. I wouldn't have said it, then: I wouldn't have used the word and would've been surprised if anyone else had, but that was what it was. I, too, wanted nothing but this: to have her back.

She was slow to divulge to me anything of life at the palace, giving the impression that nothing much ever happened there, but I was unconvinced. Was she playing it down from a respect for my feelings? Or did she judge that it wasn't my place to know? On her second morning home, I decided I'd ask: 'So, *is* the queen a laugh?'

Plaiting her hair, she glanced over, amused. '*Yes*, actually.' Sounding surprised. 'She's nice.' No more details. She crossed the two plaits over the top of her head for fastening.

'And *is* she . . . "plain"?' *Plain*-plain.

'She certainly is.' But there was no smirk, none of the sniggering that I'd have expected from her, no derision. It was offered as a statement of fact, and had the ring of a fair appraisal. She didn't elaborate.

'So, how is the king, around her?'

'He's not.' A flash of a smile in her eyes. 'He's still at Greenwich. We haven't seen him.' With a lift of her eyebrows, she said, 'He's putting off the inevitable.'

After that, she did open up a little, telling me about the various ladies alongside whom she was in attendance. What, I wondered, did those ladies make of her? Ladies who, according to her, read books, spoke French and Italian, and had complicated marital histories. What did they make of a small seventeen-year-old swamped by her notably new clothes? The new girl with no languages except English, no accomplishments, and no marriage plans.

Another couple of days went by before I dared say it: 'Francis has missed you.' The pair of us had claimed for ourselves a far, quiet corner of the kitchens, where we were gilding gingerbread medallions. I'd taken care to sound as if I were making the remark in passing; it was no challenge and she didn't even have to respond, she could let it go, she could just mirror my rueful expression and leave it with me. I'd had to voice it, though; I couldn't not. He and I were friends and I wanted to do my best for him. And unlike him, I still had her ear. And perhaps there was more to it: I wanted to dig my heels in, stop her in her tracks and bring her up against the truth of the matter because she seemed to want to pretend that nothing important had happened, that this was no stroke of luck for her but how life had always been intended to be, that she'd always been destined to go to the royal household and leave her friend and her lover behind. Not that the pair of us weren't fine in her absence. But still. Anyway, maybe – just maybe – her

response would make it easier for him. Maybe I'd have
something to take to him that might alleviate the despair
which, I suspected, persisted.

It's all new for her, it's a lot for her and she's finding it
hard.

Or, of course, *She's still our friend*. Although that, upon
reflection, would've been consolation only for me.

All she said, though, without raising her eyes from her
work, was a quiet, moderately regretful, 'I can't help that.'
I was assuming there'd be more, but there was nothing.
Nothing other than the slightest opening of my eyes and
the slightest hardening of my heart, which surprised me
because it wasn't as if I'd ever had any hopes of her.

Francis's presence around her was never pressing, but he
was always at her side in case of a thaw in her attitude
towards him. I knew no better than he did: even I was
wondering if she'd come round. Was she simply putting him
in his place, first – showing him that there'd been changes,
or that she wanted changes? Or was her mind really made
up against him? I could see that he didn't quite believe that
their affair was over, for the good reason – I suspected –
that she hadn't told him so. I doubted she'd ever do that,
however far she distanced herself. She'd make it clear, but
then leave it for him to give up on her. I had to watch the
ebbing of his hope. Once, in the privacy of our room, I
did ask her, directly: 'Is it over between you and Francis,
d'you think?'

She shrugged, unhappily, a reluctant little chuck of her
shoulders which I took to mean that she wasn't quite sure

or perhaps that it seemed to be going that way and she felt powerless to resist but, well, if circumstances changed . . .

And then the two weeks were over and she was gone, back on shift at the palace.

And Francis was gone again, even more resolutely than before, back among the duke's men. I missed him, which had the unfortunate effect of making me snappy with those who remained: Maggie, Skid and Oddbod. I'd be gone, too, sometime soon, I supposed: called home, girlhood over. This was how it'd be, soon, I realised: all of us gone.

But then one day it happened again: Francis, back again; and this time I bumped into him – literally – rounding a corner.

I laughed with the shock. 'Oh! I thought –' *you'd gone.*

He looked as if he loved being able to confound me merely by standing there: the tiny, unlooked-for triumph of it. He grinned – a glimpse of the old Francis – and performed a cheeky bow: *But here I am.*

'But here you are,' I agreed.

And so we fell into step – the whispers of my skirts, the jingling of his spurs – and from then onwards, for that week or so before Kate returned, we hung around together whenever we could, finding each other at the beginnings and ends of days. Just as before, the times when there were no other claims on us, we claimed as our own. He was busy training his new falcon, and I helped him. Of course I knew he wasn't very happy but, I felt, he might be getting closer to being happy enough. Certainly *I* was. He was such good company, but his physical presence alone could make me laugh, a mere glance at him could make me laugh: those few, endearing little imperfections of his, such as the gap between his two front teeth into which you could, perhaps, if you were careful, slip a thumbnail; and that fluffy, boy-blond hair, most unsuitable for one of the duke's men. It did cross my mind that he was lovely. But he was Kate's – he'd been so from the very beginning – even if, in the end, she didn't want him.

Then one night when I'd just bedded down and was dozing in the glow of the wick that burned for Maggie's return from Compline, a knock came at the door. It was on me like a shot; I'd heard no one on the stairs. A voice, too: '*Cat!*'

It was Francis, speaking low yet also loud. Francis, at my door during the night. My blood thundered scalding into my recesses and extremities – ears, throat, scalp, fingertips – and pounded for escape. Something of the room seemed to have taken flight, too – its solidity – because the heavy oak door couldn't even keep a mere whisper at bay.

'It's me,' he was confessing, unnecessarily, 'Francis.'

'What is it?' my own voice sounded embarrassingly querulous.

'Shooting stars, *loads* of them!' A rasp again but this time leavened with wonder. 'Quick, go and look!'

I scrambled from beneath my bedcovers to be assaulted by the cold. Grabbing my cloak, I threw it over my shoulders, whipping the candlelight around the walls. Across the room, behind the curtain, was the window, ready to yield a square of sky beyond. I dashed to the door instead, slipping my bare feet into my shoes, and opened it. His turn to jump, now, taking a step backwards into the shadowed stairwell. I could see very little of him, just the graininess in the darkness that was his hair, but even so I registered the lack of his own cloak. 'Aren't you cold?' It sounded like an accusation and he didn't respond. 'I'll come with you,' I said, passing him and pattering ahead down the steps.

The chill down in the courtyard was dense, my breaths noisy and visible on it, and the silence so thorough as to seem intent, like a live presence, stealthy. But every one of the courtyard's many windows turned a blind eye, leaving us to it. Fiercely starred though the moonless sky was, nothing in it was moving. I scanned this way and that, as if it were finite and I could search its corners. Yet, for all my craning, it was Francis's presence of which I was acutely aware – not because he was any closer to me than usual, but because in so much darkness and emptiness we were so definitely together. I half-expected to see an outline, as white as our breath, drawn in the air around us.

'Keep watching,' he promised me, 'and you'll see: keep watching and there'll be one,' as if my vigilance alone could summon it.

Then – '*Oh, there!*' – a soundless pop, a graceful little droop.

'*Shhh!*' But he was laughing.

'Did you see it, though? Did you see?' With my head tipped back, I had to flail at my side for his arm, to grab him and wring the acknowledgement from him.

'I did, I did.'

'Oh, and *look*!'

'I'm looking, I'm looking,' and his laughter billowed into the blackness.

Suddenly, though, my exhilaration shrank into the pit of my stomach because what, really, had I seen? A pinprick of light dropping down a finger's-width, then extinguished. No more than a blink, a twitch on the vastness.

And now – whole minutes passed – there was nothing at all: just the stubborn sky. And I was getting cold, really very cold: conscious, now, of how much bigger than me was the cold, of how it was bearing down on me. My breaths were being wrenched from me.

'Come here,' he chivvied, looping an arm around me, drawing me in and rubbing my shoulder, vigorous and business-like. I reeled and had to right myself but then still felt precarious, startled by new aspects of him: the hollow made by his extended, raised arm; his ribs, their tangible resilience; the nudging of his chin against my temple.

The sky stared back at us and eventually we had to accept that the show was over. His grip softened and I extricated myself, wary of overstaying my welcome. Our farewells were determinedly brisk, to dispel any sense that we'd been too close for comfort.

I returned to my room with the physical sensation of him haunting me like a bruise, and sank cloak-swaddled on to my mattress to ponder it. Something wasn't as I'd assumed. Something had until now managed to escape me – me, who prided myself on missing nothing – and now

I'd stumbled across it, I'd been tripped up and I didn't know how I felt about it.

What I did know, though, was my place. And that, I didn't resent. I could live with this development in how I felt about Francis and tell no one. It was mine, and mine alone: that was the consolation. The fact remained that he wasn't for me, he was for Kate, and what I probably liked best of all about him – a kind of consolation, too, in a way – was how he was true to her.

When she next came home, Francis absented himself. I wondered if they'd had an altercation. Anyway, he seemed to have realised, at last, that it was over between them, or at least for the time that she'd be in the queen's service. As for Kate, not once during those two weeks did she mention him to me. I suppose I could've asked her if she'd seen him at all, or if she'd written to him, or he to her; I could've asked her, again, if it was over between them. But I didn't want to dwell on it, as well as being wary, now, of showing too close an interest; and, in any case, I knew very well that direct questions would get me nowhere. She'd merely have shrugged and I'd have been none the wiser.

What she did want to talk about, her first evening home, as we played cards together in the duchess's day room, was that she'd finally met the king. 'He's immense,' she told me, thrilled, unable to stress it enough. 'He's absolutely huge, he's a giant!' And an uncharacteristically big smile showed her delighted surrender to this extraordinary state of affairs.

'All those little men running around him,' she derided, having lowered her voice and glanced across the room at the duchess, who was deep in conversation with Skid. 'Men like my horrid weedy uncle.' And back to the king: 'It's as if he's not quite human, it's as if he truly is different.' She surprised me with, '*Are* they, d'you think? Princes and kings — are they really different, somehow, underneath?'

She was serious, I saw, although I couldn't quite believe it, so I simply said, 'Well, I don't know about kings, it's Lord William who foxes me — what's *that* made of?'

But she was already on to the subject of the king's jewels and goldwork: ropes of pearls, walnut-sized diamonds, and the ring-set ruby as big as a baby's fist that he'd had chipped from Thomas à Becket's shrine when it was demolished and the saint's body chucked on to a dungheap. 'I wouldn't even be able to stand up in it all.'

'Don't worry,' I said, 'I doubt you'll have to, any time soon.'

'Sometimes I'm kneeling,' she rushed on, 'and, as he comes near, the floor sags, it's dipping from beneath my knees towards him and I'm *terrified* —' she was loving it — 'that I might just slide down it, that I might just end up there, sprawled across the floor at his feet.'

'Perhaps that's the idea.'

'He likes me, I think,' she mused. 'He spoke to me: he said, "So, you're the little Howard girl, are you?"' She raised her eyebrows: 'Well, I'm *one* of them.'

'You said that?'

'Of course I didn't. But "little"!' She snorted, and I realised with a flush of tenderness that she didn't consider herself small.

'Well, you know,' I broke it to her, 'compared to him, you *are* little.'

'Actually,' she rushed onwards, regardless, 'he's good fun.'

'"A laugh"?' I teased.

She frowned at me but I shrugged it back at her: *your word*.

'He likes a lot of fun, and it's our job to provide it. Well, there's a man to plan it all, the Master of Revels – imagine having that job! I tell you, he's in a permanent panic – but it's us who have to *do* it, all the dancing and so on. And we have to stay the course.' She raised her eyebrows to imply that this was taxing. The king, himself, didn't dance, she went on to tell me; he had a bad leg, an old injury that had never much improved, so he'd sit and watch his ladies and gentlemen.

I asked her if the queen was up to all this.

'Oh, she's game for anything, after what she's come from. She didn't even know how to dance – but we're remedying that, of course: we're teaching her, and she's really taking to it.'

Then I asked if the king liked his new queen any better, and, after another wary glance at the duchess, she muttered that a couple of the senior ladies who had their suspicions had broached it, asking the queen outright what happened whenever the king came to the shared bedchamber. The queen had replied that the king would kiss her goodnight and turn over, go to sleep. 'So,' Kate's eyes were lowered, she was making a show of carefully selecting a card, 'they said to her, "There'll have to be more than that if there's to be another heir." But they said that it was quite clear she had no idea what they meant.'

I was aghast. 'What will happen?'

She didn't look up. 'I don't know. No one knows. What *can* happen?'

'Will he take a mistress?'

'He needs a second heir,' she reminded me with a quick look. 'It's a wife that he needs.'

One morning later that week, Kate had a visitor, although the first she knew of it was when we emerged into the main courtyard. 'Christ!' she snapped backwards into the passageway and on to my foot. 'Jesus!' She flattened herself – stricken – against the wall.

My panic soared with hers. 'What? What is it?' I could no longer see past her, but before her hasty retreat I'd glimpsed a man on horseback: an impressive animal and a rider so important as to have been allowed to ride into the courtyard. 'Who is it?'

She didn't answer me; just a frantic, furious, 'Do I look all right?' as she clamped her hands to her cheeks to cool a flush.

Of course she looked all right; she always looked all right. '*Who is it?* You don't like him?'

She countered with a hard-eyed blank look: the opposite, the look informed me, was true.

This was new, though: I'd never seen her lose her composure over someone she liked. 'Who is he?' And why hadn't I known? Shouldn't I have known?

Still she didn't answer; just, 'What's he *doing* here?' Fiercely indignant – I understood, now – that she'd been cheated of an opportunity to prepare herself. Then a savage yank of my arm, 'Come on.'

He'd dismounted: an expensively dressed, conventionally good-looking man in his twenties. I could've sworn that from somewhere over by the stables came a muted, mocking wolf-whistle, but if the visitor heard it, he didn't let on. His smile was supercilious as he sauntered towards us and performed an unnecessarily low bow. 'Katherine,' and he had it sounding like a taunt.

He didn't look at me, not a glance, which was quite an achievement given how close I was to Kate; she still had me held by the arm. I was glad, though: relieved that she was bearing the brunt of that look.

She didn't return his greeting; asked, instead, 'What are you doing here?'

'Passing.' He answered deliberately flatly: a provocation; no attempt to make it credible.

Mimicking his tone, she came back with, 'This is a dead end.'

He broke into the threatened smile. 'But it has its compensations.' Then he turned to follow the servant who'd been waiting to take him to the obligatory refreshments, but called over his shoulder, 'Join me.'

Clearly the invitation was for her alone, but she gave me no choice, tugging on me and imploring me with her eyes.

And that was how I ended up sitting with them at a table in Hall. The two of them talked desultorily, almost in

code, about people I didn't know. Sitting there, elbow on
table and chin in hand, I gazed around and pretended to
half-listen to a conversation that in fact I couldn't follow
at all for perhaps as long as half an hour before the bell
began calling us to prayers and he took his leave. He and
I hadn't been introduced, nor had he even acknowledged
me.

'So, who is he?' I demanded as Kate and I hurried to
the Oratory.

'One of the Culpeper brothers.' Her voice retained that
edge of anger. 'Thomas.' Then, as if quoting: 'Gentleman of
the Privy Chamber, and favourite of the king.' She sighed,
even as she ran along. 'And doesn't he know it,' she added,
somehow both scathing and admiring.

Francis returned to the duchess's when Kate returned to
court, and he knew all about Thomas Culpeper: 'Kate's got
herself involved with a gentleman of the Privy Chamber,'
he said, bitterly, the very first morning he was back. I'd
contrived to accompany him in the direction of the stables:
I needed saddlesoap for a leather-upholstered stool, I said.
It was a blinder of a day, frost-vapour billowing from roofs
and dripping from everywhere else. If Francis was to be
believed, he knew more about this Culpeper than I did. I
was surprised enough that he could bring himself to
mention Kate, let alone admit that he'd been replaced in
her affections and by a gentleman of the Privy Chamber.
I felt for him. Wondered, too, how he knew what Kate was
up to. But, then, he was so often at court in the duke's
entourage that he probably couldn't avoid knowing.

Teetering alongside him over the slippery cobbles, I dithered over whether to play ignorant – whether that'd spare his feelings – but my instinct was that I should own up. 'I know,' I admitted. 'He dropped by.'

If I was hoping for sympathy for having had to endure Culpeper's company, I was disappointed. Francis just looked disgusted. 'He's a shit.'

'Yes,' I said, 'that was obvious.'

'Thomas Culpeper!' he despaired.

I didn't know what to say – a rush of responses came to mind, many of them contradictory.

He made it easier: 'How *can* she?'

'Well, it's just –' *what she does.* 'I mean, that's just her, isn't it.' Realising too late that this could be taken to reflect badly on him.

He didn't seem to have noticed. 'I'd've –' But he reigned himself in: I saw him do it and heard the unsaid words: . . . *gone anywhere, done anything for her.*

I spared him, looked away, across the courtyard. 'I know.'

And now he looked at me – halted, drew my focus back to him – and his frank look said, *Stupid, wasn't I.*

I didn't know how I should respond, so I said nothing and, again, looked away. Sunshine was stripping down the frost layer by layer before my eyes, everything sopping. Looking back, I discovered to my surprise that he was smiling, and I thought I understood why: I hadn't lied to him.

'Oh, come on,' he said to himself as much as to me, 'let's go and do something *nice*.'

'It's February,' I objected. 'And it's Lent.' *What is there that's 'nice'?*

'A fireside,' he decided. 'We need a fireside. Come on: my room.'

Firewood: up to his old tricks, then. I gestured towards the stables: 'But aren't you supposed to be going to work?'

He grinned. 'D'you know –' he encircled his throat with a hand – 'I think I'm coming down with something.'

In his room, we settled on cushions as close as bearable to the fire. I'd envisaged that we'd take the opportunity for some catching up after our two weeks apart, but in the event we spoke very little at first – a minimal swapping of news of acquaintances – and then not at all, captivated by the constant shifting of the flames and lulled by the heat. I'd envisaged, too, that being in such close proximity might feel uncomfortable but, eventually, it was the space between us that came to feel odd. I really don't remember either of us making the first move; it was just that we reached for each other and then there we were, holding hands. Incredibly, I don't remember even thinking about it, but simply receiving the weight of his hand and letting him take the weight of mine. I don't remember wanting any more of him; I felt as if I had everything I could ever want. And besides, he'd be there – I knew, now – when I did want more. We stayed sitting there, holding hands, until I said that I'd better go or Skid would be missing me.

We took our time, in the weeks to come, getting to know each other. Certainly he made much of getting to know me: dwelling, I felt, on the least glamorous, most incidental parts of me, my protrusions and hollows. A brush of his lips across the heel of my thumb and a little kiss to a knuckle; a breath on an earlobe and the pressing of his lips to an eyebrow, the bridge of my nose, the bud of my own top lip, then along my hairline and, when I'd untied it, to the ends of my hair. All the while he'd breathe a laugh too low to hear, but definitely there: a hum, detectable. The tip of his tongue to the inside of my wrist, dabbed on to the scribble of veins. His lips down the flank of my throat and into the hollow at the base, then along my collarbone, that most gawky of bones. Sometime he'd cup my wool-clad heel as if to demonstrate how perfect a fit, as if it mattered that my heel fitted into his palm. A dip of his lips into the arch and then to the knob of ankle bone and the well of it, which, he'd insist − as if I were disputing it − was kiss-sized.

With his scattered kisses he was busy doing, I suspected, what he hadn't done with Kate: doing anything and everything but. This, with me, was to be different. And perhaps he was taking me apart, too, piece by piece, and putting me back together again as a new me, *his* me. *You, you, you*, said each laying of his lips: *this is what you are, to me; all this*. As for me, I did at last get to slide my thumbnail between those front teeth. 'Careful,' he relished warning me: *I might bite*. A squeaky-tight fit: if I were to take it all the way, we'd be stuck.

And then, too soon, it was time again for Kate's return. We'd begun to talk about Kate while she was away − I suppose we both recognised that we'd be increasingly uncomfortable, otherwise − but never, by mutual understanding, about what she'd meant to him or the time they'd spent alone together. We were careful to talk of her as our friend, which, of course, she was. Now that she was due to come home, I was worried that Francis would back away from me, perhaps even deny me. When it came to it, though, he was respectful of her feelings but he didn't stint with me, and I loved him even more for it. Neither of us had told her what was going on between us but she'd seemed to sense it; and if she was surprised, she didn't show it. When, though, did she ever show that she was surprised? *I'll leave you two to it*, she'd say, breezily. She often referred to us as 'You two', and I would've been grateful but for the faintest unease that our affair was only happening because she permitted it.

She was with us less often, anyway, this time: she was more often dining in the duke's palace lodgings and returning late across the river. She was moving in a very different world from ours, and was increasingly at home in it. I didn't envy her, and, of course, I was grateful to be left alone with Francis.

What, though, of her and Thomas Culpeper? There was no mention of him, nor any visits from him; so, the day before her return to the palace, I braved it and asked her. She was busy packing her finery and didn't even look up when she replied, 'There *is* no me-and-Thomas-Culpeper.' I waited for her to elaborate, but of course I should've known better. So, it was to be that Thomas Culpeper was nothing to her and never had been. Well, I could certainly understand that.

When I summoned up courage, the following day, to mention to Francis that she and Culpeper had come to nothing, he was similarly dismissive. He was polishing his boots and, like Kate, he barely raised his eyes when he responded. 'Well, he can't have her, now, can he?'

What did that mean? He seemed to know something. Did he mean that Kate was getting married? Would he know, if I didn't? He might, I supposed – being close to the duke.

He must've detected that I was baffled because then he did look up at me. 'Didn't she say anything?'

It struck me that he probably didn't know that she never told me much. I suffered a flash of anger at her, that she so often kept me in the dark. And now here I was, being kept in the dark by the pair of them. I did my best to sound offhand: 'About . . .?'

'The king.'

The king could, of course, have plans for Kate's marriage, or at the very least some preferences concerning the placing of a minor Howard, either the shoring up or curtailing of certain allegiances among his nobles.

I was going to have to admit I didn't know. Offhand, again: 'What is it, then, that the king wants?'

He put down the boot and stared at me. '*Her.*' As if I were being deliberately obtuse.

I heard it only as a sound; it made no sense. 'Her?'

When he said nothing more, I laughed. 'What, as a *mistress*?' But he didn't need a mistress. *It's a wife that he needs.*

He frowned. 'Didn't she say where she'd been going, all those evenings across the river? To supper with the king?'

'Yes, but –' Supper with the duke, when the duke was hosting the king: that was what it was. 'Oh, don't be ridiculous.' I was disappointed in him, he was being dramatic, attempting to magnify his own loss: the girl he'd loved was special enough to be pursued by the king. *Kate?* Seventeen-year-old Kate with nothing, really, to say for herself? Kate, with her sideways glances. Kate, who'd never really done anything or been anywhere. Anyway, the king had so very rarely had mistresses, people said, he'd had wives instead and look whom he'd gone for: soulful Catherine, witty Anne Boleyn, and then, when he was sick of clever women, Queen Jane with her lowered eyes and held tongue. Kate had nothing in common with any of the ladies who'd turned the king's head. Not only did she have nothing much to say for herself, but – it was clear from that glittering gaze of hers – she was in no way pious.

I laughed it off. 'And where was it that you heard this little rumour?'

He maintained his incredulity that I'd not known. 'The duke; and his household's full of it.'

Well, they were all being ridiculous, I decided: over-excited, and deluded. So, I rolled my eyes, making quite clear that I wouldn't discuss it any further.

When Kate was next due home, in March, she didn't turn up. Francis told me that the duke had managed the impossible and found accommodation for her at the palace. She wouldn't be returning to the backwater in which she'd grown up uneducated, where she'd been just some girl. The duke, Francis said, was pretending that she hadn't ever been left pretty much to her own devices in Horsham and at Norfolk House but, on the contrary, had been raised by the duchess in a manner befitting a king's consort and, moreover, that she'd always been his own favourite niece. I wondered how she felt about that.

Wondering was all I could do, because no word came from her. Every day, I was hopeful that a letter would arrive: every horse at the gatehouse and every boat at the steps had me pause, expectant, before disappointment descended. I wondered if Francis might be the courier, and delved into his pockets whenever I could, anxious that he might've forgotten that he had a letter to relay. Kate had never written before – she'd never learned to write with any ease – but then there'd never been any need. I considered writing to her, but what would I say? I imagined dropping by – I'd find my way to that duke-wrangled room of which Francis had spoken – but then what? *Hadn't seen you for a while, so . . .* In my mind's eye, I saw her look of relief as she drew me aside to tell me what had been going on. Or I could offer a leading question – *How are things?* – and my carefully composed expression of concern would then enable her to unburden. Maybe I'd even go so far as to challenge her: *So, come on, then: what's this all about?* Eye to eye, as girls – as friends – should be able to do.

Every night when my own wicks were extinguished, I'd

stare across the river at the palace's glowing windows and ponder which was hers and what she was doing. If I ever did go to her, what would she tell me? That she was scared? That she was thrilled? That it was just a joke? Perhaps it happened all the time and was of no consequence; perhaps it was simply a part of life for a maid in the queen's service. I had no way of knowing.

Come May, I wasn't seeing much of Francis, either, as he hunted daily from dawn until dusk in the company of the duke. Whenever we found each other, though, he did now have news of Kate. No letter, still, but news. And what news! Kate was being given gifts by the king, and soon not just – just! – clothes and jewellery but, within weeks, a manor house somewhere, then a second, a third. Kate had tenants, she had income. I could guess how she'd be spending that money: somewhere in London, there'd be a very busy tailor. What, though, was the king getting, or expecting to get, in return?

I trusted Francis to have the facts, first hand, yet still, with the news he brought me of each gift of the king's for our friend, I'd find myself checking, *You're sure?*

Of course I'm sure! Wide-eyed and laughing, he regarded this extravagant favouring of Kate as hilarious spectacle, and in his laughter was a note of admiration as if she were at least in some measure responsible for her drastic turn in fortune. I had my doubts, though. She might well be as perplexed by it all as we were. After all, those whom the king favoured had no choice but to accept it. I doubted, too, that Francis would've relayed the news quite so happily had the suitor been not the king but Thomas Culpeper.

Try as I might, I couldn't laugh along with him because I was afraid, all the time, that she'd be uncovered. The king – for all that he was king and should know everything – seemed to be under the misapprehension that Kate was a lady worthy of his devotion. Well, I knew differently. What I knew was that she was just a girl, and, moreover, a girl who liked boys.

Francis saw her often enough at court, but only ever in passing, he claimed – making sure to appear unbothered – and at a duke-chaperoned distance. I couldn't stop myself, though: I'd ask if she'd said anything to him. His reply was always the same: that she'd asked after me.

Had she? 'How?'

'What d'you mean, "how"?'

'Well –' *I don't know* – 'what does she say?'

A shrug: '"How's Cat?"'

'And?'

'And?'

'What do *you* say?'

'Well, you know . . .'

No.

'Well, I say you're fine.'

Was I? Was I fine?

I'd ask, 'How does she look?'

A shrug. 'The same.'

But Francis was *a man*: what did he know! And although he might've considered that he knew her well, he hadn't had my years of experience of reading her. One look at her and – I was sure – I'd know what'd been happening to her and how she felt about it.

I never stopped asking him what was going to happen and he'd always say he had no idea. I'd ask what others were speculating, and he'd say they had no idea either. Not even the duke: the duke was utterly flummoxed, he said; bowled over by it, but clueless. Because nothing like this had ever happened; because this time there was the new wife, a really very new wife, married to the king a mere couple of months ago.

One day, though, he didn't say as usual that he had no idea; he said, instead, 'Word is that the king's going to go for non-consummation.'

The king was intending to have his marriage annulled?

'And then –' Francis spread his hands, which I took to imply that there'd be no obstacle to re-marriage, and his knowing smile intimated that Kate would be the bride. But the king was a towering monarch decades into his rule, he was challenger of the pope and defender of the faith, a patron of world-renowned scholars and artists, the richest man in Christendom. And for his wives he'd had impeccably schooled Spanish Catherine, French-raised and reform-minded Anne Boleyn, devout Jane Seymour with her meticulous embroidery, and alliance-building Anne from Cleves. It was absurd, surely, that he'd have any interest in marrying a little girl from across the river?

No one could tell me what I needed to know and there was no one, even, with whom I could talk it over. Francis seemed caught up in keeping tally of the properties Kate now owned, whereas I was desperate to know something of the understanding – if any – between her and the king, and how she felt about it. Maggie would know nothing and understand even less, and Skid's response to my tentatively ventured observation, once, that Kate was doing well at court was a mere, oblivious, 'I'm sure she is, dear.'

But, then, Skid, like everyone else, had a more pressing concern. There'd been no rain for more than a month – day after day, the sky burned blister-white – and the talk everywhere was of moving to residences with deeper wells. At Norfolk house, stink squatted around every corner; and a mile downriver, plague arrived in the city. Thomas Cromwell sailed into the thick of it, one June morning, and along to the Tower: the arch-fixer, and fixer latterly of the king's marriage to the plain-plain Dutch-speaker, had finally fallen from favour. Midsummer's Day, the queen herself boarded a barge, but for Richmond Palace, upriver, the pestilence in London the official explanation. Her notoriously health-conscious husband hadn't accompanied her, though, Francis reported to me, nor had her youngest maidin-waiting. The duke, too, was staying put nearby in his palace rooms.

As for Maggie and me: the following day, the duchess told us that we were to return to our homes and stay until we heard from her that it was safe to return.

Francis had gone to Norfolk on business for the duke, so we were unable to say goodbye and he'd be returning to find me gone. I had no way of getting word to him that I was leaving, and for where and why, although no doubt he'd guess. As for how long, though, no one knew – and my fear was that it'd end up being for ever, my parents finding it convenient to keep me home while they set about marrying me off. Francis would know not to risk writing to me because the arrival of a letter – indeed, my sending of one, too – would alert my parents to a situation for which we had yet to prepare them, for which it was crucial that we properly prepare them.

Up in our room, packing my case, I became distraught, which frightened poor Maggie, too, into tears: *Please, Cat, please, please stop this.* I wished I could, if only for her sake, but what was happening was more than I could bear.

Back home, the estate was parched: anxieties were running high and energies low. My parents were preoccupied with the calamity, and barely recognised that I was there. In the fields, the labourers were doing their best to beat the clods: dust hurtling all day every day into the house, but no water spare for dampening it down and wiping it away. I was crazed with that dust – each individual hair sheathed, the folds in my palms caked – and it built up at the base of each eyelash to raise little swellings so that even when I wasn't crying my eyes were red-rimmed and sore. Every day, I tried to do my bit – I wanted to pull my weight, and would've welcomed the distraction – but there was less and less that could be done: no sweeping, no laundry, and the heat put paid to any butter- and cheesemaking. So, as early as possible in the evenings, I'd retreat to my room to reel and weep in the relative cool of my linen nightshirt.

And that was how my mother found me, late one

simmering August afternoon. Halting in the doorway, swallowing her all-too-obvious irritation, she refrained from comment. She, herself, had become uncharacteristically unkempt under the desperate circumstances; the black of her gown – dust-frosted – had turned sloe-like. In her grimy hand was a letter and even from across the room, prone on my bed, I recognised my aunt's distinctive handwriting.

She said, 'That Howard girl who was with you at the duchess's . . .'

Oh God, what's happened?

'. . . wasn't she Katherine?'

I'd been living for news of Kate but now that it was here, I was afraid to hear it. My exhausted mother sniffed her disbelief. 'Well, would you believe it, but she's our queen now.'

November 7th

That desolate morning in the queen's bedchamber, lying alongside Kate, I was awake before I knew it; I'd never properly been asleep. Kate was awake, too: I knew, even though I didn't know how I knew. Her stillness, probably: the wariness and dread in it. Playing dead. I gave no indication of my own wakefulness and was fairly sure she remained unaware of it. Uninterested, moreover, I suspected: I had a sense that she'd take no account of me, this morning, for as long as she could get away with it. I was to be avoided, along with everyone else. Well, I was glad.

I lay listening for clues as to the time. The apartment was distant from workaday areas of the palace and usually the only activity detectable at dawn was that of the first few arrivals, the earliest-rising chamberers, still sleep-addled and clumsy: a shutter let swing, a door let slam. But I heard nothing, and evidently we were between clock-strikes.

Eventually, Kate rose, her brief parting of the bedhangings flinging cold air at the little of me that was exposed. Still I didn't let on that I was awake: easier not to. And anyway I wished I weren't. She busied herself at the brazier. It would've been a long time since she'd had to light a fire for herself. I lay there and let her get on with it, pretending even to myself that I was dozing.

I was thinking of Francis, of how unassuming was his beauty, of how he made nothing of it, wearing it slung over his bones as if he might mislay it somewhere if that were possible, or shrug it off should it prove any kind of hindrance, and then scamper away unburdened and ordinary. Now that he was in the Tower, that perfection of his might be suffering a different kind of disregard from his captors in their search for places to bruise or stretch, tear or burn.

There was a knock on the door and Kate's tinkering ceased. My own breathing, too, momentarily. Lady Margaret was the most likely visitor, and how I dreaded her: she, whose lover had died in the Tower. Kate called for her to come in; and hidden though I was, I sat up to attention, hauling the bedcovers with me, to eavesdrop on Lady Margaret's apologies for Kate having to tackle her own fire, and her assurances that she'd be sending someone immediately. Kate was brusque, to imply that a fuss was being made about nothing. Then Lady Margaret said that Kate's uncle, the duke, had arrived. She said it so quietly that I barely heard; and no wonder, because the duke's arrival – anywhere, for anyone – was never news for joyful declaration. He had a nose for trouble and while he might come proclaiming an intention to help Kate – and certainly he was a practical, no-nonsense man – he'd be here to sniff out the situation to his own advantage. Lady Margaret's pity was audible, and I knew, without having to see, that Kate would be bridling at it.

Lady Margaret finished by saying she'd send some ladies to dress Kate – ignoring me behind the hangings, although she'd have known I was there. Kate was specific at length about what she required to be fetched from The Wardrobe, no doubt aiming to frustrate any efforts to get her ready quickly for her uncle and also to make sure that when she did grace him with her presence, she'd appear at her most regal.

Having sent Lady Margaret on her way with the detailed instructions, she climbed back into bed to wait and warm up while a chamberer tiptoed into the room to see to the fire. I'd given up the subterfuge of being asleep.

'What's *he* here for?' was all Kate said in reference to her uncle, but it was complaint rather than speculation. Speculation was to be avoided where the duke was concerned. Only a fool would try to second-guess him.

Moments later, a tray was delivered – ale, and warm, soft white bread with cheese, and dishes of spiced preserved pears, figs, quinces. At least while we were eating we didn't have to speak to each other. I wondered if Francis was having anything to eat. Sitting in that bed with that tray of luxuries across our knees, I couldn't fathom if we were there of our own free will or were incarcerated. Eventually, the Parr sisters turned up laden with a fabulous array of clothes and a hearty pretence of cheeriness to set about the business of preparing Kate, while I stood to one side and dressed in what I'd worn the previous day.

By the time we arrived in the Presence Chamber, the duke and his two attendants had been kept waiting for well over an hour. Despite the fire and his furs, he looked so cold that I imagined there'd be a dew-drop on the end of his beaky nose. He spoke – spoke *first*, before being addressed by his queen – when we were barely through the door: 'Good morning, Katherine,' in that deceptively easy-going manner of his.

Katherine: no title. As if she were just, once again, his little nobody-niece. A slap in the face, those casual words: a big, bold slap in the face performed for the benefit of everyone in the room. She took it without so much as a flinch, standing her ground in her amethyst silk and ermine: a glorious, glowing queen, staring him down. It was a good move, showing him up as the worm that he was. For all her composure, though, she'd be trying frantically to make sense of what he'd just done. We all were, I knew: me, Maggie and Alice, both of whom were standing there awkwardly, tired-looking, and Lady Margaret, Jane Rochford, the Lizzies and the Annes. Because no one – not even the country's highest nobleman, not even the closest family member – would address the queen in the presence of others as if she were a mere girl.

Was this rudeness some kind of trick, or joke, or a miscalculation? But he was a shrewd calculator and a coward, not given to jests or misjudgements. What could he possibly know, though, that would have him publicly addressing his queen as a nobody? She *was* still queen, wasn't she? There was no way, was there, that she could have stopped being queen, as the first queen had? But the setting-aside of the first queen had taken years of court-hearings. As for the second queen, she'd been arrested, but she'd been an adulteress, or so people said, whereas the only accusation against Kate was that she'd had a couple of boyfriends before she was married. Tiny though Kate was, standing at my side, she was so very much the queen. A queen confined to her rooms, but – and this, surely, was the point – the *queen's* rooms. Firm on her finger was her wedding ring, and dazzling on her bodice was the lover's knot that, only two days beforehand, her adoring husband had given her.

The duke spoke again: 'I'm here to collect the queen's jewels.' The 'queen's jewels', the crown jewels, those which were not her own. And so he made it clear: the queen was not who Kate was. And again in that conversational tone, as if it were nothing much: as if, in his view, this was only to have been expected. *Game's over, hand back the bounty*. There was a collective intake of breath, and I glimpsed the faintest, most fleeting buckle in Kate's stance, the absorption of a body-blow. She could've demanded, *On whose authority?* But there was only one possible answer – *the king's* – because no one, surely, would arrive at the queen's rooms to strip her of her crown jewels unless on the order of the king himself. I dreaded her speaking up, dreaded having to hear it spelt out for her.

From the duke, though, I did want more. We all did: all of us hanging on his next words, craning for them, desperate for some explanation. Because what *was* this? Was it, perhaps, a temporary measure? An emergency measure until this muddle, or whatever it was, could be resolved and Kate reinstated.

But he said nothing more. Nor did she, which, I detected, he'd failed to anticipate; he'd imagined that she'd kick up a fuss, protesting and pleading, all of which he – never one to bother courting popularity – could make a show of brushing off. But she stood there – so small, not that her kinsman was much taller – with a challenge in her eyes: *Go on, then.* She stepped aside with a flourish, and he was revealed to be at a loss. He was the one who was looking foolish. She'd allow him to do whatever he'd come to do, but he'd have to do it in the face of her intransigence.

So, it wasn't going to be his show, after all. I watched him wondering what to do. He wasn't a man to throw his weight around, insignificant as it was; he was a man of words, few and unembellished though those words were. He was a needler, a wheedler. If the situation wasn't to degenerate to his disadvantage, he was going to have to make a bid for assistance, but it wasn't clear that any of us, having witnessed this disgraceful little scene so far and been emboldened by Kate's spirited stance, could be persuaded or even ordered to give it.

'Right –' This was ineffectual, intended as a prompt for the pair of men he'd brought with him, but they were hired hands with no initiative and so they stood, eyes down, awaiting specific instructions.

Kate folded her arms, her rigidity defying anyone to step forward to his assistance. Duly, no one shifted nor even, it seemed to me, breathed. A lightning-quick glance around showed me that everyone's eyes were resolutely lowered. There was a distracting fizz in my stomach, a buzzing in my ears, a tingling in my fingertips. A few more excruciating moments passed before Lady Margaret stepped into the breach with obvious reluctance – a noisy sigh – and indicated that he should follow her into Kate's private chamber. Kate made no move save a slide of her gaze in their wake. Because she didn't move, nor did anyone else: not a hair. But then, at the last moment, as they were shuffling through the door, she sprang after them, yanking me with her.

She didn't venture far into her golden room, just far enough to be able to close the door behind us, and from there we watched Lady Margaret gather the three leather cases that held the crown jewels which weren't in storage over at the Jewel House. Every movement was pointed, to signal that she was acting under duress. I was startled by the openness of her contempt, although her outrage, I suspected, wasn't at heart on Kate's behalf: I'd long suspected that, for all her apparent eagerness to serve, she regarded Kate as a bit of a nobody and a nuisance. She was making clear, though, that no man – of however high a rank – was going to get away with pushing his way into the queen's rooms and behaving disrespectfully while she was head of the ladies. I doubted the duke was much bothered, though, if he even noticed. He was more than accustomed to ladies'

indignation. I, though, was impressed. Not for want of trying, I'd never before managed to catch a glimpse of the Lady Margaret who'd suffered imprisonment for an unsanctioned love affair, but suddenly, I felt, I was seeing something of the girl she'd been, blazing and awesome in her fury. I envied her. Me, I was having difficulty breathing; I was utterly useless. I didn't even know how to breathe, let alone how I might be helpful to Kate.

The duke stood back while the cases were surrendered, sniffing occasionally and unproductively as if compelled to break the silence. Lady Margaret didn't open the cases; she left that to the men, but they made no move, they'd had no order to make a move and these were men who followed orders. She asked Kate an anguished, 'May I?' and inclined her head towards the bedroom door. Kate would've understood that it was either Lady Margaret or the duke who'd be going in there, so, although she didn't dignify the request with a verbal response, she nodded to permit it.

Lady Margaret disappeared into the airlock and in her brief absence the rest of us were suspended, no one looking at anyone else. She returned with a fourth case, then stood aside, hands clasped, white-lipped. The duke turned and stepped close to Kate. 'This?' he indicated her throat. I felt her shock and her shame: she'd tried so hard to keep one step ahead of him but here he was, catching her out, because she'd overlooked what she was already wearing.

He'd stopped short, of course; he hadn't dared touch her, but it was obvious he was itching to. If there'd been no one there to witness it, he'd probably have snatched at her throat.

'Cat,' she said, icily: summoning me to do the deed, to unfasten the necklace. I fumbled, and impatience rose like heat from her skin. I was mortified: I didn't want to be participating in this, to be easing it in any way, but, seeing as I had to, I wanted to get it over for her. When it tumbled free of its catch and fell into my hand, I was momentarily snared by its brilliance and intricacy. Just stones, I had to remind myself, and just metal. A necklace didn't matter, however much it insisted with its trickery that it did. What mattered was our lives: we should hand over these jewels and get away with our lives.

All the same, I couldn't quite stomach handing it to him so I offered it to her – her eyes flared with the diamond-light as I raised it – but with a switch of those eyes she indicated that I should give it to him. He affected nonchalance, didn't even glance down at it in his hand but passed it to one of his men who then headed with it to the leather cases. He gestured in his wake: *Open the cases.* And so the two men set to work, one of them opening a case and removing the items, laying them on a bench, while the other man noted the contents, peering and biting his lip to consider the description before scratching away with his quill.

There they were: the diamonds and pearls that had graced her collarbone on Christmas Eve, the emeralds that had spilled over her bodice one evening in York, the rubies she'd slung around her neck before an assignation with Thomas Culpeper. The two of us stood watching, unsure what else to do. Lady Margaret alone radiated a sense of purpose, bearing witness.

Then the duke turned again to Kate, this time indicating her brooch. Kate drew breath audibly, as if wounded. 'Mine,' she snapped, 'from the king,' and whirled to me. 'Tell him,' she insisted. 'The king gave me this.'

'He did,' I squeaked, rushing before I could clear my throat; and then, when I'd cleared it, there was no need, he'd taken her at her word and lost interest.

But now she'd started, she couldn't stop, and she raised her voice: 'There was no pre-contract with Francis Dereham.' Again, to me, and just as loud: 'Tell him!'

As a reflex, I opened my mouth to do it but she was already shouting over me, 'There was no pre-contract!'

Lady Margaret winced – I detected the dip of her head – and the two men froze mid-plunder. The duke alone looked unruffled; replying, with the air of a friendly, intimate offer of advice, 'Go quietly, Katherine.'

Kate spluttered an outraged laugh, the sound of which flipped my stomach and drove my nails into my palms. She lifted her chin – that Norfolk chin, a match for his – and reiterated, 'There was no pre-contract.' *As you'll soon discover.*

But he sidled closer to her and, in a voice lowered to keep it from Lady Margaret and the men, said, 'It doesn't matter. Because the king doesn't want you any more.' He spoke tonelessly, merely relating the fact. 'Because you're not who he thought you were.' Still nothing on his face: no surprise or dismay or disappointment. It was fact, his tone suggested, and no point regretting it.

But that did it. 'I am!' Kate shouted at no one in particular. 'I am!' she pleaded, screamed to the room. 'I'm *me*!'

And my heart flew to her, because, yes, nothing could be more true, she was always so utterly herself, and she should never have been made to be queen. How on earth had it happened – that she'd married the king? It was absurd, it'd been a terrible mistake and not of her own doing, and now look . . .

We had to get out of there while we could, as if none of it had ever happened. I needed to get Francis and get us back to where we'd come from. It was all over, and I was glad, I was really, truly glad of it. The duke turned from her, walked away, towards the leather cases. 'Katherine –' he sounded bored, *I have a job to do.* As an after-thought: 'Just count your blessings that this is as bad as it gets.'

Anne Boleyn: the reference was unmistakeable.

'Just go quietly,' he offered again, almost kindly.

'Where?' she demanded. I was surprised she'd asked, but she'd managed to load it with malice so that, marvellously, it chased him across the room like a threat.

He dealt with it, though, without even looking round. 'Probably to a nunnery,' adding, 'arrangements are being made,' as if she were thereby being done a favour.

After he'd gone, we heard no more for most of that day, and I didn't know whether to believe him. The king's men – Wriothesley, Cranmer, the duke – let Kate be, left her to stew. She had something to say – that there'd been no pre-contract with Francis – but they didn't seem to want to hear it. Let go, she was thrown back on her ladies, none of whom – it was obvious – knew quite how to regard her. No one had any idea what she was supposed to have done. The crown jewels had been confiscated, which was drastic, but was that the extent of it? Had the problem been the jewels themselves – misappropriation, perhaps, accidental or otherwise? Or was the confiscation a punishment for something else? The ladies who were old hands had seen queens come and go, they knew it could happen, and they knew how quickly, but they'd also have seen queens in trouble and then forgiven. They didn't yet know if they should be distancing themselves from her, and how far and how fast. As for the Howard ladies: they could only hope and pray for the best.

Kate was careful to give nothing away. What, though, *could* she have given away? She and I knew as much as there was to know, but were little wiser than anyone else in that room. We did know that the trouble stemmed from how she'd behaved with boys at the duchess's – but as to why that should matter, we remained mystified.

Kate was subdued all that day, but careful not to be sullen, making efforts to meet the eyes of the ladies who weren't family or friends and even encountering some sympathy there because of her humiliation by the duke, whom no one liked or trusted. All morning and into the afternoon she embroidered, working on a design of peacock eyes, each oval blur of royal blue and earthy pink rendered in her intricate stitches. She conducted herself as if biding her time until the situation would be resolved. Sitting beside her, making a pig's ear of a red rose, my concern was elsewhere:

I never ceased thinking of Francis. What was happening to him, and how long could they keep him in the Tower? Could he perhaps already have been released, and be making his way back?

Mid-afternoon, Lady Margaret was called to the door and returned to whisper in Kate's ear. Catching no one's eye – not even mine – Kate rose, calm and dignified. She was off somewhere, to see someone, and although apprehensive, she looked glad of the opportunity to get the situation cleared up.

When she'd gone, I left for my room, deflecting Alice and Maggie's quiet, anxious offers of company, but I was no further than the yeoman-guarded corridor when a Howard-liveried man intercepted me, come to fetch me for the Duke of Norfolk. I supposed the duchess had tipped him off – *There's that Tilney girl, she might be able to shed some light* – but what, exactly, did he want of me? I was shaking so much on my way to his rooms that I could hardly walk.

In his office, he was sitting behind a desk, dwarfed by it, hunched in furs and frowning over papers; sparing me a glance as I was ushered into a chair. Flames were fractious in the grate and the walls dense with tapestries hauled from ancient Howard-houses, harbouring decades of woodsmoke, rushes-chaff and tallow-reek. He sniffed: a hard scooping back into the beaky bridge of his nose. His attendant withdrew: the door closed behind me, and gone was the snipping of shoe-leather at flagstones, the man stepping outside to loll against a wall, eyes skyward, and drink down the fresh air.

The duke's small eyes were puddled greys and white, having the look of a substance unset. 'Miss Tilney,' that surprisingly light voice, like a boy's, although he hadn't been a boy for sixty years. Easy to imagine him as a boy, tearing feathers from a trapped bird or dragging a scrabbling cat by its tail. I wondered what he knew of me. Only as much as he needed, certainly, which was probably almost nothing, no more than my name.

'Look –' he sounded rattled, plonked his elbows on to the desk – 'this business of pre-contract.'

'There wasn't one,' and just in time I added, 'Your Grace.'

But he didn't seem to have heard. 'And now she's even claiming that he forced her, but what she –'

'Into pre-contract?' I'd spoken before I realised. 'Your Grace?' *Forced her to get pre-contracted?* It made no sense. How on earth would he have done that?

'No – to . . . to . . .' his sigh was harsh like a bark '. . . let him have his way.' Contemptuous of the euphemism. 'But the point –'

'No,' I hadn't intended to interrupt, but he'd been misinformed. 'No – Your Grace – she's not said that.'

He snapped shut his thin lips to signal how little he appreciated an interruption. Then, 'Yes, actually, she has, but –'

'Rape?' My breath delivered something like a laugh at the very idea.

He echoed with an exhalation of his own; his, though, I suspected, at the notion of Kate ever having to be forced.

'When?' I was forgetting myself, I forgot *Your Grace*.

Clearly he didn't appreciate the insubordination but he

had business to do, so he pressed onwards. 'Yesterday, to the archbishop. Then in a letter to the king.' He scratched behind an ear. 'Shameful handwriting, I have to say, and the duchess employed a tutor, didn't she?' *Tut, tut. Waste of money for girls, as I always told her.* 'But what my niece fails to understand –'

'Francis wouldn't rape anyone,' I said, because, incredibly, it seemed that I was actually going to have to spell it out to him. How peculiar, to be saying the words 'Francis' and 'rape' in the same breath.

The duke turned still-eyed, lost – *Francis?* – then blinked and resumed: 'Of course it's understandable that she'd make such a claim, under the circumstances, but what she's failing to grasp is that it'll make no difference.'

What she'd be failing to understand would be that Francis could die for it. That, though, she'd never have failed to have grasped, so she'd never have said it and the duke was mistaken or – it occurred to me – looking to stir up trouble. 'The archbishop,' he was explaining, 'will want to see this through. Doesn't matter to him who pulled what up or down for whom; what matters is that she's been around.'

Around: so judged by this man, who had taken his laundrymaid as his mistress and, rumour had it, kicked his wife to the ground when she objected, and kept kicking until she bled from her ears.

'And if she's been around, then the king will get rid of her and we conservative old Howards will fall from favour, which will please our forward-thinking archbishop no end.' A twitch of his extravagantly attired shoulders: water off a duck's back; all in a good day's Howard-work, being disliked by the Archbishop of Canterbury.

I could see why someone might say it; of course I could. Kate might've been tempted to say it, to save her skin, if she didn't give a damn about Francis. Or me: if she didn't care about me. The duke was saying, 'The only hope, now, is if she admits to pre-contract.'

He'd startled me: *hope*.

'That's my hunch, anyway,' he continued. 'Because if she was pre-contracted elsewhere, then she was never properly married to the king, and he can just forget it. No need for a trial.'

Trial?

'Just put her away. Better for his wounded pride, and, of course –' that nasty smile – 'better for us.'

Oh, yes, because one queen-niece to the scaffold was bad enough – but two, in the last five years? Well, that would be bad for business, for Howard-business, the business of being a Howard, which was, as far as I understood it, their only business.

He said, 'She just can't seem to see it, though. Won't take it from me. But you: you seem like a sensible girl. See what you can do. Talk her round.'

Dismissed. That was why I'd been summoned – *Talk her round* – and now he was back to the papers with a flourishing of his quill.

Nothing had been said about the actual truth of the matter. I stood up, then made myself ask, 'What does Francis Dereham say?' I knew to say 'Francis Dereham'; if I'd just

said 'Francis', I'd have had the blank look again – *Francis?*
– and there was no time for that.

'Oh – Dereham's quite clear,' he didn't even glance up.
'Pre-contract.'

My throat closed, stinging.

'Oh –' an afterthought – 'and talking of fuss: there's
nothing else, is there?' He cocked his head. 'No more little
surprises?'

And then I remembered what it was that he didn't know:
what Kate had been doing with Thomas Culpeper. For all
the duke's spies and his machinations, he didn't know about
that. His Howard-girl, made queen, had been slipping off
the throne whenever the king's back was turned, to pull
one of his most trusted gentlemen into her bed. My heart
was racing, pushing a laugh up into my throat because how
glorious that the duke didn't know but I did, and Francis
did. *We* knew: we two nobodies knew enough to bring his
whole house of Norfolk to its knees and quite probably
even lower.

But then again, perhaps not. Because who knew what
the duke could do? Not me, I realised: I didn't know what
he could do. If he ever got wind of it, he might be able to
see it off. A word in an ear here and there, some chummy
appeals to reason and reminders of loyalties owing, all with
his affected world-weariness, all in the name of saving the
Howards. Was it feasible? If anyone could get it played down,
keep it contained, he could. Perhaps he'd take the risk of
not fighting shy but proclaiming it instead as jolly japes, as
good old-fashioned courtly love gone mad. And – who

knew? – he might just get away with it. I really didn't know. Thomas Culpeper might walk away with a slap on the wrist, even a slap on the back.

I answered his question with one of my own: was there any news of Francis? *Francis*: hear his name.

'Francis?' Then, 'Cranmer's your man,' and back to those papers, interview over.

Well, perhaps he was. Certainly the archbishop wouldn't have any interest in playing down what Kate was doing with Thomas Culpeper, if he knew. And he'd realise that he had the wrong man in the Tower. But he didn't know, and I couldn't tell him: I couldn't send a man – not even Thomas Culpeper – to his death. All I could do was hope that the king's men would see sense, soon, over Francis, and release him.

I didn't go to my room as I'd originally intended; instead, I returned to the Presence Chamber, where I walked in on a spectacle that had me transfixed. Kate was sitting on the floor, flanked by five or six ladies: heaps of satins and silks, at the heart of which nestled the richest, darkest velvet in the colour of a fresh bruise. Tears had reeked havoc on her face, it was as raw as an exposed nailbed. Something had happened, she had the look of a child in disgrace: humiliated and aggrieved, devastated but defiant. Brazen, her defiance – *If you're not with me, you're against me* – and tiny though she was among the ladies, she was bolstered by them and shining with the drama.

No Maggie or Alice. The ladies turned their baleful faces to me as if I'd kept them waiting. I was late in on it but now that I was here, they were thinking, I'd fall into line. Panic kicked my stomach: *outnumbered*.

'More,' Kate announced to me, pitching it between keening and a rallying cry. Something had indeed happened, there was something more for me to know, something bad, and my heart thrashed around and my breath fled because, whatever it was, she was going to drop it on to me in front of everyone.

'Two hours with the archbishop –'

She didn't ask where I'd been; that was irrelevant, which was suddenly and liberatingly how it felt: forget the duke and his brief, dismissive dealings with me, his stupid misinterpretation.

'– and more and more of the same.' She was stoked up on outrage, but my heart plummeted because there was in fact nothing new and we were as trapped as we'd ever been.

I squatted down in front of her; I couldn't stay standing over her. Her eyes were slippery with tears, their rims and her nostrils inflamed; I didn't like to look, but she held my gaze, made me do it: *See what they're doing to me.* Quoting the archbishop through gritted teeth, she tipped her head from side to side to parody his concern: '"Could we perhaps go over this again? . . . You met . . . you felt . . ."' Then, furious, 'Over and over and over again, and I've told him, I've told him. What more can I say? I've *told* him *every-*thing.'

And more, too, in the duke's mistaken view: the duke, that sly-eyed, mealy-mouthed, begrudging, calculating duke with his old man's warped view of the world. But this girl, here, my oldest friend, wide open to me and blaring her grief: I didn't doubt her. And I felt for her, I felt so badly for her, for what she'd had to go through: in my mind's eye I glimpsed her sitting stunned and dismayed in front of the archbishop while he pondered and agonised; and for a second, in my mind's eye, I found myself there with her and just as stunned.

'What he wants –' a cry at the injustice of it – 'is for me to say that I was pre-contracted. That's what he wants, Cat,' she appealed for me to acknowledge the absurdity of it.

Jane Rochford gripped her hand, *We're with you.* Anne Parr wiped her own eyes. I knew I should get on with relaying her uncle's advice, I should be telling her that it'd be easier for her if she'd agree to say that she'd been pre-contracted. Then she could walk free and there was every chance that Francis would follow her.

But she was racing ahead: 'Because then I can be got rid of. Cranmer wants me to be Mrs Francis Dereham – that's who I am, as far as he's concerned. That's who I'll be.' In theory, she meant, not practice. Just for the archbishop's purposes, that's who she'd be.

And away from here, I should've been saying, by then: Just think, that's what you could be: away from here, alive.

'Not queen,' she whined. 'And' – worse – '*never* queen.' Scrubbed from official history, a mere missing year or so in the hectic matrimonial history of the king. To those in the know, she'd have been a wrong turning taken by a man newly adrift in an arranged marriage, a man who'd had his head turned but had come to see her for what she was.

How, though, really, it struck me, had she ever been a proper queen? A little over a year running around in some lovely dresses: that's all it had been, her queenship. It hadn't ever been serious, she hadn't ever been in the least like a queen. A private wedding in a tiny chapel. No coronation. She was a nineteen-year-old girl who'd produced no heirs, promoted no one, inspired no reforms or counter-reforms, and made no alliances.

'But I *am* queen.' She gave a tear-sodden, hysterical laugh: 'I *am*.'

And that, of course, was just as true.

'He can't —' Sobs wrenched her ribs and she moaned with the pain of it. Twisting up on to her knees, she grabbed my wrists: *Do something.* 'If I could just get to the king! Where is he?' she demanded of all of us, of no one in particular. 'Why is he allowing this? They've poisoned his mind against me! If I could just see him! Just for one minute, just for a word —' And she was up on her feet before anyone had realised, all of us scrambling in her wake. She paced, hugging herself, holding herself together while we stood in attendance, eyes dutifully lowered.

'I was never pre-contracted to Francis Dereham —' and his name was sing-song, as if not only the notion of pre-contract to him was ridiculous but he himself, too.

But let her, I told myself. She was distressed, furious, terrified. *Let her do this. Take no notice of anyone else, catch no one's eye.* I was unaware that I'd turned from her until she spun me back around — 'Never!' — as if I'd voiced a contradiction. And then to everyone else: 'I'd never have even considered it! Why would I? Why on earth would I?' And viciously, '*Marry Francis Dereham?!*'

The ladies' confusion was palpable: desperate to gawp at me – the girl whom, they knew, lived for the chance to marry Francis Dereham – and just as desperate to shrink away in embarrassment. I'd have to get through it: one difficult moment was all this was, in a day full of them. It'd pass before I knew it and she'd be retracting what she'd said, apologising, explaining it away, begging my forgiveness. She was a blur in the corner of my averted gaze, a whirl of embossed velvets in the late-afternoon gloom as I stood there in her cast-offs – a kirtle lengthened by a border, a bodice shorn of fur, and sleeves unpicked of pearls – allowing the terrible moment to pass.

'I was never even that interested in him,' she protested to the room. 'I was never that keen. It was all *his* idea. I *wish* I'd never listened! Why *did* I? What was wrong with me? *That's* where I was stupid, but I was so young. I should've stood up to him, I should've refused, I should never have let myself be persuaded,' she bawled, 'but I was just a girl.'

Francis was just a boy.

I didn't know I was crying until Kate's sister handed me a handkerchief. Taking it, I glimpsed Izzy's eyes: loaded with sympathy but also the clear assumption that we'd stand firm together behind Kate. With that handkerchief of hers at my own eyes, I hid my despair.

Master Culpeper . . . I never longed so much for a thing as I do to see you and to speak with you. It makes my heart to die to think what fortune I have that I cannot be always in your company . . . Yours as long as life endures, Katherine

At the end of the awful summer that I'd had to spend at home, a letter had at last arrived for me, written in Kate's own hand but formal in tone, informing me that I was required to come into her service. *As soon as you're back*, she'd added.

I resolved to be back as soon as possible, plague or no plague, although fortunately the epidemic was well on the wane by then. Naturally, my parents were amazed and thrilled, but I detected trepidation on their part – with which, privately, I felt considerable impatience. Not that I didn't understand it: this opportunity for me was so very much more than they had ever hoped for, but would take me into a world of which they knew nothing. I had no such qualms, though. My best friend was queen – how could life, at court, be anything other than easy for me?

The only immediate hitch was that I was ill-equipped. The clothes I'd worn at the duchess's Lambeth house were better than those in which I'd kicked around at the Horsham house, but they'd never do for the palace. That, we knew, even though we had little idea of what *would* be acceptable. For that, we needed expert advice, which took time to secure. Recommendations were sought, and a busy tailor had to be prevailed upon to make the trip down from London. Then, though, it was going to take him time to make the clothes. And time for my father to sell some land in order to be able to pay the bill. Meanwhile, the tailor made some inspired adaptations to my existing, serviceable summer gown, and, after he'd returned to London, sent back various stylish accessories such as a pair of beautifully decorated sleeves and a sleek French hood. Then I was ready to go – or as ready as I could be, on a limited budget and in just ten days.

Someone had done a fantastic job of dressing Kate. I first saw her as queen from the doorway of the Presence Chamber and she was the centrepiece in that fabulous room, wearing cloth-of-gold: cloth woven from real gold that had been thinned to thread. The expense and expertise that had gone into the design and making of that gown – which was clear even to my inexperienced eye and at first glimpse from across the room – was to proclaim the presence of the Queen of England. Despite its perfect fit on her, that golden gown belonged to the Queen's Wardrobe. I wish I'd been better able to heed what I was seeing: that Kate Howard didn't exist any more. Kate Tudor, the king's wife, spun from gold, was someone else entirely. Or she should've been.

'Thank God you're here,' was what she first said to me – or whispered – as if I'd been the one who'd been incommunicado, and she took me aside, guiding me ahead of her into a gallery where the panelling was so intricately carved that my fingertips had an urge of their own to explore it. Closing the door behind us to ensure we were unaccompanied, she insisted, 'I need you here,' as if she'd been denied me. Pacing, she was giving little kicks of kirtle, the colour of which – stunning though it was – was elusive, like that of an eye of a peacock feather. She was complaining that Lady Margaret had been appointed by the king as head of her ladies and had chosen her team. 'Don't leave me with them, Cat!' She said it jovially, but when I looked into her eyes there was no trace of humour. *Them*: the likes of the Parr sisters, I'd soon learn, and the Lizzies Cromwell, Fitzgerald and Seymour, all so much more practised at being in the queen's household than the new queen herself. I'd learn, too, though, that she was being disingenuous, because in fact she was far from isolated among Lady Margaret's ladies. Izzy's husband – Sir Edward Baynton, 'Bay' – was running her household, and she'd appointed Izzy and their stepmother as ladies-in-waiting, as well as an aunt and cousin. The king, too, was busy making favourites of her two closest brothers, George and Charlie.

At the time, she merely told me that Maggie and Alice were already in residence.

'Alice?' She'd taken Alice from Lord William? Poor Alice.

'Lord William's abroad. Oh, and –' conspiratorial – 'guess who's written, asking for a place.'

I was in no mood for guessing games. I'd had a long ride, my legs were shaking and there was a tightening around my eyes. She hadn't yet asked after me, and hadn't given me a chance to ask after her. I seemed to have walked in on the middle of a conversation that she was already having with me. My physical disorientation wasn't helping. I'd been taken through gatehouses and across courtyards and up stair-cases. I felt that if I could just glance from a window and see the river, I'd know where I was and be better able to concentrate on what she was saying.

'You'll never guess,' she rattled on, before providing the answer: 'Jo.'

'Jo Bulmer?' Even having to say the name was bad enough.

'Pleading for a place.' And she raised her eyebrows before letting it slip: 'Unhappy marriage.'

Four times is all I'm doing it: hanging there unsaid in the air between us, no longer a laughing matter now that one of us was married.

'But you'll say no, won't you.'

She inclined her head, teasing but also taking me to task. 'She's unhappy, Cat.'

'Not as unhappy as I'll be if she comes here.' It was the first time I'd referred to my dislike of Jo Bulmer, but I knew it'd come as no surprise to her. She'd only tolerated Jo Bulmer because she'd known she'd do her bidding. And she had a palace full of people to do that, now.

'Not your choice, though, is it?' she said, half-joking, but only half, and I could hardly believe she'd so casually pulled rank.

All I could manage in retaliation was, 'I am *not* sharing a room with her.'

That, though, she barely bothered to address. 'Talk to Bay, he deals with rooms.'

Well, if we weren't going to bother observing niceties, I could get straight to what mattered to me: 'Where's Francis?'

I hadn't known if she'd know but in fact she didn't miss a beat. 'Ireland.'

I felt as if I'd been shot. '*Ireland?*'

'Business opportunity,' she quoted. 'Just for a couple of weeks, he said to tell you.' And she rushed to reassure me: 'He's keen to make money, Cat, so he can set up a household of his own.'

A household of his own would make him a marriageable gentleman. I trusted to taking a breath again.

'And when he gets back,' she was heading back to the roomful of ladies, 'there's a place here for him.' She flashed me an amused look: 'Can't have you moping, can I. No use to me like that, are you.' Then, opening the door, 'You'll be meeting *my* husband, this evening.'

I never did meet the king; I was often in his presence but it was never my place to meet him. The first time I laid eyes on him, what floored me wasn't his size – extraordinary though that was – but that his bulk was so nakedly physical: his lips over-wetted; follicles more visible than the hairs themselves; and his lame tread so heavy. All the silks stretched over him and gold chains around him served not to distract from the flesh but to accentuate it; there was no escaping it. That first evening – and indeed *every* evening – he made a show of doting on his new wife and demanded the same from everyone else, his gaze sweeping up all others to her. Under such scrutiny, she held herself perhaps a little more stiffly than I'd remembered – although that could've been down to the sheer weight of her clothes – but otherwise she looked the same as ever: the high-held head, the stubborn Norfolk chin, the cryptic half-smile. That very first evening, I felt that I could see what it was about Kate that had attracted the king. He could've had any of the women in that room, but however modest they contrived to appear, they were intending with those demurely down-turned gazes to show themselves to their best advantage. There was none of that from Kate. I could see how he'd think that there was a kind of honesty to her. More likely, I felt, it had something to do with how – as she'd once told me – she was scared of nothing.

Her ladies hadn't taken to her, I didn't think; despite their efforts, I saw it even on that first evening. I understood how they felt because, until I'd known better, I'd felt the same. Kate appeared to give so little of herself: that was the problem. And although that was only right and proper now that she was queen, most of the king's previous queens had probably still managed to endear themselves to their ladies. The first queen, the first Catherine, so gracious and so very kind, had been much loved; and the latter one, Anne, from Cleves, cheerfully giving herself over to her ladies' guidance, had been well liked. Jane Seymour must've been harder to warm to, but her beady eye on her ladies' behaviour was because she'd wanted the best from them and perhaps thereby also *for* them. She'd been determined to make something of them, if only good Christian ladies. And Anne Boleyn? Well, the best that could be said was that her outbursts would've rendered her vulnerable. Kate's problem, I realised that first evening as I watched her through others' eyes, was that she gave the appearance of being invulnerable.

True to his word, Francis returned within a couple of weeks, on St Matthew's Day. There he was, at supper, watching for me to spot him; and when I did, my heart slammed into my throat, almost suffocating me. My gorgeous, joyful boy, even more so than I'd remembered, and despite his days at sea and on the road. A table-length away and amid bustling servers, he was laughing to see my helplessness, mouthing, *Meet me later.*

Where? I panicked that there'd be nowhere.

His response was an infuriatingly unperturbed little shrug: *We'll find somewhere.*

As it happened, we didn't need to, because later that evening was the first time Kate offered us Thomas Culpeper's bed. The king had retired early, leaving his gentlemen to be entertained in Kate's apartment. Dancing was about to begin – she was still seated, changing her shoes – when she whispered to me, 'You and Francis can have Thomas's room for the night.'

A room, the night: that was what I heard first, and – a little drunk, still dizzied by Francis's surprise re-appearance and distracted by the music that had struck up – I had enough trouble making sense of that. Had she said that the two of us could have a room? But when did lovers ever have a room to themselves for a night?

And Thomas's? I doubt I'd have known who 'Thomas' was, if Thomas Culpeper hadn't, at that exact moment, been first to step into the cleared centre of the room, reaching blindly behind him for one of the Annes.

Thomas Culpeper?

I looked back at Kate. She was watching him, too, intently.

Thomas Culpeper's room? But how would that work? 'Won't he –' mind? Be there?

She half-smiled. 'Not if he's in my room with me.'

A joke, I assumed, but she confided, 'Roch's on duty –' Jane Rochford, on sleep-in duty – 'so she'll watch for us,' and then she was telling me which staircase Thomas Culpeper's room was on, and which floor, and making me repeat it to check I'd got it. I *had* got it, but –

'And if I were you,' she said, supple shoes on and equipped for dancing, rising from her chair, 'I'd stop wasting time.'

I was still trying to think my way through what she'd said. Jane Rochford? Watch for them?

Thomas Culpeper, in Kate's bedroom?

It was a joke, wasn't it?

But her hand was on my shoulder, giving me a little shake to send me on my way. 'Go,' impatient, insistent, '*Go.*'

Had she said – ?

Across the room, Francis was teasing Maggie, the pair of them laughing and her hand held bashfully over her heart.

'Thank you,' I said, but she was already laughing it off: '*Go.*'

So we did. A word in his ear had him follow me at a discreet interval to the door and slip demurely along the line of yeomen before, unobserved, bounding down the stairs to join me in the courtyard's nearest corner. There, he swayed into me, something of the sea journey still in his limbs like an echo in a shell, and I opened my mouth to his. Despite our racing hearts we took our time, pausing several times on our shadowed route to the staircase, and once on the stairs and even in the doorway, but although I came close on each occasion to losing myself in the intriguing gentle roughness of his lips on mine and the slide of my tongue on his, something was holding me back: *Thomas Culpeper*, I kept thinking. And wondering: did Francis know? Was *I* supposed to have known? Thomas Culpeper; her room; Jane Rochford keeping watch. She'd told me as if I'd already known, but I hadn't. Had I? Then, though, the inner door in Culpeper's rooms opened to reveal the bed: a big, sheet-strewn bed like a storm-rattled boat, and, ahead, the calm stretch of a whole night on which to sail away.

In the cool light of the following day, though, I set about observing Kate in the company of Thomas Culpeper. She professed herself tired; the most she could face, that morning, was a stroll through her garden and orchard. The king remained indisposed, and only a few of his gentlemen were retained in his rooms for the more intimate duties; the others were at a loose end and they joined us. Of Kate and Thomas Culpeper, as we ambled down the yew-edged paths, there was absolutely nothing to witness. They barely acknowledged each other. Kate idled with Izzy and me, complaining of backache and waving everyone else ahead, while Thomas Culpeper larked about with her brothers and paid undue attention to Lizzie Fitzgerald. But if Kate and he failed to exchange so much as a glance, that was − I now knew − because they'd had their fill, the night before, of looking into each other's eyes.

The door to the orchard was locked, everyone except Culpeper stepping aside as Kate came through with the key. Oblivious, he was standing with his back to her, expansively relating an anecdote to Charlie, and Kate had to push past him. Watching her do it, I recalled her first touch to Henry Manox: her hand on his shoulder as she'd passed behind him, the feigned nonchalance of it and its teasing lightness. There was nothing feigned in this shove of Thomas Culpeper. She really was just moving him where she wanted him, and, I saw, she was used to doing so.

That evening, she made clear what she expected of me. There'd be no summoning of her to the shared bedchamber − the king was still unwell − and nor was Thomas Culpeper on sleep-in duty, so they were both free and she needed me to keep watch for them. She didn't have to explain that

Jane Rochford couldn't do two consecutive nights on duty: no lady ever did, so, to avoid raising suspicion, someone else would have to do it. I'd been right, it seemed, in thinking that only Jane Rochford and I knew. Kate told me to swap sleep-in duties with that night's designated lady, Lizzie Seymour, having taken care to fabricate a convincing reason. All of this was voiced as a request but was in fact an order, and, duly, she didn't wait for my response but was gone across the room before I'd had time to absorb fully what she'd demanded of me.

There was only an hour before she'd be retiring for the night and I couldn't think fast enough as to how I could stop what would otherwise happen. With time closing down on me, I found myself taken up by the pressing problem of what reason I could give to Lizzie Seymour for needing a swap. And so it ended up having happened before I knew it: Kate and I were left alone in her bedchamber. Nightshirt-clad, she was lounging on the bed, eyes closed, candlelight spangled in the gold-embroidered neckline and crowning her loose, rosewater-refreshed hair. I should've been undressing but I dithered, only too aware that there was still an opportunity for me to say something but at a loss as to what might be effective. Dithering near the door as if my proximity to it might absolve me.

Just say something, I urged myself. *Anything*. If I could get started, something would come to me. 'Kate . . .'

She opened her eyes, widened them: *What?*

But she knew damn well what. 'Please . . .' Please don't

make me say this. Please don't draw me into this. Please don't take this appalling risk.

'Oh, stop fussing.' She sat up, hugged her linen-swathed knees. 'No one knows.'

As if that were an answer. And so I was left glancing despairingly around that panelling-fortified, tapestry-wadded room, wondering and worrying. 'But how – ?'

She directed my gaze to the little door in the far wall, the door which led to a dark, narrow staircase, an escape route to which only she and, presumably, her head of household had the key. A route to which, somewhere in the courtyard below, there'd be an entrance.

My heart thundered. 'What if anyone sees?'

'No one will.' She flopped back on to the pillows, luxuriated in them. 'They'd have to be looking, and no one is.' It was breathtaking, that confidence of hers, but probably not misplaced because in the eyes of the world this queen could do no wrong. She laced her fingers over her stomach, settling herself comfortably, and said, 'He's very, very careful, because – don't forget – it's his life that's at stake.' She was impressed by that, I heard, and understandably so. She was almost certainly right, too: if by any chance he was caught on the stairs to her bedchamber, she'd be beyond suspicion and it'd be assumed that he'd intended to lay assault to her. His only hope – an impossibly slim one – would be to persuade the authorities that he'd been acting in jest, perhaps on a dare.

'Listen . . .' She gazed at the gilded ceiling, gathering her thoughts, then sighed with the effort of making herself clear to me: 'I *deserve* this.' And slid me a look that had me catch my breath. The king, her frank stare implied: think of having to endure sex with the king.

But even if by any stretch of the imagination Culpeper could be said to be compensation, 'What if you get pregnant?'

She blew away my concern on a humourless laugh. 'Oh, I *need* to get pregnant.'

My scalp tightened in horror. I'd been hopelessly naïve. She had a plan, and future kings of England were going to be descended from mindless, preening Thomas Culpeper. That was an abomination. And even if no one ever knew it from Culpeper's bragging or perhaps from the looks of the child, *God* would know. Kate would go to Hell for it. I'd go to Hell for having known of it.

Belatedly, though, I registered her look of scorn. 'Christ, Cat, do you really think I'd risk that?'

'But –' How? A half-lemon, again? Was that good enough? Although certainly it'd worked before.

She raised herself on her elbows, to stress, 'I am so careful. I have to be, with Thomas. He's not like –' she faltered, lay back down – 'some.'

Francis, she meant: I knew it, although I wished I didn't. And it was true: Francis was good with his timing. Not that it mattered much for me because if I found that I was expecting a baby, we'd just marry sooner. Francis had said, though, that he'd prefer not to start a family just yet: *Let's give ourselves time, first, to enjoy each other.* Whereas Thomas Culpeper, I suspected, would have no regard beyond his own immediate pleasure.

Suddenly she slipped from the bed and over to one of her jewellery cases; she drew from it a handful of rubies which hung dolorous in the half-light. Shaking the necklace at me, she indicated that I should fasten it for her. What was happening? Where on earth was she going – hadn't she'd only just undressed? Turning abruptly, she splashed the rubies into the air behind her so that I had no choice but to lunge and catch them. Baring her nape to me, she remarked, indulgently, 'Thomas is a horror, he likes me in the crown jewels,' and, tutting, '*just* the jewels, and – can you believe this? – preferably kneeling.'

The stones slithered over my palm, darted between my fingers, spilled on to the carpet. Cursing, crouching, scrabbled at them, I suffered a scratch from the goldwork to the tender skin between two fingers. Rising, trying again, I still couldn't manage the catch and she snatched the necklace from me, slew it around her neck so that the catch was at her throat, before – frowning at me, reproachful – fastening it herself, '*There.*'

Cowed, I retreated to my most basic concern: 'Where should I sleep?'

'Jane just takes the mattress over there –' she gestured vaguely across the room. 'Because these hangings –' and then she flapped the hand at the hangings, which were as thick as walls and would make something like a tiny room inside the bedframe.

Even so, I didn't want to chance hearing anything. It'd been bad enough when it was Francis, but *Thomas Culpeper*? I indicated the airlock between the bedroom and the golden room: 'I'll sleep in there.'

She misunderstood me. 'God, no, not in my day room, that's far too risky: a chamberer coming in extra-early, finding you there . . . they'd know I was alone, and how would that look?'

'The airlock,' I corrected.

A bleat of disbelief. 'But you can't sleep in there!'

Surely the least she could do was allow me to decide for myself where to sleep. 'Why not?'

'It's not big enough!' She was wide-eyed with the hilarity of it. 'You won't be able to lie down!'

'Not completely stretched out, but –' I was irritated, turning defensive – 'I'll curl up.' Opening the door, I displayed the space to her.

'But still –' she peered dubiously into the cubbyhole – 'I doubt you could breathe in there.'

'Well, I'll keep the day-room door ajar.'

'No,' she protested. 'You can't do it.' And, in a tone that clearly she intended to be inviting: 'Just sleep in here.' Then, as if it were reason enough: '*Jane* does.'

Jane could do as she liked; I was no Jane. 'Really,' I insisted, 'I'll be fine.' And actually I was beginning to look forward to it: a night entirely on my own.

She turned away. 'Well, I think you're mad.' Then back again, sheepish, to assure me, 'Really, honestly, I promise you we'll be quiet.'

I made sure to be in the airlock before Culpeper arrived. Kate was as good as her word, but despite hearing nothing of them as I lay there, I did have to listen to the bed – that vast bed – slamming into the wall: on three occasions during that long night and its small hours came a rhythmic battering of the panelling. I lay there in dread of those brutal slams reverberating around the palace, and in fear of the tell-tale bruising of the linenfold that I'd be able to find in the morning.

Sometimes in the months to come Kate would dismay me by claiming in her own defence that queens had always had favourites, and I'd have to bite back my response: *Favourites, yes, who compose songs and poems for you and pick up your prayer book for you when you drop it and hand you silk scarves in their colours when they ride to joust; but not a gentleman of the Privy Chamber who strips you down to your rubies and bangs your bedhead against the wall.*

I didn't have to bite it back, though. I could've said it. Why didn't I? Was it because whenever she had a night with Thomas Culpeper and Jane Rochford was on duty, I had a night with Francis? A whole night alone with Francis. I'd never known the like, before; I'd never have considered it possible.

I dreaded Jo Bulmer being involved, if she ever arrived; but so far Kate hadn't mentioned her again and I'd felt it safest to avoid raising the subject. I knew why Jane Rochford was going along with it: because she'd been taken into the queen's confidence. Jane Rochford: cold-shouldered by everyone else. And cold-shouldered, she was bored, too. What made her amenable in Kate's eyes, though, made her dangerous in mine. Susceptible to taking it too far, and to flaunting her favouring. Certainly she flaunted it to me: I hated the look she sometimes gave me, feverish-eyed, knowing and insinuating. I hated how she imagined a bond with me because circumstances had us in together on Katherine's secret. Worst of all, I hated that she knew where Francis and I were on the nights when she was on watch, often sending us on our way with, 'Off you go, you two, and enjoy yourselves.'

And what of Culpeper himself? He was the type, surely, to brag of conquests, and his liaison with the queen had the dubious honour of being the ultimate conquest. I did dare raise it, once, with Kate, although I was careful how I put it: Did none of *his* friends know?

'He's not stupid,' was all she said.

In my view, he was exactly that.

He was always on guard against losing face, though, and he'd have known that if he claimed even to the closest friend that he was sleeping with the queen – the perfect queen, the beloved queen – he'd quite likely be disbelieved and ridiculed for it. As for being discovered, he was one to watch his back, to save his skin, and there was little risk, I felt, of any ill-judged loyalty to Kate in the event of trouble, of any misguided stepping up to declare true love for her. He could be relied upon, I suspected, to be quick with denials if it ever came to it, although possibly too quick to be of advantage to her, because I doubted he'd pause to check his version first against hers.

I felt powerless to stop Kate. She was the queen, and I was only at the palace at her invitation. Her liaison with Culpeper was already well underway before I ever arrived: it was established, and had its own considerable momentum with a schedule and a route and even accoutrements such as rubies. As with everything, she had presented it to me as a fait accompli; and, as ever, despite my misgivings, I concurred.

For the months of the following summer, though, when we were no longer on home ground but on progress around the country, Kate's assignations with Thomas Culpeper were much harder to come by. The longest we ever stayed anywhere was for a few days, so we had little or no time to familiarise ourselves with the interconnections of rooms and staircases, and rarely had the relevant keys. In any case, accommodation was so stretched that, usually, three or four of us were sleeping in with Kate. Thomas Culpeper – with the rest of the king's men – was often lodging somewhere else entirely, across town or on an adjacent estate. Even if he'd been nearby, I doubt Kate would always have had the will, having travelled all day in the heat and then been at various elaborate entertainments until late in the evening.

Occasionally, though, circumstances did permit, and she'd summon up the wherewithal, and then I'd have to lie there on my mattress on the floor at the foot of her bed with my sheet pulled over my head.

As for Francis and me, we barely saw each other during those hectic months. Being on progress is particularly gruelling for ushers of the king's and queen's households, responsible as they are for ensuring that everyone has somewhere to sleep. Francis could never travel with us, always riding ahead to make arrangements, but even when we were settled somewhere for a few days his time was taken up with complaints. Everyone had something to say about where he or she had been stationed, and it was never good. They were long, long days for him, and often he'd not even make it to the evening's feast, or not until too late: turning up parched and drinking too much too quickly on an empty stomach, falling asleep at the table. He had to endure it, was his attitude; it'd soon be over.

But once, towards the end of the summer, somewhere in Lincolnshire, he and I resorted to spending the night together in Kate's room alongside her and Thomas Culpeper. I was to have been alone on sleep-in duty, that night, and Kate suggested I take the opportunity to bring Francis along with me. She gave no clue as to why she was offering. Although neither Francis nor I welcomed the prospect of being in the same room as the pair of them, for the foreseeable future it was that or nothing. In the event, it wasn't as awkward as we'd anticipated. We absented ourselves until they were settled inside the bedhangings; then, sleepy, we were subdued on our straw mattress, and too weary in any case to be self-conscious. Mercifully, we heard nothing from behind the hangings.

A week or so later, in York, we accepted her invitation again only to discover, when it came to it, that Culpeper wouldn't be joining us. Kate seemed to have known all along; she seemed unconcerned, telling us, 'You two can have my bed,' as she took hold of the spare mattress to haul it across the room. Both Francis and I protested, and our protest was genuine: it wouldn't feel right to be in her bed and we'd get no pleasure from it. But she had no patience for this, and gave us short shrift – 'Oh, for goodness' sake' – as she dragged that mattress. We were all too tired to argue, we were already there and it would have taken too much effort to effect an escape for Francis, so that was how it ended up: Francis and me in a bed prepared for the Queen of England, and the queen herself an arm's length away on a straw mattress on the floor.

November 7th, late afternoon

I knew where to find Archbishop Cranmer: his lodgings were beneath the king's gallery. I knew I'd have to go to him. Kate had lied to him about Francis, and for Francis's sake I would have to put the record straight. The duke had said that it would make no difference for Kate; but for Francis, surely, it would make all the difference. I wasn't afraid to go to the archbishop: I knew from sitting through his sermons that he was no ogre but a circumspect, reticent man.

In the event, the only problem proved to be persuading his secretary that I hadn't come with a plea for clemency; but eventually I was allowed through to his study.

'Miss Tilney.' The darkness of the archbishop's eyes was matched by shadow beneath them, and he hadn't had the attentions of a barber for a day or two – an oversight which looked outlandish on him. By contrast, his hair was as artlessly cropped as a schoolboy's, unforgiving around his anxious face.

'Ralph –' *You can leave us now.* The man's reluctance resounded in the silence before the drawing-to of the door. This room was nothing like the duke's; it lacked the wadding of tapestries, and the trestle table that was serving as a desk was piled with books. There were only two chairs but a lot of leather-covered chests. The candles were collapsed, they'd burned late and this morning someone had neglected to visit the chandlery. The fireplace gaped, cold.

He seemed wary of startling me, his head inclined and his big brown eyes beseeching. 'Ralph says you have something to tell me.'

So here it was, my moment. I cleared my throat and made myself do it: voiced my suspicion that the queen had suggested that Francis had 'forced her'. Forced her to do what, I didn't specify, hoping hard that he wouldn't request an elaboration.

Polite concern from him: 'And you believe this not to have been the case?'

I confirmed, 'It wasn't the case.'

'Thank you,' he said, earnestly. 'That's useful.' But clearly the opposite was true because the thank you was too quick, too smooth and, although I didn't understand why, I knew at once that Francis would be staying in the Tower. My pulse turned hectic because *why*? Why had telling the truth made no difference? What on earth could I do or say that *would* make a difference?

'Did she?' I heard myself pressing him.

'Did she?' he echoed, just as surprised, searching my eyes with his own.

'Say it.' That he'd forced her.

'Oh.' He spread his long hands in a gesture of helplessness: You know I can't say, you know I can't discuss the particulars of the case.

No matter, I told myself; I'd said what I'd come to say. I'd told the truth. I'd done it; I'd done what was right even if it seemed to have made no difference. *Leave it, and go.* But I couldn't hold it back: a wail of despair: 'Why is he in the Tower?'

The archbishop leaned forward in a bestowing of yet more concern. 'To enable us to continue our enquiries.'

But, 'Into *what*?' Unfortunately, this came as a whine. 'Because he's *told* you.' And I told him again: 'They had a romance, he didn't force her, they weren't pre-contracted, and then it was over.'

Something shone fleetingly into his eyes – scepticism? – and a realisation passed through me like a shiver, escaped me like a laugh: 'You think it's still going on?' That, I'd not anticipated, but of course, it made sense: something, at last, that made sense, because if they were suspecting him of an affair with Kate, then no wonder he was still in the Tower.

'As I say, we're continuing our enquiries.' His eyelids low over those cow-eyes.

'But of course it's over!' Too loud, and I, myself, flinched. 'He and I are getting married!'

He mustered a smile, which was more of a wince.

'*You're* married,' I accused, not knowing quite why I'd said it, quite what I meant by it. *Priest-man: you're married.*

He sucked on his top lip.

Listen, 'Can't you just let him go?' A turn of a key: that was all it would take.

Still, though, the sorrowful look.

'But he's done nothing wrong,' I insisted. 'He's . . .' and the word that came was 'good.' *Good: isn't that something that you – Archbishop – can understand?* 'He . . . fell for a girl –' which was exactly what it was, a falling – 'when she was . . . free.' When she was no one and it didn't matter. 'And then, later, it was over.' *Can't you see?* 'He's loyal, is Francis,' I pleaded, 'and he's honest. He's not the problem.'

'And the problem is . . .?'

What did the archbishop mean by that? How should I know what the problem was? What was at issue here was precisely that I didn't know. I'd told the truth and nothing had changed. His question was genuine, though, to judge from the widened eyes and lightness of tone; he was laying himself open to my response. And it occurred to me that I did know, or at least I did have an idea. I recalled what the duke had implied: 'You think Kate's not the right queen for England, because she's a Howard.'

He dismissed it with a small, exasperated, self-deprecating noise, a shrug of a breath: *As if it's up to me.* Which didn't entirely convince. Then he made to rise with the aim, presumably, of showing me the door.

'Francis isn't the problem,' I repeated. Francis – what he did, back in the old days at the duchess's – was irrelevant.

Slowly, he reversed his rise, sitting back down. 'So, who is?' he asked me, gently.

I was thrown: how had we got to that? I couldn't think back to what it was that I'd just said. Whatever it was, though, he'd misunderstood me.

'Miss Tilney?' That apologetic inclination of the head, again.

Thomas Culpeper should be in that dungeon in Francis's place, but if I breathed a word of it, he'd die. And Kate, perhaps, too. And perhaps Francis and me, for having known and allowed it – helped it, even – to happen. Although perhaps not Francis, because they wouldn't have to know that he'd known. If they questioned him about it, he'd deny it. Not for his own sake, but for hers. Obviously he'd given no word of it so far. They could do whatever they liked to him and he'd probably still deny that she was sleeping with Thomas Culpeper. For her sake.

I didn't answer the archbishop's question, but asked him one. 'Did she say it?' About Francis.

But she couldn't have done, could she? We were supposed to be going off into the future, the three of us, to be happy. That was the idea, the plan, that was what we'd always said, what we'd joked about, what we'd agreed: Francis and me to marry, and our children to be brought up in Kate's household.

The archbishop didn't respond, initially. Not a single blink of those big, sad eyes; nor, even, it seemed to me, a breath. He was reluctant to let me turn his own question around. And – I could see – he was thinking. Eventually, though, he bent down in his chair – one easy sweep – to lift the lid of a leather chest and take from it a piece of paper which he placed gently on the table in front of me. Having surrendered it to me, he sighed wearily and sat back, closed his eyes, frowning as if troubled by a headache.

But then I found I couldn't look at it, whatever it was. It held an answer to my question. Those pitying eyes would open again in no time and he'd watch me reading it, and suddenly I couldn't bear that. Then, though, as if he understood, he snapped up from his chair and stepped to the window, standing there with his back to me. That long, black back. Released from his scrutiny, I glanced down at a letter. It was unmistakably Kate's handwriting: her scrawl, which had always looked so jolly and, as far as I knew, had never before been put to any serious use. I scanned the letter, spotted what I was looking for: *Francis Dereham by many persuasions procured me to his . . .* Reading the words, I was conscious of whispering them as if I were a child, tracking them, anxious that the meaning might give me the slip. Calm, was how I felt as I read, but my cheeks were ablaze.

I addressed his back: 'Did you make her write it?' I was merely making my own enquiries, not lobbing an accusation. I was confident that he'd tell me the truth or at least that I'd be able to detect if he didn't. He replied with that sound again – a shrug of a breath – but the pitch was lower, derisory, despairing: an admission, *No, of course not, because – you said it yourself – I think she's the wrong queen, so why would I want to help her make excuses for herself?*

'It's a lie,' I confirmed.

'I know.'

'You let her say it, though. Write it. To the king.'

He turned, with a little upwards throw of his hands: *She can do as she likes.* 'And the king –' he stopped, it didn't need saying: the king's no fool, there was no danger that he'd be taken in by it.

She'd said it, and she'd written it down for the monarch to read. She'd signed Francis's death warrant, in effect, for a chance at a future of her own. Well, her future – if she ended up having one – would meet no obstacle from me: I'd leave her to it, I'd never see her again, I'd leave this room and turn into Fountain Court rather than Inner Court, fetch some belongings, go down to the river, go to London, and work something out from there. I could do it, I could; surely it could be done.

I checked: 'It won't help her?'

'No,' he sounded regretful. 'It won't help her.'

For nothing, then, her betrayal of him.

'And you did tell her that?'

He nodded.

'But she was still willing to try.'

He allowed, 'She's very frightened.'

'We all are.'

'What *is* the truth, Miss Tilney?' That tentative incline, again, of the head.

'You don't care about the truth.'

'Actually, it's all I care about.' Rueful again, as if admitting a weakness.

So I reiterated: 'The truth is there was no pre-contract, just a romance, and he didn't force her, and it's over now and he and I are going to get married. That's the truth.'

'That's the truth about Francis Dereham.' He linked his hands. 'But what's the truth about the queen?'

What 'queen'? It was all over for her, as queen. Which would mean – it occurred to me – that Thomas Culpeper probably wouldn't want her, either; he'd wouldn't want anything to do with a disgraced queen. No man would. It was all over, for her. 'There *is* no truth about the queen,' I said, which sounded wrong, didn't make sense. I shook it away. I didn't want to think about her. 'Let Francis go,' I pleaded. 'He's innocent: you know that much.'

He draped those long, delicate hands over the back of his chair. 'The problem is,' he confided, 'that we have a very, very hurt and angry king.'

Not good enough: 'He shouldn't be angry at Francis; Francis isn't who he should be angry at.'

'Oh –' *don't worry* – 'he's angry at the queen, he's furious with her. But she was his little rose, and someone –' *in the king's view* – 'is responsible for the rot.'

Rot: I recoiled. 'Not Francis.'

'No.' He withdrew from the chair, half-turned to the window, gazing away. 'Someone else?'

Nothing at all entered my mind; I kept it clear. I could do it, I told myself: I could know nothing. It was crucial that I knew nothing, although I did wish the archbishop knew. Francis's and my problems might well be over if he knew.

He glanced back to me; just a glance. 'You're frightened.' He was sympathetic.

Of course I am. Tears trembled in my eyes but I held my tongue; he'd get nothing from me, I'd fall into no traps.

He returned to his chair, edged around it before sitting down, and there were those great dark eyes again. 'What's frightening you?'

'I'm not frightened.' I swiped at a stray tear.

'Concerned, then.'

'Anyone would be concerned,' *given the circumstances.*

He sighed, sadly. 'Anyone would, yes. But you?' So soft a voice. 'What's your particular concern?'

'Same as anyone's: what'll happen.' He could make of that whatever he liked.

'To the queen?'

I said nothing.

'To you, then?' Those eyes. 'If you tell me what you know?'

How did he know that I knew something? *Did* he know?

When I said nothing, he said, 'Well, as for the queen, she can throw herself on the king's mercy, which she's already doing, and, frankly, I don't think it can get any worse for her. And who knows?' He brightened a little. 'It might even get better, in time.'

Could that possibly be true?

'But you: you're frightened for you?' Full of concern. 'Because you've known about something?'

Still I said nothing. He was so close, I was stunned.

'You, alone, know?'

He didn't have to know that Francis had known, and anyway Francis would deny it; Francis was safe.

'Is there anyone else I could try?'

Try: that was all it would be. He made it sound perfectly reasonable.

'Miss Tilney? Is there? Anyone, for me to try? Because if there is, a name will be all I need from you.'

I couldn't look at him.

'Do you understand? A name, and then you'll be free to go.'

To try, was all he'd said. That was all: trying was all he'd be doing. Just a name, nothing else, no information.

'Miss Tilney?'

He could try and still fail. Kate could deny everything, and they'd be hard-pressed to come up with any proof to the contrary. But they'd no longer have any interest in Francis. Francis could go free. So, I looked him in the eyes and said it: 'Lady Rochford.'

He recovered himself almost instantly. Stupid Jane Rochford, who'd been so helpful in the downfall of his beloved, clever, reforming queen, Anne Boleyn: he didn't like Lady Jane Rochford, was what I'd seen.

He bit his lip, nodded. 'I could, I suppose. Yes, I could . . . try Lady Jane.'

Silence; but inside, my blood shrieked and roared and I feared that I was about to drown in it.

'Here's what I'm going to do –' he was speaking quickly and lightly, proposing a solution to a problem that he was keen to present as no problem at all – 'I'm going to ask

Lady Jane to come and talk to me.' And then he surprised me with: 'Will she tell me what she knows, do you think?' The bitten lip, the wide eyes: it was an honest question. He really did want to know from me what he might expect, how he might proceed.

I was about to say that I didn't know, when I realised that actually, I did. 'Not at first.' In time, though, yes, and probably very little time.

'But what should I ask her about, d'you think?' That same pleasantly practical tone. 'Where, perhaps, should I start?' A simple matter of procedure. 'A name,' he suggested. 'Just a name, Miss Tilney. Just as somewhere to start.'

Somewhere to start. That was all. 'Thomas Culpeper.' My stomach flipped as I said the name.

'Our very own Thomas Culpeper?' I heard the considerable effort in trying to keep it casual. Thomas Culpeper: the king's favourite.

I said nothing; I'd already said more than enough.

'Our very own Thomas Culpeper,' he said to himself, and nodded as if he might well have known it all along.

The archbishop had said that I was to go back to the queen's rooms and carry on as normal: that was how I'd escape suspicion. It would take a while, he explained, for him to question Jane Rochford and then for Culpeper to be called in. Meanwhile, I should give nothing away. But – I'd pressed him – what about Francis? How, and when, was Francis's freedom to be secured? He'd reiterated: Francis was out of his hands; he could only do so much, but he'd do his utmost and he anticipated no difficulties – not now, he implied, that there was a bigger fish to fry.

As for me, though: I'd never be implicated. Jane Rochford, under questioning, would be the one to confess to having encouraged the queen's improper behaviour and she'd inform on Thomas Culpeper. The archbishop would be doing the questioning and if and when she cited my role, he'd omit to make a note of it; and, if necessary, he'd explain and ensure that anyone else – such as Wriothesley – did the same. I was to be protected. I had his word.

Go, he'd advised me, but go back to the queen's rooms and act normally. Easier said than done, as it happened. Emerging from his study into the palace's inner courtyard, entangled in skeins of rain, I felt incapable of taking another step. I was shaking, and then I retched. This was a fever, I told myself: I'd worried myself ill and was in need of my bed. When I reached my room, I asked Thomasine to take word to the queen's rooms that I was unwell.

And there I lay, under my blankets, reminding myself over and over again that all I'd done was give the archbishop two names. I'd told him absolutely nothing: just given him two names. The rest would be up to them – Jane Rochford, Thomas Culpeper, and Kate – and they'd play it down. They could make it a simple tale of poetry-composition and prayer-book retrieval; they'd do fine, they were accomplished at deception. Anyway, I didn't care what they did or how they did it. All I cared about was that Francis should be free. He'd done nothing wrong and he should be free.

When Alice came in, late, I pretended to be asleep and endured her clodhopping attempts at tiptoeing – thankful, for the first time ever, that I'd been allocated a room with her rather than with Maggie, because I would've found it much harder to keep from confiding in Maggie. In the morning, I maintained my pretence of sleeping until she'd gone. I couldn't lie low for much longer, though, I knew, and within the hour I was composing myself at the door to the queen's Presence Chamber.

Inside, there was no one but Lady Margaret, sitting on a stool at the unlit fireplace, chin in hands, looking like a ragdoll despite her luminous abundance of plush grey silk. She raised her eyes – which looked pink, but they often did – to mine, and shunted them to the far door: Kate's day room. So, that was where everyone was. Why not her? She unsettled me, perched there, resolutely expressionless, and I was only too happy to oblige, to pass through that chilly room with its reeking ghosts of sea-coal smoke and wick-flare.

However awkward the atmosphere awaiting me in the day room, it'd be preferable. Pushing open the door, I antici-pated candle-burnish and a haze of brazier-warmth, a cluster of ladies feigning nonchalance over their embroidery with a dream-wracked dog at their feet. But again a cavernous room glared back at me, the golden magnificence of this one tarnished by unmitigated November murk. Something must've happened: there'd been a catastrophe while I'd slept and everyone except Lady Margaret – arch-survivor – had succumbed. But then I recalled the yeomen guarding the apartment: all present and correct and in rude health. And back beyond them, the courtyards had been peopled as usual. Only the queen's retinue had vanished. Why? Where was Alice, who'd gone ahead of me? The archbishop had said that nothing would happen quickly; and even when it did, would it really be as drastic as this – every last person gone?

One more room for me to try – Kate's bedchamber – and there was Kate. Alone, unfortunately: I hadn't anticipated that I might have to be alone with her. I was unprepared and, reeling, cursed my lack of foresight. Trapped on the wrong side of that door, I switched those silent curses towards her, as if she'd somehow snared me. I was trying and failing to discern if she knew yet that Culpeper was under suspicion. Soberly attired, she was standing at the far side of the stripped bed holding an armful of clothes, a couple of leather cases open in front of her on the mattress. She glanced up, expectant, but clearly I wasn't who she'd expected to see and – to my momentary relief – her attention dropped back to the task in hand, those cases. I was confounded to recognise her plain black gown from our time at the duchess's. It was worn differently, though, from at the duchess's: no turned-back cuffs, no raised collar. Worn as the duke, who'd paid for it, would've wished. The dress was the only respect, though, in which she resembled the girl from the duchess's: I was taken aback by her papery skin, dead-fish eyes, and a blueness to her lips as if she were suffering a lack of air.

How had that old black gown turned up here? In one of those cases? What was happening? I stayed by the door, trying to make sense of what I was seeing: was she unpacking, or packing? She'd been folding something and now she laid it in one of the cases. Packing, then. Going. But where? Well, wherever she was heading, she was on her way there as plain Katherine Howard. Going back, then – to the duchess's? Back from whence she'd come. Was that possible? And under what terms? She was packing her own cases and she was taking her time about it, methodical despite her obvious exhaustion: no sign of compulsion, no evidence of her being under arrest. By the look of it, she was free to go, and I dared to hope that it was all over, that this was the extent of it – this packing up and leaving, this returning – and now we could simply go our separate ways. I only wished it had happened sooner.

She remained unforthcoming and the silence was turning heavy, so I had to ask her: 'Are you going back to the duchess's?'

She remained busy. 'Syon.'

That, I wasn't expecting, and missed, which she detected, so she repeated it.

'– Abbey?' The only Syon I knew of: the old abbey, ex-abbey. Distant, secure, and respectable. Not, then, surely, her choice? I recalled what the duke had said: *a nunnery*. From there, though, when the furore had died down, would she go back to the duchess's?

Matter-of-fact, briskly packing, she explained, 'They know about Thomas.'

I should've come straight back at her with an expression

of surprise: *How?* Played the innocent. But I found I couldn't say anything, was seized up, unable to breathe.

She raised a nightshirt to shake it free of creases. 'You always said they would.' *And I always said, But you're not going to tell anyone, are you.*

I was right, though: they would've known about Culpeper, in time; they would've. It could never have stayed secret, under the circumstances; it'd merely been a matter of time. The only surprise was that she and Culpeper had got away with it for so long. How dare she expect sympathy from me. She was about to discover how it felt to have her lover in a dungeon. 'Well, just don't own up to very much,' I managed, linking my hands to steady them, to keep a semblance of calm.

'No,' she agreed, but obviously half-heartedly, making a show of humouring me.

At that, I felt a second flush of fury: *Oh, don't give me that, don't act so put-upon; you've lied before, no doubt you can do it again.* She could talk her way out of anything; she always had. And, after all, Syon was where she'd be: not in the Tower.

Suddenly, from her, 'Are you feeling better?' although she still didn't pause, still didn't look at me.

I'd forgotten that I was supposed to have been ill. 'Much better, yes, thanks.'

She said nothing.

And that was when I realised that she knew: she did know what I'd done. *But you'd have done the same*, I wanted to yell at her. Indeed, she'd already done it: protected her

lover at the expense of mine. *Did* she know, though? The
certainty vanished in the same instant, leaving us just as
we'd been: Kate packing her cases, me stuck there by the
door. I cast around, panicky: *where was everyone?* 'Who's going
with you?' Because surely she'd be going accompanied to
Syon, surely she'd have attendants?

She closed the lid on one of the cases, began buckling
its strap. 'I'm allowed to choose four ladies, and I'm taking
Maggie, Alice, Izzy and Anne Basset.'

Not you.

So, there it was, loud and clear. There we were, afraid to
look each other in the eye. When I did dare look, I found
that she too had relented, her gaze softening as she ventured,
'Cat, Francis'll need you here when he's released.'

But, actually, Francis would be fine; he and I were going
to have all the time in the world. Standing across the bed
from her, I realised that Kate had never intended any harm.
She just hadn't thought; she never did. She was a girl who
couldn't help but turn heads, she was a girl of no ambition
who'd become queen. She was a girl who couldn't help
herself. It was she who'd need me. *Don't you ever go through
anything like that again on your own.* In spite of everything,
my heart welled and I said, 'But if you need me –'

'– I don't.' She dropped her gaze, letting me go, shaking
her head as she lifted the cases from the bed, ready to leave,
to pass me on her way to the door. 'I don't.'

Afterword

Francis Dereham was never released. On December 1st, 1541, he and Thomas Culpeper were arraigned at Guildhall. Both petitioned the king to be merciful, to commute the punishment to beheading, but whereas clemency was extended to nobleman Thomas Culpeper, commoner Francis Dereham faced the full penalty for treason: to be hanged, drawn and quartered. The men died at Tyburn on December 10th.

Both men had maintained their denials of adultery with the queen – although Francis Dereham confessed to a sexual relationship with her before she was married – and despite Lady Rochford's incriminating accounts of the queen's assignations with Thomas Culpeper, no evidence of any overtly adulterous act was ever uncovered. The men were convicted of presumptive treason: Francis Dereham's coming into the queen's service, given his past relationship with her, was suspected to have been ill intentioned; and Thomas Culpeper, too, it was accepted, was hoping for sexual intimacy with her.

Katherine Howard never stood trial. For three months, she lived in relative comfort at Syon, her fate uncertain. At the trial of Francis Dereham and Thomas Culpeper, it was recorded that she had 'led an abominable, base, carnal, voluptuous, and vicious life, like a common harlot, with divers [several] persons . . . maintaining however the outward appearance of chastity and honesty,' and, three weeks later, at the trial of various Howard family members and others, it was asserted that she had 'traitorously retained the said Francis, and one Kath. Tylney, who was procuratrix between them and knew of their carnal life, in her service . . . and appointed Kath. Tylney one of her chamberers, and favoured them and gave them gifts, employing the said Francis in her secret affairs more than others.'

So many members of the Howard family and of Katherine's maids and ladies-in-waiting were under arrest by December that the Tower failed to hold them all, and other arrangements had to be made for their detention. One of the prisoners was a woman cited in the letters and records of this time as 'Kath. Tylney'; Wriothesley wrote of her in a letter, 'My woman Tylney hath done us good service.' At a trial on December 22nd, all these prisoners were found guilty of misprision of treason, and sentenced to the forfeiture of all their goods and to perpetual imprisonment. However, they were all released in the coming months.

Katherine Howard was taken from Syon to the Tower on February 10th, 1542, and the following day her death warrant became law. She was beheaded on February 13th, followed by Lady Jane Rochford.

'The brilliant spectacle of her career soon faded, leaving nothing but a king grown suddenly grey and aged and a law declaring it to be treason for a lady to marry the king unless she were a virgin, which, it was noted, rather limited the number of candidates.'

Lacey Baldwin Smith, *A Tudor Tragedy:*
The life and times of Catherine Howard, 1961

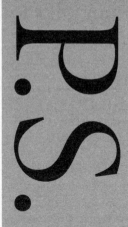

P.S.

Ideas,
interviews
& features ...

About the author

About the book

Read on

Suzannah Dunn talks to Sarah O'Reilly

Who, or what, made you a writer?
Oh, so many factors, as you'd expect. Here
are some: I'm the eldest of four children but
the others are much younger, so I spent a lot
of time in my own company. I had a typical
1970s primary school education ('creative')
and whilst I struggled terribly with maths, I
got a lot of praise for my creative writing, so,
I was well disposed towards it, and – like
many children – grew up thinking of myself
as a potential writer. Furthermore, I come
from a long line of self-employed workers
and could never imagine myself working for
anyone else!

But my impetus as a writer comes from an
oral history angle (putting it simply, my
interest is in people's lives, not books). My
mother, who talks endlessly, directed most of
it at me when I was a child because I was the
eldest. She was a great collector of people's life
stories. We did visit the local library sometimes
but, beyond that, we had no books at home
and I don't remember ever being read to. Even
now, although I love a good book, I'm still
primarily a talker and listener (I'm trying hard
to avoid the word 'gossip' here, as you can
probably tell . . .).

Later, when I started writing, the world was
a much kinder place for new young writers
than it is today due to economic factors. There
were no riches to be had, but it was possible,
with luck and state benefits or part-time
work, to have a life as a new author. I don't
think that's the case now.

You said once that you would never write about Katherine, the fifth wife. What changed your mind?

Because I was so sure that I was never going to tackle Katherine, she could serve as light entertainment for me when I was recovering from writing my last novel, *The Queen's Sorrow*. I settled down for a little light reading about her, but within half an hour I realised I'd been missing a trick. I'd been thinking of her as a 'silly little girl' but she was clearly rather more complicated than that. And the shape of her story too: that's a gift, for a novelist; that utterly unanticipated, precipitous fall.

The verdict of history on Katherine appears to be that she was out of her depth in Henry's court and too generous with her favours. What persuaded you that her story needed to be told?

My considered opinion is that this – the 'silly girl' view – is unsophisticated, and fails to grasp the complexity of Katherine and the situation. It's glaringly obvious to me that Katherine was a sexually confident young woman (in her sexual relationships with men – started when she was thirteen – she always had the upper hand, chose her lovers and moved on when it suited her) to whom her own small circle of friends and acquaintances were in thrall. That's far more interesting than the 'silly girl' story we've tended to be fed, and, if you accept it, the whole arc of her rise and fall makes sense in a way that, with the 'silly girl' view, it never quite does.

Suzannah Dunn talks to Sarah O'Reilly *(continued)*

You view the Tudors with a distinctly modern sensibility. Can you explain how this came about?

Well, I view them with *my* 'sensibility', which is inevitably 'modern'. Certainly I took a definite stance with the first novel, *The Queen of Subtleties*, because of who I was writing about. Anne Boleyn was *the* modern girl of her generation. She was confrontational and out-spoken, and her language so shocking on occasions that ambassadors would flounce offended from her presence. She was notorious, *in-yer-face*. Well, I'm not going to convey that with the odd 'Christ's foot', am I? And my job as a novelist – my job above everything as a novelist – is to convey a character: I need the reader to really know what Anne was *like*, to *be there*, not viewing her down the wrong end of a telescope as someone skipping about in a big dress, having hissy fits. She was far, far more powerful than that.

My argument is this: we don't know how people spoke in those days. We know how they wrote – or how some of them wrote – but no way is that ever the same as how people speak. For instance, does anyone really think that Tudor people didn't use contractions? I mean, why do characters in many so-called historical novels tend to say, for example, 'Do not' rather than 'Don't'? Even if we accept that people did often speak more formally to each other, did they always? I am not claiming that the Tudor nobility spoke as I have them speak in my novels; I'm just saying that we don't know how they spoke, so I have licence, in my novels, to have them speak as I wish. ▶

◄ In *The Confession*, you don't write about the more obviously dramatic moments in the story: the deaths of Culpeper and Dereham, for example, or Katherine's beheading. Why not?

It never occurred to me to put them in! I think – now that I'm thinking about it – that perhaps that's because, well, a beheading is a beheading is a beheading. I mean, what would it show you? You know it happened to them, but that's not their story. *Their* story – what's individual to them – comes before that; it's the story of their lives, not their deaths. ■

Small is Beautiful

By Suzannah Dunn

OH IF I had a pound for every time I've been asked, 'Are you going to work your way through all the wives? Are you going to do them all?' Certainly that wasn't my intention when I began with Anne Boleyn for *The Queen of Subtleties*: I was simply trying to write a novel about a fascinating character with a fascinating story who just happened to have lived and died about five hundred years ago.

Those five hundred years did give me problems but in the end I really enjoyed the reading and research, and welcomed the challenge of finding how best to use, in a work of fiction, what I'd learned from the history books. So, I decided to see if I could stay within that period for my next novel, and, as a kind of joke with myself (I know, I know, but I lead a quiet life . . .), turned my attention from the wife with the big story to the wife with, apparently, no story: Katherine Parr, who 'survived'. What I discovered was that the year and a half or so that she 'survived' were – mostly unfortunately for her – jam-packed with story.

After that, I didn't do a wife, I did a daughter, and chose the unpopular one: Mary Tudor, 'Bloody Mary'. An added contrariness of mine was that I knew next to nothing about Mary's reign and, in a way, didn't want to know much more. I did find that novel gruelling to write, not only because of the sheer volume of reading that I had to do but because of the grisly nature of much of the subject matter.

Reeling from Mary, I turned to Katherine Howard for a little light relief (no jokes, please, about not being the first to do so). I was merely reading about her: I had absolutely no intention of writing about her, or, more accurately, had every intention of never writing about her. I mean, why bother? As I understood it, she was a teenage nonentity, only briefly queen, who, stupidly, had an adulterous liaison with one of the king's favoured young gentlemen. Inevitably, her transgression was uncovered and she died for it. It's a story, yes, but not one, I felt, that would keep me interested while I wrote a novel about it. There was no mystery: nothing about which to speculate, nothing to try to understand. She simply did something foolish and suffered the consequences. Anne Boleyn, Katherine Parr and her best friend Catherine of Suffolk, Mary Tudor: these were complicated women with complicated personal and public histories, and whilst being very much of their – fascinating – age were also deeply against the grain of it. But Katherine Howard? Nope: couldn't get excited about her.

Still, she'd be good for a laugh (er, well, if we overlook her appalling fate), and after Mary Tudor a laugh was definitely what I needed. So, off I went, one post-Mary day, to a coffee shop, and sat in a sunny courtyard reading an account of Katherine Howard's brief, uncomplicated rise and fall. Within minutes, I was captivated. Eking out a couple of double espressos (there are only so many one can safely have, aren't there?), I read then and there to the end. What gripped me was that although she was undeniably in many ways an uncomplicated character – a ▶

7

Small is Beautiful *(continued)*

◀ conservative gal with very limited life experience even by the standards of the day, and no discernible interests beyond clothes and boys – she was very much star of her own little show, a position she attained and maintained against all the odds. She wasn't physically striking: small, not beautiful or probably even pretty, and, being relatively impoverished, probably not well dressed. She wasn't educated – barely literate – and she doesn't seem to have been clever or witty. She was never favoured by anyone with any clout (on the contrary, she was the tenth child of the hapless, derided, sidelined second Howard son). And her upbringing among many other girls in her step-grandmother's household, bang opposite the king's favourite, flashy palace at Whitehall, might as well have been in the middle of nowhere, so isolated and desperately old-fashioned was it. During those dramatic few years of profound social and cultural change, Katherine's girlhood with the Dowager Duchess of Norfolk was practically medieval.

So, how did this clueless little nonentity, at the age of thirteen, turn the head of her twenty-year-old music teacher, then, in time, dump him and move on to others, having plentiful sex in the girls' dormitory at the Duchess's, before, at the age of, perhaps, seventeen, capturing the heart of the middle-aged, much-married king? And how and why, then, did she get her friends to risk their lives so that she could continue with boys as she always had? In her own particular way, albeit small, she was clearly a singular and powerful girl: singular and powerful in a way that's wonderful for a novelist because, for novelists, I think, small is beautiful. It's the big stories that are easy: to a great extent, they tell themselves. The story of Katherine Howard – making it utterly convincing, making it 'real' – would be a considerable challenge, I realised.

I have on my wall a Holbein sketch of a plain girl who, it's said, might well be Katherine Howard sometime before she became queen. She wears no particular expression – by which I mean she's neither smiling nor looking serious (nor startled, as a few of Holbein's girls and women do) – yet every time I come into this room and look at her, I see something different. Sometimes she's faintly smiling, sometimes mildly bored, other times hopeful, occasionally calculating, occasionally wistful, often knowing, and sometimes she's the very picture of innocence. Well, Holbein was no fool, was he? There is – there was – a lot to Katherine Howard, none of it evident at first (or second . . . or third . . .) glance. ■

The Mysterious Face of Katherine Howard

By Sarah O'Reilly

IN THE TOWER of London on the last night of her life, Katherine Howard made an extraordinary request. She wanted the block on which she was going to be beheaded the next morning brought to her chamber so that she might 'make a trial of it' and 'place her head on it by way of experiment'. [1] Even in the face of death, this was a queen who cared about the spectacle she would present to her curious public: Katherine was a woman to whom image and appearance mattered.

How ironic, then, that today art historians are unable to agree on the identification of a single picture of the woman who took such care over the face she presented to the world.

Maybe we shouldn't be altogether surprised. Katherine's reign was short, and ended in disaster. What reason could there possibly be for anyone to *want* her portrait, after such a spectacular fall from grace? Even the Howards removed her picture from their family gallery after the execution. It is as if she just vanished.

And Katherine was someone who inspired love at first sight. Her grandmother, the Dowager Duchess of Norfolk, heard that 'the King's Highness did cast a fantasy to Katherine Howard the first time that ever his Grace saw her'.[2] No wonder scholars and art historians have tried so hard to find images of this enchantress.

The first portrait to be identified as Katherine (in the early eighteenth century) was a tiny miniature – only two inches across – painted by Hans Holbein and now in the

Royal Collection. It depicts a woman with smooth auburn hair, parted in the middle, wearing a square-cut dress, edged with a broad band of gold and jewels, and a French hood studded with pearls and gemstones. Her dark eyes are framed by hooded eyelids, and she fixes the viewer with a quizzical stare.

In Henry's time, the miniature portrait was the prerogative of the ruling dynasty. There were only two artists in his court with the skill to paint these tiny jewel-like artefacts, and neither ever divulged the secrets of their art to an apprentice. It was a highly exclusive, and therefore highly coveted, form. And there were (and are) not one, but two versions of Holbein's 'Katherine' miniature, which suggests that the sitter was someone of exceptional status. Could the woman in the picture be Henry's fifth queen?

One clue that it might be are the fabulous gems that adorn her. An inventory of Queen Katherine's jewels reveals she amassed a treasure trove of riches: a trimming 'of goldsmith work enamelled and garnished with 7 fair diamonds, 7 fair rubies and 7 fair pearls'; a necklace 'containing 29 rubies and 29 clusters of pearls being 4 pearls in every cluster', and a pendant 'of gold having a very fair table diamond and a very fair ruby with a long pearl hanging at the same' were just some of the baubles heaped upon Katherine by her doting king, and all of them can be seen on the sitter in the Holbein miniature. [3]

But it's not the only plausible contender for ►

11

The Mysterious Face of Katherine Howard *(continued)*

◄ a portrait of Katherine. In 1910 art historian Lionel Cust identified a woman, shown in a portrait in the Toledo Gallery, Ohio, as Katherine. Known as the 'Toledo type', the picture shows a pale-skinned and dark-eyed lady with a pronounced nose, dressed in black. Cust pointed out the similarity between the 'over accentuated chin' of the sitter in the Toledo type and that of the woman shown in the Holbein miniature. Though he was |chivalrous enough to admit that the upper part of the face in the Toledo type was 'well-formed', he suggested that the jawline was a Norfolk one, strong and powerful, of a type which can be seen in portraits of Katherine's uncle the Duke.

But by far the most important piece of evidence for Cust was that the Toledo portrait was an exact match for (and in fact was the original of) another picture, owned by the National Portrait Gallery in London, which the Gallery had already designated as being of Katherine Howard some ten years earlier.

This might have ended the debate, had it not been for the fact that by 1949 the NPG had decided that its portrait was not of Katherine after all, thereby removing the central plank of Cust's argument. Today it's still unclear what evidence (if any) there ever was to support the claim that it depicted Henry's fifth queen.

More recent historical research has further disproved the identification, by showing that the portraits both came from art collections owned by branches of the Cromwell family, at whose head had sat Thomas Cromwell, Earl of Essex. Cromwell had been Henry VIII's closest and most trusted adviser until Queen Katherine inadvertently brought about his demise. That being so, why on earth would the Cromwell family have 'cherished, multiplied, and handed down to posterity' (as art historian Roy Strong puts it) a portrait – and its copy – of the woman responsible for their ancestor's untimely end? Strong also points out that the dress worn by the woman in the portraits – black, with cut sleeves that reveal rich gold fabric underneath – appears to be of a style which only came into fashion after Katherine's execution.[4] So Katherine faded from view again.

Or not. Whilst accepting Roy Strong's argument in her book on Henry's six wives, the historian Antonia Fraser did offer up another tantalising glimpse of Katherine in what she called the 'one permanent monument' to her. It's not a conventional portrait at all, but a stained-glass window in the chapel of King's College, Cambridge, the college founded by Henry VI in 1441. Stained glass was a powerful decorative art of the Middle Ages and a succession of kings from Henry VI to Henry VIII ensured that the chapel's windows would record and promote their families. Henry VII studded the windows with hawthorn bushes that symbolised his victory at Bosworth Field; his son Henry VIII used them as a canvas on which to record his achievements, depicting himself on them as Moses, as David brandishing the head of a Goliath (a thinly veiled image of the Pope), and as Solomon. And it is next to Solomon ▶

The Mysterious Face of Katherine Howard *(continued)*

◄ that Fraser thinks we might see a glimpse of Katherine, in the figure of the Queen of Sheba that kneels before him 'with her short nose and full lips, sensual and suppliant, presenting gifts'.[5] Is she right? The depiction certainly chimes with the motto Katherine adopted on her marriage to Henry ('Non autre volonte que la sienne', meaning 'No other wish but his').

A portrait of a woman in disguise, preserved on a brittle, vulnerable medium: for Katherine, in whose life story there are so many gaps, and whose hold on the crown proved so fragile, it is perhaps the most fitting memorial. ∎

1   Quoted in Antonia Fraser, *The Six Wives of Henry VIII*, published by Weidenfeld & Nicolson, 1992, p.353 and in David Starkey, *Six Wives: The Queens of Henry VIII*, published by Chatto & Windus, 2003, p.683.

2   Quoted in David Starkey, p.649.

3   Quoted in David Starkey, p.651.

4   Roy Strong suggests that the only securely dated portrait which showed a fashion of this style was Holbein's portrait of *Christina of Denmark*, painted in 1538. From this he concluded that the sitter in the Toledo type must have been a lady who was twenty-one in about 1535 to 1540; too old, in other words, to be Katherine who, it's believed, never lived to see her twenty-first birthday.

5   Quoted in Antonia Fraser, p.332.

Spread the Light

'There are two ways of spreading light: to be
the candle or the mirror that reflects it'

EDITH WHARTON

From Socrates to the salons of pre-
Revolutionary France, the great minds of
every age have debated the merits of literary
offerings alongside questions of politics,
social order and morality. Whether you love a
book or loathe it, one of the pleasures of
reading is the discussion books regularly
inspire. Below are a few suggestions for topics
of discussion about *The Confession of
Katherine Howard*.

Cat Tilney feels a 'pang' when she thinks of
how Katherine lost her mother at the age of
three. How sympathetic do you find
Katherine's character? How much of her
behaviour can be explained, or excused, by
her upbringing?

How would you describe life at the court of
Henry VIII? To what extent does it compare
with Katherine's life in the household of the
Dowager Duchess of Norfolk?

How harshly should Katherine be judged for
her unfaithfulness to Henry? In her marriage,
is she a victim of her family's ambitions, or
the author of her own downfall?

Does the novel cast new light on the private
lives of sixteenth-century women? How
surprising do you find Katherine's and Cat's
behaviour around men? ▶

Spread the Light *(continued)*

◄ Why do you think Suzannah Dunn chose to convey her historical characters using contemporary vernacular, and how does it affect your reading experience?

What do you make of the character of Francis Dereham, and his relationships with both Katherine and Cat?

How responsible is Cat for Katherine's downfall? What would you have done in her position?

Of all the characters, who do you feel most sympathy for at the end of the novel? ■

If You Loved This, You Might Like...

Other novels by Suzannah Dunn

The Sixth Wife

Katherine Parr, Henry VIII's sixth and final wife, survived their four turbulent years of marriage. But when the handsome Thomas Seymour wins her heart, mere months after the old king's death, their hasty union undoes a lifetime of caution. For Thomas is ruthlessly ambitious, and to achieve his own ends is willing to betray his wife . . .

'My, what a story . . . delightfully vulgar and utterly compelling'   *The Times*

The Queen of Subtleties

The story of Anne Boleyn is well known. Henry VIII divorced his longstanding, long-suffering, older Spanish wife for a young, black-eyed English beauty and in doing so severed England from Rome and, indeed, the rest of the western world. Then, when Henry had what he wanted, he managed a mere three years of marriage before beheading his wife for alleged adultery with several men, among them his own best friend and her own brother.

If You Like This, You Might Like ...
(continued)

Told by two women – Anne Boleyn, the king's mistress and ill-fated queen, and Lucy Cornwallis, the king's confectioner – *The Queen of Subtleties* tells Anne's story as it has never been told before.

'A stunningly refreshing way of retelling an old story. I often abandon historical novels nowadays, but I really could not put this one down. It brings Anne Boleyn to life as never before and, probably for the first time ever in fiction, Henry VIII emerges as a truly credible character in an authentic setting'

ALISON WEIR, author of
The Six Wives of Henry VIII

The Queen's Sorrow
These are desperate times for Mary Tudor. As England's first ruling queen, her joy should be complete when she marries Philip, the dashing Prince of Spain. But despite her ardent devotion, he's making it painfully obvious that he cares little for his new wife – and her struggle to produce an heir makes him colder towards her. Lonely and depressed, Mary begins to vent her anguish on her people – and England becomes a place of cruelty,

persecution and fear. Mary's fall from grace is seen through the eyes of Rafael, a Spanish sundial maker who is part of the Prince's flamboyant entourage. He becomes the one person that she trusts, but his life – and new-found love – will be caught up in the chaos that follows . . . ∎

Suzannah Dunn
Answers Your Reading Group
Questions

What made you decide to tell Katherine's story from the point of view of her lady-in-waiting, rather than in the first person?

I had some very good advice from my agent: 'Don't just re-tell history as we already know it. Look at it through someone else's eyes.' Then, when I was reading letters written by Katherine Howard's interrogators, I came across this cryptic, chilling line: 'Mistress Tilney hath served us well'. I knew that at least one of the Tilney girls – Catherine – had grown up with Katherine, and accompanied her to court. Katherine Howard was betrayed by someone close to her, but we don't know who or why. As soon as I read that line, I had my story.

Do you think Katherine's story is relevant to today and modern experience?

Well, girls are girls, it seems – wherever and *when*ever they are. For me, Katherine Howard and Cat Tilney's complex friendship is instantly and intriguingly recognisable. Indeed, when I was first reading about Katherine Howard, my reaction was, 'I *know* you – I was at school with you', as it were . . . and it's a reaction that I've had since from readers, too.

You have written about several of Henry's wives – which did you find the most interesting character?

They're each interesting in different ways. You might think that Anne Boleyn would win hands down – bright and ambitious, uncompromising, outrageously forthright. But the sixth wife, Katherine Parr, is fascinating: a clever and always so very cautious woman of a certain age who, within six weeks of the king's death, chose (and it was definitely her choice, she was the one with the wealth and power) to marry a most unsuitable man, a playboy who duly was her ruin.

Katherine Howard, though, is the one who has, unexpectedly, got under my skin, precisely because she didn't initially seem to be a big character – but appearances are deceptive, and that apparent simplicity of character was cover for conduct far more daring and outlandish than anything ever even contemplated by those other two queens.

We loved the historical setting of this book. What do you think gives the Tudor period such enduring appeal?

Well, the period isn't known to historians as 'early modern' for nothing! Whilst being intriguingly different from our own (as 'early', of course), the Tudor era is also recognisable to us as we were beginning to be 'modern', unlike the medieval period which remains alien.

To take just one example: the increase in social mobility – remember Thomas Cromwell, who became the most powerful man in England, was reputedly the son of a butcher. It's a world that we both know and don't know, and, as such, is particularly satisfying for us, I think.

How much research do you need to do for your novels?

My research is two-fold. First, and obviously, I have to research the details of daily life (which, admittedly, I seem to find hard to retain! I have to go over it again – what people ate, what they wore, how they spent their days – for each novel). Secondly, I'll read as widely and deeply as possible on a character, weighing up the various historians' accounts to try to reach an accurate picture of him or her. That's very important to me; I know that my job as a novelist is to make things up, but I do try to stay true, as it were, to the real people.

What are you working on now?

I'm investigating a little known but devastating scandal that happened in the Seymour household when Jane (later to become the third wife) was a teenager. Jane is the least visible of the six wives, and I'm beginning to understand why that might have suited her very well.

To find out more about Richard and Judy's Summer Book Club go to
whsmith.co.uk/richardandjudy